I0659490

# A CROWN IN TIME

## Also By Cidney Swanson

### The Ripple Series

Rippler
Chameleon
Unfurl
Visible
Immutable
Knavery
Perilous

### The Saving Mars Series

Saving Mars
Defying Mars
Losing Mars
Mars Burning
Striking Mars
Mars Rising

### The Thief in Time Series

A Thief in Time
A Flight in Time
A Sword in Time
A Crown in Time

### Books Not in a Series

Siren Spell

# A CROWN IN TIME

## Cidney Swanson

Copyright © 2018 by Cidney Swanson
Cover art © by Nathalia Suellen. All rights reserved.

All rights reserved, including the right to reproduce
this book or portions thereof in any form whatsoever.

This is a work of fiction. Names, characters, places,
and incidents are products of the author's imagination
or are used fictitiously. Any resemblance to actual
events or locales or persons, living or dead, is entirely
coincidental.

ISBN 978-1-939543-51-6

For Sarah,
who promised researching
history was the fun part,
and who was right.

## Prologue

### The Previous October

Nevis, driving north out of Florida on the I-75, wasn't thinking about terrorists taking down the power grid. He was having trouble with coherent thought. What on God's green earth had he just witnessed?

Three hours ago, he had watched as two people appeared between equipment that had been spitting blue fire in Arthur Littlewood's clandestine laboratory. Two people who had not been there a moment earlier. He saw them appear out of nowhere and slump to the ground. What had he seen? One thing was for sure: he was glad no one in that room knew he'd seen it.

Gripping the wheel of his rental car, Nevis made a mental shortlist of possibilities.

Deep-cover government agency technology.

Terrorist activity.

Alien technology.

Honestly? He had no idea what he'd just seen. But he was pretty sure that whatever it was, Jules Khan's death was mixed up in it. A shiver ran down Nevis's spine. Littlewood hadn't seemed like a killer. Neither had the young woman from Santa Barbara. Julie? Jillian? But Everett—the young man who'd opened the door—was he some high-level assassin sent to eliminate Khan when Khan had demanded hush money? But Everett could barely defend himself in a fist fight.

Nevis blinked as a new possibility presented itself.

What if his assailant had *pretended* to be unable to defend himself? Everyone at that lab had been intent on preventing Nevis from seeing anything, that was for sure. He shuddered, remembering the flashes of light. The two people who had appeared out of nowhere.

Nevis had FBI clearance for another two days. Maybe less than that. He'd blocked calls from his SAC, after passing the county sheriff back at the complex where Littlewood's secret lab had been located. He tapped his fingers against the steering wheel. He wanted answers. What had he witnessed? Something big, that much was clear. Littlewood had said his work was government funded. Okay. That was a place to start. Find out more about Littlewood's funding. What branch was it from? How long had he been getting it? These were things that would be a lot trickier to find out two days from now when his clearance was revoked.

That decided it.

Exiting the freeway, Nevis pulled into the parking lot of the Valdosta Walmart Supercenter. He needed to figure out his next move. If Littlewood's funding was governmental, then maybe the reason Nevis had been ordered to back off was because the FBI itself had been told to back off. The forces behind a secret

2

of this magnitude must be powerful. And deadly.

Nevis swallowed and then reached up to loosen his tie. He shifted his seat, tipping it back to a more comfortable angle. As he did so, his keys shifted in his pants pocket, jabbing his thigh. Except . . . his keys were in the ignition. He reached into his pocket.

Oh.

It was the thumb drive he'd picked up in front of Littlewood's clandestine operation. Could it belong to the professor?

Nevis's heart began to beat double-time. Although he had to turn in his badge and gun, handing the thumb drive over to his SAC wasn't a remote temptation. He fired up his laptop, inserted the drive, and examined the contents, encountering equations, theories, diagrams, and equipment lists that were meaningless to him. But what was *not* meaningless were the names.

Five hours later, Nevis had an address in Missouri. He'd used his FBI access to locate the possible whereabouts of someone calling himself Ken Julius, a name he'd found on the thumb drive in a list of aliases once under consideration by none other than *Jules Khan*. Whoever this Ken Julius living above a coffee shop in Kansas City was, he knew something.

Nevis swallowed again. He should maybe consider adopting an alias himself.

Nevis would never know the complicated path by which the thumb drive had landed in his possession. But he did know one thing: he'd seen two people appear out of thin air, and this thumb drive contained scientific papers and schematics and blueprints that referenced time travel as though it were an actual *thing*.

Benjamin Nevis had questions. Lots of questions.

If time travel were possible, what would that mean for humanity? Or, closer to home, what might it mean for Nevis? For six years, Nevis had replayed the horrible day when his former boss Lewiston had double-crossed him and gotten away with millions. The day that had nearly ruined Nevis's career and led to his sister's death. *If only he could turn back time,* had been his constant refrain. Now by some crazy chance, he'd found someone who might, with the right persuasion, be able to do just that.

And so, thirty-one hours later, on a hot, sticky morning outside a hot, sticky coffee shop in Kansas City, Nevis waited until a compact man in need of a haircut stepped out with a cup of coffee and a day-old doughnut.

"Hello, Jules Khan," said Nevis.

The man dropped his doughnut, but not, fortunately, his coffee, and glared at Nevis.

"Who the hell are you?"

Nevis flashed his badge without a verbal response, allowing the question to hang unanswered for a moment before offering his most genial smile. "I'm the man you're going to have an extended conversation with, regarding the contents of this thumb drive."

Khan's face turned pale. "That's mine."

"It *was* yours. It's mine now. But if you tell me everything about the time machine you invented, it could be yours again."

Khan swallowed, his Adam's apple bobbing up and down. "What do you want to know?"

# 1

## · *HALLEY* ·

### December, Present Day

Halley was ready for a change. She stood in the darkened living area of the latest hotel efficiency suite she shared with Edmund, watching colorful Christmas lights as they blinked on a twelve-inch artificial tree. It was a portable and therefore a very practical tree. Since the first of December, Halley and Edmund had lived in three similar hotel units, following the filming of a movie that had barely wrapped on Christmas Eve. They'd paid out of pocket to stay here tonight, the 25th. Edmund had already gone to bed, exhausted from staying up late the night before to finish Halley's present.

It had been a good Christmas. Cozy. Peaceful. They'd slept in, dined on craft services leftovers, and exchanged gifts. Halley's eyes fell on Edmund's gift to her, a hand-made wooden baby cradle. The timing was . . . serendipitous. For the past month—since they spent Thanksgiving alone, in fact—Halley had been reconsidering the lifestyle that meant she was always on the road, always at someone else's beck and call, at all hours, and without any permanent home.

A little over two years ago, when pregnancy had become a possibility, she'd gone on the pill. There was no *way* she could run wardrobe for major motion pictures while enduring morning sickness and exhaustion, not to mention a belly that would seriously hamper her ability to dash around fixing the twenty to thirty wardrobe "emergencies" typical on any given day.

No, the pill had been an awesome solution.

Somehow, though, she hadn't managed to tell Edmund of her choice that first month of sharing his bed. Or the second month. By the time a year had passed, it would have been awkward to bring it up, what with Edmund thinking she wanted a baby and trying to cheer her up each month when her period arrived. Edmund had always wanted to be a dad. Until recently though, Halley hadn't wanted to be a mom.

She crossed to the plastic tree, reaching for its light switch. Now the room was dark except for the glow put out by a few LEDs. A blue TV button light lit the cradle's smoothly polished surface. Edmund was a true craftsman. Halley smiled and ran her hand along the glossy top rail.

What would it be like to settle down and live in the same place for more than six weeks at a time? To have a backyard where they could invite friends over for Fourth of July? She'd accepted her next job, a shoot of Shakespeare's *As You Like It* reimagined in the Florida Everglades, because it would put her closer to the people she loved—to the ones who were family even if they weren't blood-related. But what would it be like to own a condo in Wellesley, Florida? Or buy a house there, close to Jillian and Everett, DaVinci and Quintus? She and Edmund had saved enough for a modest down payment. What would it be like to have a *home*, or even . . . to have Edmund's baby?

Halley nudged the cradle, setting it gently rocking.

It was time for a change. It had been a long time coming, but she finally felt ready, and so for the first time in over eight hundred nights of sliding under sheets to join Edmund's enticing body, Halley didn't take her pill.

## 2

### · KHAN ·

#### December, Kansas City

Jules Khan hurled the whiteboard eraser across his laboratory.

What was wrong with Space-time?

For the past week, this had been his question. It was all he could think about. It had started three weeks ago, although he hadn't known anything was "starting" at the time. He'd been sitting at his desk, awaiting results of a time machine trial. To pass the time he'd been online, reading news about some seemingly unrelated thefts of valuable historical artifacts, which had vanished as if by magic. Khan had become more interested when he read that each of the items in question had been purchased from an estate in Montecito, California. Further investigation showed the estate in question had been that of the late Jules Khan, a duplicate self created through the vagaries of space-time. But then an alarm on the machine had started blaring, and he'd thought no more of the vanishing valuables.

Until last week.

Last week Khan had been standing by the singularity device, trying to figure out why it seemed to be drawing twice the power it ought to draw on each of seventeen trials he'd run. Why would his machine draw extra power?

As he puzzled the problem, Khan had absentmindedly reached in his pocket for a stone he kept with him. The stone—a small piece of Rome's *Via Sacra*, had been his one memento from a visit to 53 BC using his former advisor's time machine. Well, the stone had been his only memento aside from a hulking Roman soldier, whom Khan had obviously *not* kept.

And then, as Khan stood there, listening to the machine's roar and worrying the stone in his hand, his memento had vanished.

*Vanished.*

Not fallen, dropped, slipped, or slid out of his grasp.

Vanished.

Khan had immediately halted all operation of the machine. Either something was wrong with space-time, or with his machine. But space-time operated in predictable ways, in accordance with Khan's first and second temporal laws. If something was wrong, it had to be operator error. So what had he miscalculated?

"*Nothing*," he said out loud. His voice echoed in the cavernous warehouse space he'd rented eight months ago, before Nevis had turned up. At first, Khan had been thrilled to meet Special Agent Benjamin Nevis. Nevis had possessed—and shared— the one thing Khan needed most: a thumb drive containing schematics for building a singularity device. Khan had rebuilt the device to spec, correcting earlier errors introduced *before* he'd gotten his thumb drive back. He'd done everything precisely. Triple-checked his work. There was simply no logical explanation for the problems with space-time or rather, with his machine.

Nevis, for all that he claimed to know a little physics, was no help at all. Lately, Khan had even begun to doubt he was a current FBI agent. Not that it mattered. Either way, Nevis had him under his thumb.

Khan examined his work on the whiteboard, daring an error to reveal itself. He must have missed something. He should recalculate. Grabbing a sweater Nevis had left unattended, Khan used the sleeve to erase the diagram on the whiteboard. What was he missing?

He pinched his eyes shut and then opened them again, staring at Nevis's sweater. Dry-erase ink had transferred itself from the whiteboard to the sweater. Khan released a single grunting laugh. Teach Nevis to leave his things lying around. How was Khan supposed to work in these conditions?

That was the *real* problem. Khan knew damn well he was capable of building a functional singularity device from the information on the thumb drive. He knew it because *he'd already done it*. Or at least, a version of himself had done it. When Dr. Arthur Littlewood had accidentally transported Jules Khan from 2001 to 2018, Khan had learned of the existence (and death) of a separate version of himself who had remained behind in 2001. Space-time apparently abhorred the void that would've been left if a person or object wasn't duplicated, to exist in both times. The alternative Khan left in 2001 had abandoned academia, built a time machine, and amassed wealth in Montecito. This was how Khan knew he had it in him to build a machine from the instructions on the thumb drive. The other Khan had already done it! He'd built a machine and operated it very profitably for almost seventeen years.

If his other self had done it, then so could he.

This was all Nevis's fault, Khan thought, glaring at Nevis's sweater. How was anyone supposed to work with an armed FBI agent watching his every move? Khan heard the distant industrial flush of the lab's only toilet. Nevis's bathroom visits were practically the only breaks Khan got from the man's onerous presence. He waited for Nevis's second flush. His disgusting, why-did-he-need-it, second flush.

Khan set Nevis's sweater back down, hiding the marker ink inside a fold.

He knew why he was having so much trouble figuring out the problem with space-time. Or rather, with his machine. Who could be expected to do their best work under constant threat of exposure and imprisonment? While Nevis pretended they were colleagues (*as if!*), Khan understood the nature of their relationship. Nevis was blackmailing him. If Khan didn't build the machine and do whatever the hell else Nevis demanded, Nevis would tip off the FBI or CIA or Homeland Security. One or the other of those organizations would then take a careful look at Khan's falsified ID, which Nevis said wouldn't stand up to those levels of scrutiny. Khan might fantasize about running away and starting afresh, but he knew better than to believe he could outwit the powers Nevis would bring to bear on him if he *did* run in his current penurious state.

No, he needed to get the machine operational and steal obscene amounts of valuables from the past and convert these to cash, which would allow him to flee to some country without extradition where he could . . . start all over again.

Khan groaned. Some prospect.

The toilet flushed a second time.

Then again, if it wasn't a great prospect, at least it beat life with Benjamin Nevis.

Lately, Khan had begun to wish he could consult with Arthur Littlewood on his problem. Had Littlewood perhaps encountered these troubling "disappearances"? And never bothered to mention it? During Khan's tenure as postdoc, Littlewood had never so much as hinted at "object impermanence." Of course, so far as Khan knew, Littlewood had only made a handful of trips to the past, and only one or two retrievals. Littlewood was probably as ignorant as he was.

But Khan did wish they could discuss the matter, researcher to researcher. The problem with working alone was that he was . . . *alone*. If there were physics conundrums—as clearly there were—Benjamin Nevis was not the sort of person one could turn to for a little brainstorming. The toilet flushed a third time.

"Really?" Khan muttered to the empty lab.

Then he turned back to the whiteboard. If he was ever getting out of here, he had problems to solve.

Why was the machine drawing twice the power it should?

Why were *some* (but not all) duplicated objects retrieved from the past disappearing?

Where did these items disappear *to*?

And, worst of all: would he, a duplicate himself, be next?

# 3

## · HALLEY ·

### February, Florida Everglades

Halley set the carefully rinsed plastic stick on the bathroom counter beside its twin. Two positives. One positive and it might've been a fluke, but two meant she was definitely pregnant. Tears welled in her eyes. Edmund would be thrilled. Was this why she'd been so hungry lately? She was eating for two! She wondered if pregnancy might also explain her recent headaches and this morning's scratchy, dry throat. She had so much to learn . . .

She couldn't wait to tell Edmund. She switched to washing her hands, admiring her wedding ring as she scrubbed. Halley smiled at the practical low-set ruby. They'd had to alter her ring once she'd found that her original pronged setting injured the delicate fabrics she worked with as a wardrobe mistress. The ruby itself had been plucked from an Elizabethan necklace once belonging to Edmund's mother. A beautiful stone, it had languished unseen on the backside of the necklace clasp. The Elizabethans loved such secrets in their ornaments, unknown to everyone except the lovers who exchanged them.

Now she and Edmund would share a far more important secret! Well, until she started to show. Wrapping one of the pregnancy-test sticks in a tissue and tossing it, she stuck the other one in her pocket to show Edmund. How should she make the announcement? Over a romantic dinner, maybe? Valentine's Day was in a week. But could she wait? She didn't think so.

But when she stepped out of the bathroom and into the sitting area of the efficiency hotel suite, she realized Edmund was on the phone, talking to DaVinci.

He smiled warmly at Halley and said to DaVinci, "Halley is here. I shall convey you onto the speaker."

That smile . . .

Did Edmund suspect what she'd been up to in the bathroom? She couldn't tell him now with DaVinci listening in. Edmund needed to be the first to know. *In private.*

"Hey, DaVinci," said Halley.

"Halley! Hi! Quick question. Remember that sarcophagus in Montecito? Belonging to Jules Khan? *Dead* Jules Khan, I mean."

It was how DaVinci distinguished between the two versions of Khan.

"The Egyptian casket made of pink granite?" Halley remembered it. It was hard to forget anything to do with the basement where both she and Edmund had nearly been killed. By *dead* Khan. She still had nightmares where she was trapped in that basement.

"Yeah, I remember it.'

15

"I don't suppose you happened to take any pictures that would show it, for the purpose of estimating its size?"

Halley frowned. She'd taken a few pictures of the futuristic lab equipment for DaVinci, who'd been heavily into steampunk art at the time.

"It's probably in the background of some pictures."

"Can you send them over? I told Dr. Littlewood I would ask."

"What does Littlewood want with that sarcophagus?"

"He got a call from Dr. Khan's former lawyer."

"Jesús Torres?"

"Yes. Mr. Torres says the sarcophagus sort of disappeared recently, and he contacted Littlewood after remembering Littlewood had removed, you know, all the time machine stuff from the basement."

"So Torres wanted to know if Littlewood helped himself to the sarcophagus too?"

"I guess so. Which he didn't, obviously, but I guess Dr. Littlewood got to thinking, and between him and Everett, they're convinced the sarcophagus would never in a million years have fit up those stairs. So I said I would ask if you had pictures."

"I'll send some over."

"I wish you'd take a break and drive up here instead," said DaVinci. "We miss you! It's only, what, an hour and a half from the Everglades to Wellesley?"

"They're keeping me busy," Halley said apologetically. "Four hundred costumes—"

"I know, I know. Maybe I'll drive down instead."

Halley swung her head fast to check with

Edmund on this. *Ouch!* Her headache was worse. She winced audibly.

"Wow, that excited to see me?" asked DaVinci.

"Sorry, sorry. It's just another headache."

"More cranky actors who can't handle corsets and codpieces?"

Halley grunted out a small laugh. "They're not *all* cranky."

"This is your third headache this week," said DaVinci. "You need a break."

"It is her fourth," said Edmund.

"Four headaches in one week?" asked DaVinci. "That's not good. Maybe it's a hormonal imbalance. Have you thought about getting off the pill? Lot of women's headaches disappear when they go off it."

Why did DaVinci have to bring up birth control? Especially now of all times? Halley's stomach clenched, and she smiled nervously at Edmund.

"Listen," Halley said to DaVinci. "I should go. Super busy today."

"Okay—talk soon!"

The phone went silent.

Halley glanced to Edmund. His hands were clenched, and a frown furrowed his brow.

Gravely, he asked her, "Wherefore did DaVinci speak of the pill?"

# 4

## ·HALLEY·

February, Florida Everglades

"Do I misunderstand DaVinci?" Edmund asked Halley. "Does she speak of something other than a preventative to offspring?"

Halley tried to think of an answer that wouldn't end with the two of them squared off in opposite corners regarding reproductive freedoms. It was incredibly ironic that the subject would come up today, of all days.

Edmund had been so perplexed the first time he heard of the pill. "Wherefore should a husband and wife not desire children?" he'd asked Halley. At one point, he'd compared the invention of the pill to that of a medicine intended to lessen the tastiness of food. She hadn't bothered trying to explain that there was probably a market for medicine like that. There were things Edmund just didn't get. The pill was one of them.

"My love?" His words brought Halley back to the present.

"Yeah. DaVinci was talking about *that* pill." Halley could hear how defensive she sounded, but how could the topic *not* put her on the defense?

"Wherefore have you hid this from me?"

"It's not important," said Halley. "I'm not even taking the pill anymore."

"Not of import?"

Edmund's indignation was overblown, like Halley had feared.

"How can you say this? It is of great importance," he insisted.

"I knew you'd be like this, which is exactly why I didn't consult you about my decision," she snapped back.

"Your decision?" Edmund's nostrils flared. "How is't you have construed this as a decision in which I play no part?"

"Because it *is* my decision. This is the twenty-first century, and if I don't want to get pregnant, I don't have to."

He stared at her like she'd slapped him.

Halley turned away. "I *knew* you wouldn't understand."

"How am I to understand those things that you hide from me?"

"This isn't about you—"

"I can think of nothing pertaining more to us both—"

"It's *my body*!"

Edmund's face flushed faintly. His voice softened. "Thine, which thou didst invite me to share, even as I have given my body to thee, because it is thine."

Now Halley felt like she was the one who'd been

struck.

Silence hung thickly between them, like velvet curtains at a theater.

"I didn't mean for you to find out like this," she said at last.

There was a chill in Edmund's voice when he answered her. "Indeed? Didst thou intend I should find out in some other manner?"

Halley flushed deeply. Edmund was completely infuriating at times like this. Of course she hadn't wanted him to know, because he would take it exactly like he *was* taking it, like some personal affront, when it wasn't about him at all.

"Not wanting to discuss something with you isn't the same as planning to hide it forever."

"Well my lady. . ." Edmund's voice trailed off. His lips pinched together and he bowed perfunctorily. "I pray you will forgive me. I find I am in need of air."

"Edmund . . ." She wanted to tell him to sit down. She wanted to ask for a re-do. "It's just . . ."

He stood stiffly at the door. "My lady?"

Halley shook her head. What was the use? He wanted to storm off? Fine. She wasn't going to stop him. The man was more stubborn than an actor trying to fit in too-tight jeans.

"Just . . . stay off the highway shoulder," Halley said, turning slightly away from him. "Cars aren't expecting pedestrians out here in the middle of nowhere."

"I shall in this, as in all things, attempt to conform to thy desires."

She'd heard this before. She hated when he said it. It was his most formal ending to their rare spats. She turned back to tell him they needed to talk, but he was already gone.

The door closed with a heavy *snick*.

As Halley sank onto the hotel couch, the plastic pregnancy test stick popped out of her jeans pocket. The plus sign looked like it was judging her.

Her eyes brimmed with tears. This morning had completely derailed. A fat tear dropped onto the back of her hand. Pulling out her phone, she texted DaVinci.

*Are you still up for that visit?*

5

· *NEVIS* ·

December, Kansas City

Benjamin Nevis knew himself to be a patient man. Six years had passed since he'd first resolved to track down his former SAC and brother-in-law Lewiston to pay him back. It was thanks to Lewiston that the FBI had regarded Nevis with suspicion, ever since the incident where Lewiston had made off with $7 million in unmarked bills. Lewiston had wrecked Nevis's brilliant career, eventually landing him in Florida where he'd been fired and forced to turn in his badge and gun.

If that wasn't bad enough, Lewiston was also partly responsible for the death of Nevis's only living relation, his sister Karen. She'd divorced Lewiston after he'd fled with his millions, and then she'd had to tackle cancer without insurance. She had lost. It still kept Nevis awake nights. For six years, the thought of paying Lewiston back, or better still, stopping him mid-heist, had been a fantasy in Nevis's mind. To think that all the times he'd wished he could reverse time, it had been possible! Or it would be, once Khan got the time machine running.

Even though he'd waited to pay Lewiston back for six years, Nevis was finding it harder and harder to remain patient. It had been October when he'd handed Khan the thumb drive, and now it was nearly the new year. Nevis asked Khan every day—sometimes more than once—for a progress report. Khan, hardly the model of diplomacy to begin with, had begun to snap at Nevis. Or to ignore him. It didn't take extraordinary powers of observation to figure out Khan was keeping information back. There were times Nevis wanted to break his weaselly little neck. At these moments, Nevis had to place his quite-capable hands behind his back and step to the other side of the lab for a few hours. Of course, as soon as he drifted back to look over Khan's shoulder, the cycle began again.

Lately, though, Nevis had begun to wonder if Khan might work more efficiently without constant supervision. Or rather, without *observable* supervision.

So, during Khan's fourth of January trip to Costco to restock the supply of frozen breakfast sandwiches, frozen burritos, frozen pizza, and frozen taquitos that made up their diet, Nevis set up surveillance. After this, he began to absent himself from the lab, renting an office in the warehouse next door, from which he could observe Khan in secret.

He learned a few things within days.

First, it was apparent Khan was still troubleshooting the machine's operation, exactly as he claimed. Second, when he was alone, Khan operated the machine almost daily, but it was as though he'd hit a roadblock, because Khan had yet to send himself anywhere. (And you could bet Nevis would race over when he did!) But the roadblock to travel was surely a significant one. To Nevis's face, Khan would only confess he was still working the problem.

Khan was hiding things. Probably many things.

Well, was that a huge surprise? Nevis couldn't think of any invention in humankind's history to rival this. Neither the combustion engine, atomic weapons, nor the personal computer presented such potential for shaking up the course of human development. But if it was exciting, it was also unnerving. To place this kind of power in the hands of people like self-absorbed Jules Khan, or even nervous Arthur Littlewood? The idea troubled Nevis. These weren't the guys you wanted poised over big red buttons of any stripe. The thought made him feel vaguely protective of humankind. After a few days, he realized the feeling was familiar. It was this same feeling that had driven him to a career in the FBI: the desire to serve and protect.

Technology such as this belonged in the hands of the United States government. Behind locked doors. Lots of locked doors. Which was precisely where former (and . . . future?) FBI agent Benjamin Nevis would make sure it ended up. Just as soon as he'd used the machine to repay Lewiston.

# 6

## · HALLEY ·

February, Florida Everglades

Edmund hadn't returned in the hour and a half it took DaVinci to drive down from Wellesley.

"I left right away," said DaVinci, hugging her friend. "I was painting, and I didn't even wash my brushes. Just stuffed 'em in Ziploc bags."

"Thank you," murmured Halley. The two settled onto the efficiency suite's unyielding living room couch.

"Okay," said DaVinci. "So tell me everything. Did Edmund not know about you being on the pill?"

Halley tucked a decorative pillow behind her back and sighed heavily.

"I take it that's a *no*?" asked DaVinci.

"I *used* to be on the pill. I quit taking it almost two months ago. I just . . . never got around to telling him."

"Yeah. Oh boy."

"It's not like it was any of his business," snapped Halley.

DaVinci raised an eyebrow.

"It was my decision."

DaVinci held up her hands. "Okay. I'm not arguing, but I'm going to point out that a seventeenth century Englishman might not see eye to eye with you on the issue, and that means not telling him is kind of a big deal. You know?"

Halley broke eye contact and rested her head on the back of the couch.

"I knew you'd take his side."

"Whoa, whoa. I'm on *your* side. Team Halley all the way. If you want to take the pill, *take the pill*. But if you've been hiding it from Edmund, well, girlfriend . . ." DaVinci shook her head sadly.

"I wasn't *hiding* it, per se. I just—"

"—hadn't gotten around to telling him, I know," said DaVinci. "But you've been married for how long?"

"Fine. I get it."

She was being terrible. DaVinci was on her side. She'd just said so. So why did she feel so defensive? Halley reached for her wedding ring, twisting it round and round.

"Hal?"

She looked up. DaVinci was staring at Halley's wedding ring, looking alarmed.

Halley looked down at her ring. She blinked. Twisted it around. "The ruby . . ."

Her ruby stone had fallen out.

"No, no, *no!*"

This had to happen today? Really? On top of everything else? Tears formed in her eyes and then spilled over her lower lids.

"Is this the universe trying to tell me something about . . . my . . . marriage?" Hiccup-y sobs broke up her last two words.

DaVinci threw an arm around her. "Come on. Let's find that stone. I think you could use a distraction right now."

Four hours later, though, they were no closer to locating Halley's missing stone. Worse still, Edmund hadn't returned. Halley tried texting him and got an "undeliverable" message.

"He might have turned his phone off," suggested DaVinci.

"Does that make messages undeliverable?" asked Halley.

"Got me." DaVinci's stomach growled noisily. "Okay. So seriously? What's a girl got to do around here to get some dinner?"

Halley scrounged up a bag of tortilla chips, some salsa, beans, and queso, and soon the two were lamenting how far they were from their favorite taco truck in Santa Barbara, where they could've gotten *real* salsa. They opened a second bag of chips, finishing those too, and still Edmund didn't call, text, or return to the hotel.

By 11:30 that night, both girls were working hard at not worrying.

"He's never refused to talk to me," said Halley. "We've had disagreements, but usually I'm the one who storms off."

"I'm sure he's fine," said DaVinci. "He's probably hitchhiking to Wellesley to talk to Everett. He just needs time to . . . to process everything." DaVinci hesitated. "Hal—you do get that this is a big deal for

Edmund, right?"

Halley frowned, nodded, and teared up again.

"Look," said DaVinci, "I support you taking birth control if that's what you want, but maybe you guys can talk through your decision *together* when he gets back."

Halley was on the point of telling DaVinci that she was *pregnant*, but the thought of telling someone before she told Edmund? She couldn't. He needed to be the first to hear. This thought, of course, only made her cry harder.

"Hey, hey, hey," murmured DaVinci, rubbing her back. "Everything's going to be fine. I'm here. Edmund will probably call in the morning. He just needed some space. It's going to be okay. Come on. We're going to bed." Saying this, she steered Halley to the bedroom and settled her underneath the comforter.

As soon as DaVinci climbed in bed, she pulled her charge cord from her purse and plugged her phone into the bedside outlet. "Hey, here's a thought. Didn't you tell me Edmund's even worse than me about charging his phone?"

"He's the worst."

"Well, there you go. Mystery solved. His phone is just dead."

A tiny smile. "I'm sure you're right," said Halley.

Exhaustion took over and Halley fell asleep soon after, although she woke several times in the night to check her phone for messages, just in case. At 5:30 AM, knowing Jillian would be awake, Halley sent her friend a text.

*Any chance Edmund's contacted you or Everett or*

*Quintus? He disappeared yesterday and we haven't heard from him since.*

Jillian responded immediately. *Oh my gosh, Hal! So sorry. Give me a quick minute and I'll check.*

Five minutes later, Halley's phone rang. Was it Jillian or Edmund? She fumbled for her phone, swiping to answer the call, but it wasn't anyone she expected.

"Hello? This is Halley."

"Ah. Yes. Halley."

It was . . . Arthur Littlewood. Halley waited for him to explain why he was calling, but there was only silence on the line.

"Um, so you called me?"

Beside her in bed, DaVinci blinked and rubbed her eyes.

"Ah. Yes. Jillian tells me Edmund is missing."

Halley swallowed hard. Her throat felt like it was on fire. She grabbed a sip of water before speaking.

"Yeah. We argued, and he left the hotel to take a walk yesterday, and he hasn't come back yet."

"Oh dear," said Littlewood.

"'Oh dear' *what?*" demanded Halley, sitting upright.

"It's just . . . well . . . I have a terrible feeling I may know something concerning his, ah, absence."

7

· *KHAN* ·

February, Kansas City

Left to his own devices, Khan might never have worked up the courage to contact Arthur Littlewood about the disappearance of objects from the past. But Khan was *not* left to his own devices. His devices were continually being encroached upon by Benjamin Nevis.

"I'm running out of patience, Khan," Nevis said. "I want this machine up and running. I think you and I both know it's time to turn somewhere else for the answers we need."

"Littlewood won't tell us anything," Khan said glumly.

"Everyone has their price."

"And you think you've discovered Arthur Littlewood's?" Khan's tone was laced with derision.

Nevis had no answer. Of course he had no answer. Nevis knew he was the *last* person Arthur Littlewood would speak to. Well, if the truth were told, Khan might tie for that position.

And yet, if Nevis really was desperate enough to risk contacting Littlewood, then Littlewood would quickly figure out Nevis had set up shop with Khan. Littlewood might even attempt to bring the law down on both their heads.

"I'm calling him now," said Nevis, reaching for his cell phone.

"No! Wait! You have no idea what you're doing!" Attempting to reign in his fears, Khan said, "Just let me think for a minute."

He rose and paced, considering his options. He knew Nevis well enough to be sure he would do what he threatened: contact Littlewood for assistance. This meant that when it came down to it, there were only two options: allow Nevis to contact Littlewood, or contact Littlewood himself. Which was safer? Khan thought that, on the whole, he preferred a world where Arthur Littlewood was ignorant of the Khan-Nevis connection. And now that he considered it, was it, perhaps—just *maybe*—possible this meeting could go well?

If Khan begged his former colleague for forgiveness—to let bygones be bygones—the two of them could tackle the problem together. In fact, Khan had good reason to think Littlewood would see this as his problem, too. Nevis had mentioned a hulking soldier from ancient Rome, which meant Littlewood had befriended the duplicate Roman. Khan knew Littlewood: if Littlewood had taken the Roman under his wing, he would try to protect him, which included *protecting him from disappearing.*

This meant their interests were aligned.

Khan hesitated. He didn't trust Arthur

Littlewood, but he knew Littlewood would find it hard to turn down the chance to compare notes, to toss hypotheses back and forth with an equal. Perhaps. *Perhaps*...

When Khan spoke again, his mind was made up.

"I will go to Littlewood and allow him to believe I've seen the error of my ways. I will apologize and ask his forgiveness."

"I'd like to see that," muttered Nevis.

"No! You cannot 'see that.' He can't know that you and I are working together. It would ruin everything! It's imperative Arthur Littlewood sees me as a starving, frustrated, repentant colleague who's run out of options. That's the only way I'll succeed in regaining his trust. Believe me—I know his weakness for aiding the . . . *unfortunate*."

Nevis folded his arms and paced. After two excruciating minutes, Nevis appeared to have reached the conclusion Khan was correct.

"Very well," said Nevis. "You work things from your angle."

Khan's brow furrowed. What other angle was there? He didn't actually need to know. He needed to fix things with Arthur Littlewood, and fast.

He placed a call, unsurprised when Littlewood didn't pick up. He left a message. And then, he waited for a response. And waited. And waited.

No one was more surprised than Jules Khan when, on the eighth of February, almost a week after the recorded message, Arthur Littlewood called back to arrange a meeting.

8

· *NEVIS* ·

February, Kansas City

Nevis refrained from taking any steps on the third of February, the day after Khan had left a message for Littlewood, requesting a meeting. He didn't do anything on the fourth or fifth of February, either. But on the sixth, after watching Khan (via surveillance camera) do nothing more than pace the lab and occasionally stare morosely at the time machine, Nevis had had enough.

Sure, he was concerned about screwing over Lewiston, but he was also thinking about what sort of job he'd request in exchange for bringing the FBI the biggest discovery in its history. Or did he want to approach the CIA instead? A time machine was a history-changing invention.

One thing was for sure: he wasn't leaving a secret like this in Khan's hands.

Khan wasn't just going to roll over and give up the machine, though, which meant Nevis couldn't go to the government until he was fully able to operate—

and even troubleshoot—the machine.

Something even Khan couldn't seem to do at the moment. It didn't look like Arthur Littlewood was calling back, either.

Nevis needed to explore other options for getting information from Littlewood. Briefly he considered abduction and interrogation, but he knew he had neither the stomach for it nor the requisite skill set. No, what he needed was access to all the information stored on Littlewood's computer network.

Nevis had once been a trusted agent, working documents fraud and cyber-threats. Before losing his clearance, Nevis had copied contact information for every felon who wasn't currently locked up; several had received lighter sentencing in exchange for information, and Nevis was only too happy to work with one of them to obtain a fake badge, because you never knew when a badge might come in handy. Nevis had not, however, expected he would ever need to contact anyone from cyber-threats.

"Never say never," he muttered, sliding his thumb down his phone screen.

The first hacker Nevis contacted was a bust. She had overreached and landed herself behind bars for ten years. His second contact, one Odo Wilkerson, was available for a meeting, via secured chat, at Nevis's earliest convenience.

Odo nearly turned him down.

"Are you for real?" asked the hacker.

"Yes," replied Nevis.

"How do I know this isn't a sting?"

"I'm not in the FBI anymore."

"Ex-FBI agents aren't the best clients. Besides, it's

too easy. It's so simple I would probably die of boredom two minutes in. Dude. Seriously. Find another hacker."

"I'll pay you in cash—"

"*Um*, duh. You think I take credit cards or something?"

"If that's what you'd prefer—"

"No. I'd prefer Numenorean coins. If you happen to have any of those lying around."

"Newmin—"

"Never mind dude. Pay me in gold dust and we have a deal."

"Gold . . . dust?"

"My girlfriend wants gold dust for some Pinterest project. We got a deal or not?"

Nevis hesitated. He wasn't sure where to find gold dust.

"Oh my God, dude. I can literally feel myself growing old here. Yes or no?"

"Yes." Of course yes. He would ask around. Someone would know how to acquire gold dust.

9

· *HALLEY* ·

February, Florida Everglades

Halley felt sick to her stomach when she'd finished the call with Littlewood. If what Littlewood told her was true, Edmund wasn't just missing: he might be gone from their timeline. She wanted to take everything back from yesterday, to start all over again. If Littlewood was right, if space-time had pulled Edmund out of her timeline? It was too awful to consider. How would they ever find him? And if they couldn't, how was she going to face her life alone?

She couldn't live without Edmund, let alone raise a child without him. Hand on her belly, Halley told herself to calm down. To take the next steps. Call in sick to work. Eat something. Take a multi-vitamin. And drive north to Wellesley, *stat.*

"I couldn't really hear that conversation," said DaVinci. "What was Littlewood talking about?"

"I'll tell you on the drive. We're going to Wellesley."

"Got it." DaVinci hopped out of bed and pulled

on the same clothes she'd worn yesterday. "Let's go."

"Actually, give me a minute? I'm starving," murmured Halley. She had no idea how she could be hungry under the circumstances. Because she was pregnant, maybe? She had to eat, for the baby's sake.

While stuffing her overnight bag, Halley downed a protein bar she could barely swallow thanks to another dry, scratchy throat.

Within ten minutes, though, they were in DaVinci's car and on their way. Only at that point did Halley explain what Littlewood had told her about Edmund's disappearance.

"Two months ago, Littlewood thought he'd misplaced one of the manuscripts they brought back from the Great Library of Alexandria."

"Yeah, I remember Quintus saying something about that." DaVinci shook her head. "Classic Arthur Littlewood."

"Right. He *thought* he'd misplaced it, based on his forgetful habits. But then he and Everett realized there were three manuscripts missing, and at least two of them hadn't been taken out of their climate-control storage, like, *ever*."

"Oh my gosh, if Jules Khan is up to his old tricks stealing things—"

"No, no," said Halley. "It's worse."

"Worse than Khan?"

Halley swallowed and then winced, reaching for her throat.

"You okay?"

"Scratchy throat. I must've slept with my mouth open."

"Or it could've been all those tortilla chips. Here.

37

I made coffee while you were packing. Drink this."
DaVinci handed Halley the coffee. "And then, for the
love of cadmium white, tell me what could be worse
than Khan."

"About a week ago, Littlewood gets a text out of
the blue from Khan, saying they need to set up a
meeting."

"Wait—did Khan steal the missing stuff or didn't
he?"

"He didn't. But Khan has been seeing the same
thing Littlewood noticed. Things that were duplicated
and brought here from the past are . . . *disappearing.*"

"O-*kaaay*," said DaVinci, lingering on the second
syllable. "So now we think it's some kind of . . . time
warp thingamagizmo?"

"Khan and Littlewood think space-time is . . .
acting up or something. They're meeting later today to
discuss things." She twisted her wedding ring, feeling
more hopeless than ever.

"Meeting. Today. With Khan." DaVinci arched a
skeptical-looking brow.

"Yes," said Halley. "In a neutral location, with
Quintus there as . . . security."

"Oh. *Oh.* Well, if Quintus is security, I guess we're
safe enough. But still. *Khan?* Really? Ugh."

"I know, but if there's even a chance he knows
something we don't—"

"Right. Of course." DaVinci shook her head and
blew out a long breath. "Never thought I'd be glad to
see Jules Khan."

After that, DaVinci was silent for a minute, taking
everything in. Then she struck the steering wheel.

"Your wedding ring ruby! It's from 1598. Did

space-time take it, too?"

So far, Halley had held it together. She'd had to, to get DaVinci up to speed before they all gathered with Littlewood, but at the mention of her ring, Halley's calm disintegrated. Large tears fell from her eyes.

"Oh, girlfriend," said DaVinci. "I'm so sorry about your ring."

A small and somewhat hysterical laugh escaped Halley's mouth, and then, she managed to choke out what DaVinci hadn't yet pieced together for herself.

"It's not—" She swallowed hard, trying to contain her rising panic. "The ruby isn't . . . what I'm worried about."

"What then?"

"*It's* . . . Edmund."

"Oh no." DaVinci's face paled. "Space-time took Edmund?"

# 10

## · GEOFFREY ·

### February 1601, London

Geoffrey Philemon Aldwych stared gloomily out of the stone manor, ancestral home of his forefathers. It was not an inspiring view; his third story bedroom window overlooked the midden heap. A fitting view, maybe, for a younger son with no prospects. His entire life was shite, so why should his view not include it as well?

If only his older brother would die. Nay—for even in death Edmund's offspring would defeat Geoffrey. Sour-faced Edmund, God-fearing Ned, had produced offspring. Geoffrey found it hard to believe, but the two boys delivered to Ned's wife in as many years indicated his brother had somehow managed to discover a route between Maria's thighs. One child and it might've been contestable. A bastard, maybe. Two—and two who looked so like Edmund? It was proof.

"Proof the universe doth conspire against me," muttered Geoffrey.

He turned from the unhappy prospect of the

midden heap. Edmund expected him to aid with the sheep today, or there would be angry words. Edmund in a temper was something Geoffrey preferred to avoid. However, if he went to London instead of assisting his brother, Geoffrey could avoid all of it: his brother, his brother's temper, *and* the sheep. Now that he thought of it, Geoffrey felt the desire for a different kind of mutton. A buxom lass who would part her legs for a penny and tell him what a handsome man he was, such a large, comely, desirable, pleasing man.

He slid from his bed and shoved his feet into boots polished with a care that was not in evidence in the rest of his wardrobe. His doublet was missing buttons, and his codpiece had a hole in it, the woolen stuffing showing brightly white against the black. He did not mind having attention drawn to his member, but not in this fashion. He grumbled against the laziness of servants meant to look after his clothing. Never mind that as oft as not Geoffrey retired in his clothing, rendering it inaccessible for a needlewoman's attentions. Noting the curtains enclosing his bed had a black border, Geoffrey seized his dagger and cut a jagged square of the black cloth. This, he stuffed in into his codpiece, effectively disguising the presence of the hole. Perhaps at the brothel he could tease Nell or Nan into a good enough humor to mend the tear, after he'd dipped his quill in the inkwell of course.

Slipping his dagger back into its sheath, he then strapped on his rapier, tied his cloak jauntily over one shoulder, and strode out to the horses. From thence he rode the seven miles to town, to the narrow lanes of London's finest houses of ill repute. Well, perhaps not *finest*, but fine enough for Geoffrey.

He sank onto his accustomed stool, tired after his late hours last night. Perhaps he ought to fortify himself so as to avoid the humiliation of finding himself not . . . up to the task. Signaling for ale, he glanced around the inn. It was crowded for so early an hour. Or perhaps it wasn't early after all. The gray sky hid the sun and hour from him alike.

Geoffrey sipped his ale quietly, listening in on several of the conversations before choosing one upon which to focus his attention. The group of men were strangers to him, except for Nicholas Rowntree. Nick was one of Lord Devereux's men. The four at Nick's table were arguing the merits of two of London's troupes of actors. Nick was for offering "the job" to the Lord Chamberlain's men, while two of the others argued different players would do the job with less questions asked.

"And the fewer questions the better, eh, lads?"

"But if the theatre standeth empty," argued Nick, "it matters not how well they play their parts. We must persuade the Lord Chamberlain's men, who can draw greater numbers."

Geoffrey continued eavesdropping, gradually ascertaining Lord Devereux wished to see *Richard II* played, to the end that it might stir Londoners to rebel against their queen. Geoffrey had small love for his queen. He had room for only one great love: *self*-love. Thus, when the talk turned to how the Lord Chamberlain's Men might be persuaded to put on the play, and when money was proposed as a universal solver of problems, Geoffrey stood and joined the group.

"I know the Lord Chamberlain's Men. I can

persuade them to perform this play."

He had their attention.

"It is not a popular play," he said. "However, for the right price, they will do it."

Twenty minutes later, Geoffrey found himself in possession of fifty shillings, and a threat against a bodily part of which he was very fond, should he consider pocketing the shillings for his own use.

"We know where thou dwellest," said Nick Rowntree.

Nick was not smiling. Nick did not threaten idly. And Geoffrey was not pocketing the money for his own use.

However, by the time he reached the tavern preferred by the Lord Chamberlain's men, he had determined to hold back ten shillings for himself. Forty was still substantial sum, and moreover a sum he felt certain they would accept.

There was however, another request he would make of them: and if he paid them *five* and forty shillings, might not he be allowed to strut upon the stage as an actor? Not as Richard of course—too many speeches. A duke perhaps, or an earl. Yes. He thought he could manage an earl quite well. It was as close to an earldom as he was like to get. Damn Edmund, the second earl of Shaftesbury. And damn his two sons as well.

# 11

## · *HALLEY* ·

### February, Wellesley

Halley and DaVinci joined Jillian, Everett, Quintus, and Dr. Littlewood in Wellesley, Florida, above the basement laboratory, in what had become a cozy art studio for DaVinci. DaVinci had hauled several "free to a good home" couches from the sidewalks in front of USCF student housing after graduation last year, making the space far more inviting than the lab.

"So where do we think Edmund went?" Halley demanded, almost before everyone had sat down.

"We don't know," Littlewood admitted glumly.

"There are a limited number of possibilities," said Everett.

"*So*," said DaVinci, "do we get to hear these possibilities?"

"Well," said Littlewood, "our guesses are based upon our hypothesis that matter is never simply lost."

At the word *lost*, Halley swallowed hard, which sent pain shooting down her throat.

"So Edmund's not *lost*," said Jillian.

"Good heavens, I should think not," said Littlewood. "That would fly in the face of all we know about—"

"Did he go back to 1598?" asked Halley.

"Ah. Perhaps," said Littlewood. "Or perhaps he will have returned to early 1601."

"1601?" asked Halley, baffled.

"He's been here two and a half years," explained Everett. "So he may have returned two and a half years forward of where he was inadvertently duplicated, which would make it February, 1601."

Halley nodded. "Okay." It was a start. 1601. They had a date.

"But, ah, purely hypothetically speaking, there is another issue," said Arthur Littlewood. "We are guessing based on space-time's other behaviors that matter is not simply lost, but we don't know it for an absolute certainty. Do objects and, ah, *persons* travel somewhere or do they simply disappear? If our preliminary conjecture is correct, our outlook on chaotic isotemporal return pockets is at least . . . *hopeful*." Arthur Littlewood sighed heavily and set his folded hands in his lap, looking anything but hopeful.

A movement in the corner of her eye caught Halley's attention. Everett had removed Jillian's balled fist from her lap and taken it into his hand. Halley would have given anything to feel Edmund's hand in hers right now.

"The question is this," said Everett. "If objects—well—let's use Edmund as an example. If he has returned to the past, are there now *two* Edmunds in the past?"

In her mind's eye, Halley saw two Edmunds, one

on each arm. She couldn't decide if that was horrific or kind of sexy.

"How else would it work?" asked DaVinci.

"We don't know, but two of any of us would create the potential for the disruption of the historical timeline as we know it," said Everett.

"Not to mention confusion for those involved," said Jillian.

Quintus straightened. "Should I find myself returned to ancient Roma once more and discover that my other self lives, I will fall upon my sword in a remote location, so as to preserve the continuity of time."

DaVinci backhanded his shoulder. "You'll do no such thing!"

Quintus looked as though he was preparing to reply, but Jillian cut him off.

"There are additional implications for Everett if he vanishes," she said, gazing at him. "If he returns to 1918, and there aren't two of them . . ." Her voice trembled. "That is, if he were 'merged' to the Everett who exists in 1918, both of them would die in 1918."

Everett nodded, his eyes fixed on his shoes.

"Please," said Littlewood, "let's not get ahead of ourselves. We have yet to run an experiment which proved one thing or another conclusively."

"Quintus and I returned to the Great Library in Alexandria to look for our missing manuscripts," said Everett.

"What did you find there?" asked Halley. If the manuscripts had returned to the library, would that mean there was hope for finding Edmund in the past as well?

"We looked for our manuscript a few minutes prior to the time from which we first removed it to confirm it still existed, which it did, and then we traveled back a second time to a few minutes *after* the time when we'd first removed it. On that journey as well, we found only one version on its shelf," said Everett.

Littlewood spoke. "But I've felt all along that it's equally or perhaps even *more* likely items will return to their original time *plus* the time for which they have been 'duplicated'—that is, for manuscripts we've kept for a year, they will return one year forward of where we first got them."

"Did you go and look there? Or . . . then?" asked Halley.

"We did," said Quintus.

"But our findings were again inconclusive," said Littlewood.

"How many copies did you find in the plus-one-year, er, past?" asked Halley.

"In one instance, we found one manuscript," said Everett.

Littlewood added, "Which is impossible to identify as original or duplicate or . . ." He shrugged helplessly.

"In another case," said Everett, "we found no manuscript. Which could have meant someone had removed it."

"Or even lost or destroyed it," said Quintus.

"Rendering our experiment once again inconclusive," said Littlewood.

"Is it possible the duplicate copy that vanished doesn't exist anywhere?" Halley asked softly.

"Ah. Yes. Well," said Littlewood, "at this point, we simply don't know."

"However," said Everett, "while experiments on inanimate objects will tell us little, if we were able to speak to Edmund in 1601, we'd have some answers."

"If there were two of him, each would surely notice the presence of the other," said Quintus.

"And if there was only one of him," said Everett, "it would be a matter of . . . which Edmund was there, and did he recognize us or not."

Littlewood's watch alarm sounded shrilly. "Ah. It is time to meet with Jules Khan."

The group piled into a van belonging to Quintus and drove to Our Lady of Mercy Catholic Church for the meeting. Quintus seemed to have decided Littlewood needed some prepping.

"You frequently display nervous mannerisms," said Quintus. "I must advise you to conceal your nerves, as this may assist you to baffle and defeat your enemy."

"Right," said Halley, " but at this time, Khan isn't our enemy."

"*Yet*," said DaVinci.

"Our situation," said Everett, "has put us in a position where we have no choice but to consult with Dr. Khan, but I don't trust him farther than I can throw him."

"At least he won't get to snoop around the lab," said DaVinci.

"Father Joe permits our use of the Sunday School classrooms for just that reason," said Quintus.

"Not to mention, to encourage you to not accidentally-on-purpose kill Khan," murmured

DaVinci.

"I have already vowed I will not kill him," said Quintus.

"I'm sure you won't, babe, but I'm sticking by your side just in case he presents too tempting a target," replied DaVinci.

Quintus nodded curtly. "While I may wish to end his miserable life, I recognize we must consult him if we are to learn more concerning these disappearances and how to prevent or cure them."

"Totally," said DaVinci. "Our need for information is an excellent reason to avoid manslaughter."

The group arrived and then stood waiting outside for Khan in the balmy afternoon breeze.

At four-thirty, Jules Khan turned into the church parking lot.

"Everyone remember," said Jillian, "we're not mentioning where Everett and, *er*, Edmund are from."

Halley didn't think this was important. What did it matter if Khan knew they'd brought people from the past? The only thing that mattered was getting Edmund *back*.

Khan approached them, looking every inch a puppy with its tail between its legs. Or maybe, thought Halley, he looked . . . *scared*. Especially once he spotted Quintus, who was currently making fists, like he was restraining himself from anything worse.

The group moved to the fourth through sixth grade Sunday School classroom. No one had thought to bring adult-size chairs into the room. DaVinci, Halley, and Jillian fit in the small chairs just fine, and Littlewood and Khan were slight of build, but Everett was large, and Quintus looked particularly uncomfortable in his small red plastic seat.

"Well, then," said Arthur Littlewood, "here we are." He ran an anxious hand through his hair before catching Quintus's eye, at which point he dropped his hand and laughed nervously. "Jules, I believe you, ah, had things you wished to discuss with me?"

"Yes," said Khan, slowly. "But first, please allow me to make a sincere apology to the young man I inadvertently, *er*, brought to this century."

"His name is Quintus," said DaVinci. "And you totally owe him."

"I forgive the consequences of your error," said Quintus, glaring as though forgiveness were the last thing on his mind.

It was certainly a qualified forgiveness, thought Halley.

Khan hemmed softly, looking away from the Roman and back to Littlewood.

"Right," said Littlewood, clapping his hands softly together.

"As I wrote," began Khan, "I have observed several alarming anomalies in the past month. Objects obtained by my . . . *duplicate self* have been reported as stolen—"

"We don't think they were stolen," said Littlewood.

Khan hesitated. "I don't either. But . . . what brought you to this conclusion?"

Littlewood detailed his own list of items from the past which had vanished, notably leaving Edmund *out*.

Where was Edmund right now? She felt slightly sick to her stomach. She was exhausted. She had a headache and her throat was dry. Were all these things side effects of pregnancy? Couldn't life maybe slow down for one second so that she could research being with child?

*Of course not.*

She retrained her attention on Khan and Littlewood.

The two were discussing the nonlinear nature of the disappearances—how objects that vanished did so in a highly chaotic fashion, following no pattern that might link length of time in the modern world to either distance traveled through time or even the chronology of the objects' removals from time.

"Prior to these incidents," said Khan, "everything we've observed has behaved in so regulated a manner. We don't have many data points, admittedly, but perhaps by combining our data, we can begin to see a pattern that is now hidden from us."

"We need more than some stupid pattern," snapped DaVinci. "We need a solution."

"We also need to determine," added Quintus, "to where and to when things are vanishing."

Everett chimed in. "And will they return, or is disappearance a permanent condition?"

"We are at a loss," said Littlewood. He looked hopefully to Khan. "Unless, Jules . . . ?"

Khan's eyes darted nervously around the room, and then he seemed to make a decision to share something. "My thinking is that by examining the fluctuation of the second order energy-time term in the conservation equation, it is conceivable that an isotemporal return pocket could coalesce around a shifted entity."

"Do the equations support this?" asked Littlewood.

Halley soon stopped listening to the discussion, lost in thoughts of her last conversation with Edmund. The angry words she'd spoken. How upset he'd been. She shouldn't have shouted at him. She shouldn't have hidden things from him. She would have given anything to have him back in the room to tell him she was willing to try to understand things from his point of view. She couldn't imagine the next nine months of her life without him. And after her pregnancy came to term? How would she manage alone? How could she be a mother without him at her side?

DaVinci gave her a sharp nudge in the ribs, and Halley turned her attention back to Littlewood, who seemed to be answering a question Khan had raised.

"I'm afraid it's not that simple," said Littlewood. "The system is highly nonlinear and chaotic so the appearance of an isotemporal return pocket could be pseudo-random."

"For the non-scientists," said Jillian, addressing Halley, Quintus, and DaVinci, "he's saying things are vanishing randomly—not first-in, first-out. And that a chaotic and non-linear system could account for this."

"Yes," agreed Littlewood, "but what I don't understand is where the energy for the return is coming from."

While Littlewood was speaking, Halley's attention had drifted to Khan. Because of this, she noticed that Khan's face paled as Littlewood admitted his confusion about the source of energy. Did Khan know something he wasn't telling them?

Littlewood, not observing Khan's demeanor,

continued. "Unfortunately, there is only one thing which the data tell us clearly these temporal return pockets, and that is that they are unpredictable.

"There is a slight possibility . . ." Khan broke off, frowning.

"Is there something you're keeping back?" demanded Halley.

"It's just . . . I've been working on an experimental device—"

"Please tell me you're not building a time machine," said DaVinci.

Khan said nothing.

"Oh my God. No. Just . . . seriously?" DaVinci threw her hands up, got up from the red plastic chair, and began pacing next to the windows on one side of the classroom.

Khan cleared his throat. "There have been . . . in my work . . . anomalies . . ."

"Good grief, man!" Littlewood was yanking his hair straight up from his scalp. "If you know something, tell us."

"I don't want to jump to conclusions," replied Khan. "I need to spend some time digesting your ideas, and then we should consult again."

"I could go back with you," offered Littlewood.

"No!" Khan looked appalled. Or terrified. Halley wasn't sure which. "I mean, that won't work right now. Bad timing. Maybe another time."

After a few more questions from Littlewood, every last one of which Khan demurred from answering, Khan declared he needed to leave.

"Or I'll miss my return flight," he said, eyes darting around nervously.

Halley wanted to call him on it, demand proof in the form of an airline ticket, but Littlewood seemed ready to call it a day.

"We'll stay in touch," said Littlewood, running a hand through his messy hair.

"Of course," Khan said, a little too quickly. "Of course."

Halley frowned. Khan was hiding something. Or a lot of somethings.

As soon as they heard Khan's car leave the parking lot, she was the first to speak.

"What's he hiding?"

# 12

## · HALLEY ·

### February, Wellesley

Halley's question of what Khan might be hiding from them was met with awkward silence. With Khan, who knew? Only one thing was certain: he would act in an ethical manner only for as long as it served his purposes.

"Maybe we should be asking ourselves what he hoped to gain today," suggested Jillian.

"And whether or not he gained it," said Everett.

Halley and Littlewood nodded in tandem while DaVinci emitted an exasperated sigh. Quintus looked gravely out the window to where Khan had driven away.

"I told him prior to our meeting I could no longer admit him to the lab," said Littlewood, "so he came here for something besides an, ah, glimpse at what we've been up to since he and I parted ways."

"That's true," said Everett. "So he was hoping for a different kind of information than what he could gain by a look at our facility."

"He was scared," said Halley, with a quick glance at Quintus.

DaVinci, also looking at Quintus, patted his bicep. "Good job, babe."

"No, not that kind of scared," said Halley.

Quintus raised one eyebrow.

"I'm sure he was totally scared of you, Quintus," Halley said, "but there was something else too."

"I think it's pretty obvious," said Everett. "He's scared of the same thing we are: are those of us displaced from time going to end up like Edmund?"

Like Edmund.

Halley felt her calm veneer about to give way to a new round of tears.

"We still don't know if that's what happened to Edmund," said Jillian, pointedly making eye contact with Halley.

Halley let out the breath she'd been holding. She had to keep it together. Crying solved nothing, and they had a lot of solving ahead of them. She took two calming breaths and then shared a discovery she'd made while Littlewood and Khan were dialoguing.

"I discovered something about Edmund. Well, his phone. It's . . . *gone.* I tried locating it with 'Find my Phone' and another GPS app on his laptop, but . . . there's nothing. It doesn't exist. Period."

"Ah," said Littlewood, fixing his gaze on the polished floor. "So he is gone. I think we must assume the disappearance preserves some sort of stability, however chaotic."

Halley didn't think she could stand getting bogged down yet again in another hypothetical discussion of space-time. They needed to discuss Khan first, and finding Edmund immediately after.

"So here's what I think about Khan," she said. "I agree he's afraid he'll be next. I know we didn't discuss it, but how could he not be worried about that? And I think the device he mentioned is his way of trying to make sure he sticks around. Like, so he can duplicate himself or something."

"Oh," said DaVinci, nodding. "Classic mad scientist, right? Make sure you live eternally or whatever."

Littlewood frowned. "The idea is not without merit, but Khan assuredly knows he cannot achieve any connected sort of existence, which would be the only kind of immortality he would wish for. Duplicate selves would have separate motives and agendas and might even conspire against him. I think additional selves would be the very last thing Khan would want."

"So do you *not* think he's building a time machine?" asked DaVinci.

"I think we can assume he has," said Littlewood. "And we can assume he's using information he got from me to do it, just as his other self did in 2001."

"And if he came to you *now* because he's afraid," said Everett, "what might that mean?"

"What if . . ." Jillian broke off, her brows pulling together. "Okay, this might sound a little out there, but what if you built a machine incorrectly? Could you, I don't know, 'harm' space-time? Like a chef introducing botulism into a restaurant kitchen?"

"He completely freaked out when you said something about energy," said Halley. "I was watching him pretty closely, and that was a turning point for him. He clammed up after that."

"Energy? Well that certainly bears thinking about," said Littlewood, frowning. "Although as to Jillian's question about 'harming' space-time, no, that isn't a possibility. In that analogy, space-time would be more like the stainless steel counters than the food."

"The counters could *harbor* bacteria but not be harmed by it," said Jillian.

"Well, all analogies break down, of course . . ." Littlewood seemed to lose the train of his thought.

"But none of this gets us any closer to finding Edmund," said Halley. It was like they were all watching a building burning down and discussing the colors of the flames instead of how to rescue the people trapped inside. "Where is he? How do we figure that out? How do we rescue him?"

Her voice cracked on the word "rescue." Where was Edmund? Was he afraid? Alone? Had he . . . *ceased to exist*?

"Halley is right," said Everett. "Our first order of business is finding Edmund."

"Ah," said Littlewood. "Yes."

Halley held her breath, waiting for him to continue, but it was Everett who spoke next.

"What we must learn is where objects and persons go when they vanish," Everett said.

"Not only Edmund, but Everett and I stand to lose much if we cannot make this determination," added Quintus.

"*Um*, excuse me, but we *all* have a lot to lose here," DaVinci murmured.

Quintus continued. "We must determine whether we can retrieve people lost in this manner."

"And having done so, can we prevent the process

from repeating?" said Jillian.

"I need to understand where the energy is coming from to effect the transfers from one temporal plane of existence to another," muttered Littlewood. "We need to devise an experimental method whereby—"

"With all due respect," said Halley, "you've run experiments. What we need to do now is launch a rescue."

# 13

## · *GEOFFREY* ·

### February 1601, London

Geoffrey Aldwych had frequented the tiring house in back of the Globe Theatre on several occasions, but until now, never during a performance. And today, the seventh of February, 1601, not only was he on the unaccustomed side of the stage, he was there as a player, expected to shortly deliver his single line of, "Aye, my lord," along with a bow and hasty retreat.

The hastier the better.

He would have liked to make his retreat *now*, abandoning any present or future interest in the actor's life, which he had up till now desired. He peered from behind the curtain that blocked the audience's view of the cramped backstage area. If he was hoping the glimpse of audience would draw out bravado from his inmost depths, he was sorely disappointed. The view of a theatre, more full than empty, had the opposite effect, and he was seized with an even stronger impulse to flee.

"Five minutes," said the stage manager.

Geoffrey was going to be sick.

"If thy stomach is in rebellion, see thou quell it *now*," muttered the manager as he brushed past Geoffrey. "And away from thy garb."

He'd been found out. The embarrassment was sufficient to restore some measure of courage. He was an Aldwych, and noble born. Geoffrey adjusted his rapier and his codpiece. And cursed loudly.

"'S'blood!'"

"What ails thee now?" asked Moll, a pretty fixture at the theatre who had twice rebuffed his advances.

He pointed to the codpiece covering his crotch.

"I've told thee already thou shalt ne'er lodge thy rapier—"

"You mistake me," said Geoffrey. He tugged at a piece of woolen stuffing that had worked through a hole in his codpiece, bright white fuzz against a sable background.

Moll shook her head while raising her eyes to heaven. "If thou wouldst but leave off touching thyself—"

"Will you mend the hole?" he demanded, face burning crimson.

Moll considered his crotch. "I suppose we cannot have thee parade onstage thus."

He began to undo the ties that held his codpiece to his hose.

"Nay, thou need'st not un-man thyself," Moll said with a smirk. "I can sew you together while you stand."

She was laughing at him. Geoffrey couldn't remember what he'd seen in her.

The entire time she sewed, she made remarks

upon his size and how she had no fear, at least, of pricking him with her needle, so slight a man was he. When he grew silent, however, she seemed to think she'd gone too far.

"Now, then. Let us change thy sable doublet for one more befitting 'Sir Piers Exton, *rebel*,'" she said. With this, she handed him a scarlet-lined cloak in exchange for his dull one.

He mumbled his thanks, agreeing the scarlet lining *was* nicer. And anyway, Moll's jibes had taken away his earlier nervousness. Perhaps that had been her intention. Perhaps she wasn't so bad after all.

By the time the musicians struck their first notes, Geoffrey was resigned to the fact he must appear onstage, which was a far cry from his initial enthusiasm for the undertaking, but was much better than being sick in the wings. He could do this and then be done with it forever. In fact, maybe he would turn shepherd after this. Shepherds never had to appear in front of any assembly more terrifying than sheep. The next time his brother needed help with the sheep, Geoffrey vowed to assist without complaint. Or at least, with less complaining than was his habit.

The stage manager had reduced Geoffrey's appearances onstage to one scene only. Backstage during nearly the whole performance, he was frequently in the way of actors entering or exiting the stage, but at least he had a good view of the entertainment. And it *was* good entertainment. At the opening of Act 4, the scene where King Richard II was made to renounce his crown, a brawl broke out in the audience between supporters of Lord Devereux and supporters of Sir Robert Cecil. Two hulking actors leapt from the stage, rapiers drawn, threatening the brawlers away from the front of the house so that the deposing of the ill-fated king might be accomplished.

In spite of the goodly entertainment, Geoffrey had never been more glad to hear the applause signaling the end of a performance. He followed the actors on the blustery afternoon to their favored tavern, the Mermaid. Inside was warmth and camaraderie. In a fit of gratitude—either for having been included onstage or because he would never again have to be onstage, he paid for a round of canary for everyone. As canary cost several times what ale did, his generosity made him popular, and a few rounds in, he even persuaded himself his earlier cowardice as an actor would go unnoted.

The noting of his cowardice, however, was not what he ought to have been worried about. He ought to have been concerned about the testimony of two fellow actors, who reported Geoffrey had brokered the agreement between the Lord Chamberlain's Men and the Percy brothers for the production of *Richard II*. By the morrow, it was whispered, and then shouted, that the play had been intended to rouse Londoners to support the deposition of the current monarch Elizabeth I.

Geoffrey ought to have been concerned about being branded with the epithet *traitor* rather than that of *coward*. Unfortunately, by the morning of February 8, 1601, when Sir Robert Cecil had the mayor and heralds denounce Lord Devereux as a traitor, Geoffrey was passed-out drunk, beyond caring about being branded with any epithet.

# 14

## · GEOFFREY ·

### February 1601, London

Geoffrey awoke to the sound of someone shouting. At him. He blinked and the world seemed to reel, so he squeezed his eyes tight shut. The someone continued to shout. Geoffrey caught a few of the words: *apprehended . . . name of . . . Majesty . . . traitor . . . confined . . .* And then the ground seemed to slip away from under him.

His eyes flew open and he realized he was being bodily raised by others, his hands secured behind his back. A rough push between his shoulders propelled him forward, out of the alehouse, and into a rude conveyance. Within, similarly bound, he recognized Charles and Joscelyn Percy, alongside Nick Rowntree.

The cart lurched forward.

The contents of Geoffrey's stomach lurched forward too.

Rowntree protested. "Thou degenerate, fat-kidneyed, cot-quean!"

The Percys, white-faced and silent, seemed not to

have noticed.

With his stomach somewhat emptied, Geoffrey spoke. "Wither are we bound?"

"Her Majesty intends to offer us lodging within the Tower," replied Rowntree.

Geoffrey's stomach lurched again.

"Have a care, thou rank-scented dullard!" snapped Rowntree, whose boots were now besmirched.

"Upon what charge are we to be confined?" asked Geoffrey, eyeing Charles and Joscelyn. He feared his countenance must resemble their pale ones.

"We are to be examined," said Rowntree, "that Her Majesty's Privy Council might determine whether we are traitors to the Crown or no."

"I'm no traitor," protested Geoffrey. He called to the driver. "Sirrah! Un-cuff me at once. I am Her Majesty's loyal subject!"

The cart driver paid him no mind. Rowntree gave an accusatory glare.

"I am no traitor!" Geoffrey insisted to Rowntree.

"And thou hang'st not, I'll skewer thee myself!" growled Rowntree. He then began a mumbled litany of complaints against *actors*.

From this point until they crossed the drawbridge to enter the grounds of palace and prison, the Tower of London, Geoffrey held his peace.

However, upon being installed within a private cell in Beauchamp Tower—dank, cold, and smelling of things Geoffrey had rather not contemplate—he began to call loudly for pen and ink. For the first hour, no one answered him, but eventually the jailor who brought his supper of pease porridge and ill-looking water said that he might know where pen and ink were to be found.

"Please, my good man," said Geoffrey, although the jailor looked neither good nor manly, "bring it to me at once. My brother and his family will be sick with worry, not knowing where I am." The truth in this declaration was stretched as upon the rack. "I beg of you, a pen."

"I own no pen myself," said the jailor, "having no use for one. However, if you were to part with that scarlet-lined cloak, I might beg a pen of the constable's deputy."

"Curse you for a cozener!" cried Geoffrey.

The jailor shrugged and turned to leave.

"Nay! Wait! I spoke in haste," said Geoffrey. His only hope lay in writing to Ned. "It is only that I mistook the exorbitance of items purchased within these walls, which must of course be more costly than items got outside. I am sure thy expenses are similarly exorbitant, else thou wouldst not have asked."

The jailor offered him a thin-lipped smile.

"Here. It is thine, as a gift," said Geoffrey, passing the cloak to the serving man. After all, the garment wasn't even his to begin with.

An hour later, the man returned with . . . a pen and an inkpot. *Only* a pen and an inkpot.

"Where is the paper thou didst promise?" asked Geoffrey, with a degree of politeness he did not feel the occasion warranted.

"I agreed to trade your cloak for a pen." The jailor's voice was as oily as his face.

"Of what use is a pen with no paper?" demanded Geoffrey.

"I wot not," replied the jailor, turning to shuffle off.

"Wait!"

The man turned.

"What price do you ask for a sheet of paper?"

The jailor smiled. "I might exchange that ring you wear—"

"Done!" Geoffrey wrenched the ring from his finger and held it out. "Only please delay not. My brother—"

"Aye, aye. Thy brother knows not where ye are to be found." The man departed with Geoffrey's ring and a grunt of satisfaction.

An hour later, when all was dark, Geoffrey began to despair of paper ever being brought to him. Moreover, should it be delivered now, he would have to undertake negotiations for a candle, as the room had none. He shivered. The room was not only dark, it was chill. He had no fire, although there was a fireplace and even a chimney such as those the previous Earl of Shaftesbury had installed throughout Hensley Manor. What would a fire cost him, he wondered?

From a distance less remote than Geoffrey would have liked, screams and pleas could now be heard. He tried plugging his ears with wool from his codpiece, which had sprung another leak, but the wool did nothing to shut out the noise. Eventually, however, the tortured soul must have confessed, for the screaming ceased. A few minutes later, Geoffrey's paper was delivered, and negotiations for a candle were begun, for which Geoffrey found he must pass through life without his second-best doublet.

"I say, fellow," said Geoffrey, "are these negotiations lawful, whereby you relieve me of my garments?"

"Once thy brother the earl hath pledged thy keep, we need bargain no more." The jailor smiled and spat. "Unless thou wouldst buy back from me what thou didst sell."

Having said this, the man began building a small fire for Geoffrey, who now realized he'd bought a candle he might have done without. He sulked but made no further verbal attacks on the man who had the power to spit in his pease porridge, or withhold it altogether.

Alone at last, and dressed only in shirtsleeves and fitted deerskin breeches over a pair of mouse-colored hose, Geoffrey began his letter, wondering what it would cost him to have it delivered.

*Dear brother Ned,*

*I am apprehended under false accusation of treason . . .*

## 15

### · EDMUND ·

February 1601, London

Shifting, Edmund kicked at the covers that twisted around his legs. The bed was of the sagging variety, having doubtless been slept in by so many guests that a furrow had been worn into the mattress. He sighed. Halley's job in the Everglades lasted another three weeks. Well, he'd encountered worse mattresses in the 16th century. He shifted again, sinking into the trough. Then again, perhaps he had not.

He closed his eyes and tried to force himself back to sleep, but he was thirsty, and Halley was snoring lightly, both of which were bringing him to more complete wakefulness. The snoring was . . . *odd*. Halley was a very quiet sleeper. He nearly reached out to nudge her, but then decided against it. If she awoke, she would not thank him for it. She would be angry—

His eyes flew open as yesterday's discoveries came flooding back into his mind. The pill. The secret Halley had been keeping from him for months—or longer. The remembrance of her duplicity brought him more fully awake. There would be no more sleeping tonight.

Throwing back the heavy bedcover, he sat up and swung his feet off the side of the bed. Where he encountered . . . a heavy fabric preventing his exit. Had Halley wheeled a garment rack into their bedroom? It wouldn't be the first time. He shoved himself farther down the bed to avoid rattling the costumes. But here too, were more heavy fabrics. Something shifted in his mind as he recalled his bed in Hensley Manor, hung round with thick curtains. He could almost recall the ever-present scent of wood smoke that penetrated every fabric—God's wounds! Smoke! Something was burning in their hotel room. He pushed past the fabric, landing bare feet on . . . an icy *stone floor?*

This was not his hotel room.

He glanced at the light source to his left: a fire, burning low, with glowing embers. And to his right . . . his eyes traced the faint outline of the great window of his bed chamber in Hensley. Good God!

He must be dreaming. He had somehow, through the frustrations of the day, dreamt himself into the world he had once known, and sometimes still yearned for. Yesterday, for instance. When he had learned of Halley's deception, how he had wished himself far from her century with its pills and contrivances. How he had yearned for a simpler life where a man might, by the sweat of honest labor, provide a home for his family—*his family*—and for those who depended upon him for their own livelihoods.

He sighed. A dream, then. How real the fire felt as he approached it. Its heat penetrated his jeans—

how strange that he was wearing 21$^{st}$ century garb in this dream! It was not a choice suited to this place. His tee shirt, in particular, was not up to the task of keeping him warm in the frigid stone building. His eyes caught on an antechamber—his dressing closet— and he strode to it, grabbing his fur-lined cloak. In defiance of fashion, he turned the collar upward, buttoning it like an old man, before sinking into his chair before the fire.

He stirred the embers. The dream was so seeming real. In a moment he would awaken to find himself in a hotel room in the Florida Everglades, yearning for a past long gone. The door creaked open and a servant entered, carrying kindling and a large log.

"Good morrow, my lord," whispered the servant.

It was the younger sister of the girl he had rescued the day he first met Halley. What was her name? Joan? Jenny? He frowned. Paused. How would he know the rescued child had a sister, much less an idea of what her name might be? More dream illogic, he supposed. He returned the child's greeting.

"Good morrow to thee."

This elicited a wide grin from the girl. She was missing several teeth. There had been an incident, Edmund recalled, with a horned ram. But how did he know this? Unless . . .

Unless this *wasn't* a dream.

But what else could it be? Time travel? He'd been nowhere near Littlewood's time machine recently. It had to be a dream.

The girl swept ashes into a bucket, built up the fire, and departed with a bow.

"On her way to my brother's chambers,"

murmured Edmund, certain of her next task. He felt a brush of longing for his brother Geoffrey. How he had missed all of them.

And how hungry he was. He did not normally feel hunger in dreams. Now, though, he felt as if he could consume an entire loaf of bread and a wheel of Mistress Cartwright's excellent cheese. And why not? After pulling on his sheepskin boots, fleece-lined for warmth, he strode along the halls he remembered so well, seeking passage to the larder. Various members of his household bowed in deference as he passed, and he greeted each by name.

It was not until he located bread and cheese and began eating that the back of his neck prickled with unease. He could *taste* the wild-yeast tang of the bread. Food never had flavor in his dreams. Texture, perhaps, although often it was the *wrong* texture: meat that chewed like cake, cake that became dry dust—these were "normal" in his dreams. But this cheese tasted like *cheese*. A most excellent and well-aged cheese.

His neck prickled again. This "dream" had none of the qualities of a dream.

He tried to recall his last thoughts prior to awakening in his 16th century bed. Sunshine. A warm February afternoon. Fatigue. He had been walking along the highway, sorting his thoughts—

He stopped chewing. *Halley!* If this was no dream, what must his wife be thinking? But if he was *here* and . . . and *now*, Halley did not yet exist. The thought filled him with dismay. If the past had somehow reclaimed him, would that mean Halley would never have met him? He wished suddenly that he could speak to her— even for a handful of seconds, to tell her he loved her.

To say he was sorry for how they had parted, nay—to confess it had been childish of him to have stormed off rather than to have listened to her. The thought that in some far-flung future, she might believe he had abandoned her? It was too horrible to contemplate.

He swallowed suddenly, a too-large portion, and felt his throat constricting in protest. These sensations, too, were not normal in dreams. He looked about him, in desperate hope the larder would transform into a field with oaks, or that he would find himself now on the deck of a ship at sea. But this dream had not shifted location even once, thought such was customary within the landscape of Edmund's dreams. He closed his eyes tightly, willing the scene before him to change.

His eyes opened. The scene had not shifted.

"Ale, my lord?" asked Nan. *Nan!* It was the rescued girl herself, except that she looked older than she ought to. Was this a bit of dream illogic after all?

"Nay," he said on a sudden impulse. "I'll take coffee this morn."

Nan stared at him, perplexed. "Cough-fee, my lord?"

"Ale," he said, covering quickly. "Some of your cousin's small beer." How did he know she had a cousin? Or that her cousin brewed small beer?

But dwarfing these questions was the one he could not answer: wherefore had he arrived here, in Hensley Manor, in the 16$^{th}$ century?

# 16

## · *EDMUND* ·

### February 1601, London

Edmund strode along the dim corridors toward his chambers, feeling a heaviness he had known only once before, and in another century far from this. When first he had realized that staying with Halley meant the loss of everything he knew, of every plan and every acquaintance—that it meant adopting an entirely different life, he had felt a measure of despair. Was he now to experience this a second time? He had grown accustomed to life in the 21st century. He had a good life there. A *wife* there! And friends. And plans. Must he once again face the wrenching sensation of belonging to a place where, also, he did *not* belong?

He arrived in his chambers. If he had truly slipped backward in time, his first order of business was to don clothing proper to this time. If he should encounter the Edmund of this time whilst he was dressed in such outlandish garb, what would that Edmund think? He would suspect devilry. His cloak and boots had thus far hidden from view his jeans and tee shirt, but were he to mount a horse or engage in labor requiring him to throw back his cloak, his odd clothing would appear impossibly strange.

He could not risk meeting the Edmund who belonged here, or being further mistook for him. He would have to leave. But that would mean living as an outlaw vagabond, liable to whipping in whatever town he should try to find labor or shelter. London would be safest . . . He grimaced. He had no love for the great city, far from the fields and flocks he loved here. The sea, then? Aye, that had been his dream once. But who would vouch for him? He would have to sell himself into indenture, and at unfavorable terms, too, as a man with no family, no past, no connections.

It was too much to consider all at once. First things first, as Halley was fond of saying. He must change clothes. This would warm him, too. It was February in Florida. Here, all felt cold as an English February.

Debating between velvet and woolen hose, he chose the woolen as the warmer of the two. It was a day for quilted breeches, too. He replaced his fleece lined boots on his stockinged feet. Had he a hat with earflaps hidden herein? He would have preferred a beanie, but only laborers wore such. Ah—there it was, an old-fashioned cap of his grandfather's, replete with earflaps. He tied them under his chin, noting the slight itch of the woolen ties. His linen shirt felt rough to his skin after years of tee shirts. He eyed his starched ruff with hesitance. Nay. He could not bear the feel of it, the stiff edges biting into a neck that had gone ruff-free for close to three years.

Suddenly he recalled sitting beside Halley as she

sewed a ruff last week for her Jacobean-era movie. He had told her he remembered when his mother had first placed a small ruff on him, and how he had disliked it. His heart pinched at both memories. What must Halley be thinking of his disappearance?

No. He had to stop dwelling on that life. It was a luxury in which he could not indulge—not if a rapier-carrying Edmund lay around the next corner. It was then Edmund realized there ought to have been, well, *three* in the bed he had recently left. Himself, the other Edmund, and his wife Maria. Good God! Maria . . . He'd been in bed with someone else's wife. Had the other Edmund been there too?

He knew himself to be something of a late riser. His other self must be abed still, for when had he last awoken in time to see a servant making up his fire? He shook his head as if to clear it. "When" was a very confounding question at present. So where was this other Edmund?

Hastily, he donned his third-best doublet and buttoned all four and twenty brass buttons. And then, over everything, he donned his rabbit-fur-lined cloak once more. His other self would understand.

Would he not? He ought perhaps to converse with himself. He knew himself to be rational and sympathetic to those needing assistance. No sooner had he thought this, he caught a glimpse of himself in the reflection of the dressing room window. What he saw made him feel ill. Had he, indeed, donned his old life so quickly? The symbolism struck him as hard as that horned ram had struck the serving girl. He looked every inch the Earl of Shaftesbury, not Edmund, husband of 21st century Halley. Was it so easy to throw aside that life? His eyes fell to his wedding band. *What must Halley be thinking?*

No. No, he was not throwing aside that life. He was only trying to stay alive in this one. Well, he was warm now at least, from the struggle of donning so many layers. Just before he left the antechamber, a sheet of paper caught his eye. He picked it up. It was a playbill, a notice stolen from London by his brother Geoffrey, advertising a performance of *Richard II*, "Including that Moste Infamous scene of his Deposition from ye Throne." He had not attended, he thought dismissively. But it was as if the thought belonged to someone else, a tickle of memory not his own. Good God, he could almost remember having told Geoffrey he would not attend, could almost recall Geoffrey's petulant reaction. From whence had he acquired the "memory"?

As he stepped back into his bedroom, silent but for his wife's snoring, he felt he must know how many persons lay in his bed. He approached the bedstead and drew back the curtain, peering inside the curtained bed. He saw no "second self"; the bed held only his wife, Maria. She always looked so lovely in the mornings. Unlike other women, his Maria had no need to paint color on those cheeks, those thick lips. Ah, those lips . . .

Edmund stepped back, startled by the recollection of the feel and taste of those lips on his. How could this be? He must be remembering Halley's lips. He stared at this *other* wife, blowing out a long-held breath.

Hearing him, Maria stirred. She turned and smiled at him just as a cry from the passageway caught their attention. Another scream, followed by laughter, high and shrill—a child's laughter.

"Husband, wilt thou . . ." She did not finish her sentence. Edmund saw she was pregnant. *Heavily* pregnant. Yes. Of course she was. He knew this. Her time was approaching. She wished for him to attend to their child. *Children.* They had two. Maria, his wife Maria, wished for another minute to lie abed before the labors of the day commenced. This, also, he knew without being asked.

"Of course, my love," he heard himself respond. "Rise thou when thou art ready." And then, because he needed an answer, he asked a question. "Thou mayst think it strange that I ask, but had I any plan to depart Hensley today, of which thou wert aware?"

She smiled lazily. "And I so near to delivering thy child? I should have divorced thee for departing today, as thou well know'st!"

"Of course," replied Edmund smoothly. He had not planned a journey. He never would have done so. He would have remained here, within call of his wife. Did that mean there was only . . . *one Edmund?* Had the other been obliterated by his reappearance? Ought he to feel guilt for having usurped the life of another? For having obliterated it?

"Husband?" Maria interrupted his thoughts, and he realized she was awaiting further response.

"Of course," he said. "Thou shouldst have divorced me, and I should have deserved it!" He kissed her hungrily before guilt made him break off, but within that kiss he had felt the shape and tenor of their relationship—her quick wit and his ready answers. The knowledge wafted through him, familiar as a top-forty pop song. Was he only imagining it, or had he stolen the memories of some Edmund now gone forever?

"The children, my husband," said Maria.

Glad of the reprieve from his confusion, Edmund crossed out of his bedchamber and into the passageway. Childish shrieking echoed off the high ceilings and down the passageway. And then Edmund saw him: Thomas, his eldest son.

In his mind's eye, he saw the Wikipedia entry for *Edmund Aldwych, Second Earl of Shaftesbury.* He had examined it so many times, it had seared itself into his memory.

*Children:*
*Thomas, 1599-1642*
*John, 1600-1666*
*Charles, 1601-1616*
*James, 1601-1609*
*Betsy, 1602-1679*
*Margaret, 1603-1691*
*Anne, 1604-1654*
*William, 1606-1607*
*Another James, 1609-1611, born the year the first James died of fever*
*Valentine, 1616-1700*

Swallowing, he bent to catch the boy running pell-mell toward him. He had a son. An heir. Here there were no preventatives to offspring. Here, he was a father!

"Papa!"

Hugging the boy to his breast, Edmund closed his eyes and swung the child round and round. His eyes watered with tears of gratitude. And of remorse, and of confusion . . .

But of one thing he felt certain: *he was home.*

# 17

## · *EDMUND* ·

### February 1601, London

Edmund kissed the warm, untidy hair of his eldest son.

"Papa! Down! Down!" cried Thomas. "Me *wite!*"

"Thou canst write?" asked Edmund. The wriggling of the child in his arms felt so familiar, as if the two had embraced hundreds of times and not this once.

"Now papa!"

The child's voice, shrill and piping, caught at Edmund's heart. There was nothing to be done but find pen, ink, and paper so that the boy might demonstrate his great achievement.

Tongue angled out the left side of his mouth, young Tom dipped the goose quill and began to write.

The first mark *somewhat* resembled a "T." Several marks followed, and they grew less and less like actual letters, but the boy's pride was unmistakable.

"I *wite!*"

"Aye, Tom. I have known old men whose hands

do shake with palsy that cannot write so well as thee."

"Aye!" Tom commenced writing additional "letters."

Edmund stared about him at the familiar hanging tapestries, the familiar stone carving over the great fireplace. He glanced up to the musician's gallery and felt his heart skip beats. There, he had been wed to Mistress Halley. There, he had pledged to love her and only her till death should part them. His heart felt split in two, pulled in opposing directions.

*What was he doing here?*

And also:

*How could he be anywhere else?*

"Papa!"

Edmund turned to his son.

"What is't, child?"

"Not child," declared Thomas. "Not baby. Johnny baby."

"John is indeed but a babe compared to thee," spoke Edmund.

"Papa, *amo, amas, amat.*" Thomas grinned up at Edmund, all white teeth and pink cherub cheeks. "*Amo, amas, amat.* I talk Latin."

"Even so," laughed Edmund, swinging the child up from where he stood on a chair, demonstrating his great size.

"*Bwek*fast!" Thomas wriggled free again and ran toward the kitchens at the rear of the manor house.

From the other end of the hall, Edmund saw his wife approaching. Maria was beautiful. How could he doubt his place was here, beside her? He glanced up to the musicians gallery again, feeling emotions that pulled him back to Halley. But he was *here*, not with

Halley. He must govern his thoughts. He dropped his gaze from the gallery.

Maria was lovely, in spite of her great girth. Upon one hip was straddled a boy of less than two years of age, if Edmund was any judge. *John.* He knew his son, just like that. And in his wife's belly, *Charles*, whom family would call *Charlie*.

He was a father, and would be shortly again. The rush of pride he felt was at once tempered by profound humility: how could he have been given so undeserved a gift? But then guilt pricked at him: what of the Edmund who had lost all this? Whose existence had been extinguished by his own inexplicable appearance? He did not belong here, no matter how many "memories" he might think he'd recalled.

And then, swinging like a plumb bob, Edmund felt shame for having desired anything but Halley. How could he do so? He was Halley's husband. He owed her his life, his possessions, his body, and his devotion. His gaze fell on the woman approaching him, and new confusion filled him. If he owed all that to Halley, what of Maria? If his appearance had banished the Edmund formerly here, was it not *his* duty now to provide Maria what she was owed?

The baby on Maria's hip shrieked loudly, drawing Edmund's attention. It was John. His son, John, who needed and deserved a father. The child wriggled, demanding to be let down to see his papa.

"Off you go, my ruffian," said the boy's mother.

*The boy's mother.*

His wife. Maria. Who needed and deserved a husband.

A memory flickered through his mind. He'd been

sitting with Halley, looking at his Wikipedia page. "M-A-R-I-A-H," Halley had said. "That is how we would spell the name nowadays, to match the way it was pronounced in that era."

Edmund's jaw tightened. Halley would have many things to say, seeing him here with Maria, but the spelling of her name wouldn't be among them.

"This child had best prove a girl," said Maria, patting her belly. "I've no stomach for more boys."

Edmund smiled tensely. It would be another boy. While deciding whether to suggest this possibility or not, Edmund squatted, arms open to catch John. The boy was barreling toward him, his fists raised and aimed to strike a part of Edmund's body not best suited to receive a blow. Thinking quickly, Edmund caught John in his arms.

Edmund breathed in the scent of his boy, chamomile and sticky fingers and dirt—*Edmund's* dirt: the earth of his ancestral lands. Even before the title of earl had been granted, these lands had been tended by generations of Aldwychs. The dirt under his son's fingernails represented Edmund's destiny, and one day, John's too. The estate would go first to Tom, who would die without heir in 1642, whereupon John would become lord, entrusted with care of the estate. Something caught in Edmund's throat at the thought of what it meant to live as lord of his lands, but almost at once, his reverie was interrupted by John screaming for his breakfast, which was only to be supplied at his wife's breast.

Maria waddled toward her family, breathing heavily. "Assuredly it is a girl," she said to her belly. "See what mincing steps I take? 'Tis the influence of a daughter."

"I see a wife who would hasten the hour of her labor with much walking and carrying," said Edmund. There was approval in his tone of voice, as if he knew he himself proud of her, for never using pregnancy as an excuse to avoid daily labor.

"I will hasten this one's arrival by whatever means I may," said Maria.

Having said this, she reached for a small purse tied to her gown and withdrew a letter. "This was delivered for thee, husband, but a moment ago." The look on her face had turned, and Edmund thought he recognized it. This was a look she wore when his brother had committed some transgression or other.

"Is't from Geoffrey?" he asked.

"Who else?" Maria handed over the letter.

Edmund broke the crude seal, evidently made with candle drippings and Geoffrey's own thumbprint, and read the contents.

"Christ 'a 'mercy," he whispered. Blanching, he looked up at his wife. "Geoffrey has been seized and lodged in the Tower. He hath brought upon himself and the Aldwych name the charge of traitor."

At this, Maria sank heavily, catching her fall with one hand outstretched to the floor, the other clutching her swollen abdomen.

# 18

## · HALLEY ·

### February, Wellesley

Halley stared Arthur Littlewood down, daring him to contradict her declaration: *What we need is a rescue attempt!* Anything short of an all-out rescue attempt was unthinkable. Edmund was alone, who knew where, and their final conversation had been an argument. She hadn't even had a chance to tell him they were pregnant.

Littlewood became preoccupied with the fuzz on his lightweight wool cardigan. Everett was gazing out the Sunday School classroom windows. Quintus had begun polishing his sword—his all-purpose indication he was ready for action. DaVinci and Jillian offered sober half-smiles. To Halley, these varied responses were as good as an invitation to continue.

"Okay," she said, "so here's what we're going to do. I'm driving back to the set of *As You Like It* where I'm going to liberate some late-Elizabethan-era costumes." Struck with a vague sense that heavy lifting and pregnancy didn't combine well, she turned to

Quintus. "I'll need you, too. The costumes can easily weigh fifty pounds each."

Then she addressed Everett. "Let's all get back to the lab. I want you and Jillian and Dr. Littlewood to work out Edmund's most likely location, and by the time Quintus and I get back late tonight, I want a plan of action for the . . . rescue." Her eyes brimmed at the word.

Littlewood tugged at his hair. "Well, ah . . ."

"That was not a request," snapped Halley. She swiped her eyes with the back of her hand.

She needed to pull it together. And maybe dial it back a notch, based on Littlewood's hair-tugging.

"I mean, what do you guys think?" she asked.

"It is a sound course of action," said Everett, rising and patting Littlewood's shoulder. "Arthur, let's revisit those ideas you had about isotemporal pockets . . ."

When they reached Littlewood's lab, DaVinci suggested an alteration to Halley's plans.

"I'm going with you and Quintus," DaVinci said. "I have zero contributions to make to iso-whatsits, but I have an excellent eye for fashion."

A grunted laugh left Halley's throat.

"What?"

"We'll just ignore the fact that your fashion sense doesn't extend back four centuries," said Halley.

DaVinci shrugged. "I know some art history. And besides, I've already decided Quintus should go with you to find Edmund, in case you need a swordsman, and if Quintus goes, I want to have a say in his hotness factor, because, babe," here she turned to Quintus, "you are going to be smokin' wearing your doublet and hose."

~ ~ ~

The drive from Wellesley to the costume trailer in the Everglades took ninety minutes. After that, it took Halley two hours to gather costumes that didn't have obvious signs of the 21$^{st}$ century, like plastic "jewels" or so-called invisible zippers. Another hour was eaten up convincing her wardrobe assistant that he could handle things while she took a few days personal leave, and then they had to drive back to Wellesley.

All told, it was 1:30 in the morning before they made it back to Jillian's apartment. Halley couldn't remember *ever* having felt so exhausted. When DaVinci asked her if she might be coming down with something, Halley nearly confessed she was expecting. Instead she blamed it on her poor sleep the night before.

"But I'm fine," she said to DaVinci. "Really."

"And that sore throat you were complaining about earlier?" demanded DaVinci.

"Oh. *Um* . . . I maybe swallowed a tortilla chip funny yesterday."

"I hate that! Like when you don't chew it enough and the stupid thing claws its way down your throat?"

Halley winced a bit at the description's accuracy.

Jillian had waited up for them at her apartment, although Everett had fallen asleep in an overstuffed armchair.

In hasty whispers, Jillian managed to convey the plan.

*"It's a go. We're convinced Edmund is in 1601 and not 1598, because of how space-time preserves a linear passage of time, from the point of view of the traveler."*

After that, Jillian got even more technical, and Halley stifled several yawns.

"*Sorry,*" said Jillian. "*You could use a good night's sleep more than my explanations.*"

Halley could've used one of Branson's throat-soothing tisanes too, but she didn't want DaVinci *and* Jillian worrying she was sick, so she just nodded, stretched out on the couch, and started planning how to tell Edmund they were having a baby.

## 19

### · HALLEY ·

February, Wellesley

Back at Littlewood's lab the next morning, there were negotiations to be entered into. The professor was wringing his hands over sending anyone but himself into harm's way.

Halley spoke up. "I have to be the one who goes back for Edmund," she said. "I know the customs better than any of you."

"Not to mention the language," said DaVinci, "after listening to Edmund's freaky speech patterns for so long."

"You cannot be permitted to travel alone," said Quintus sternly.

"*Babe*," said DaVinci in a whisper. "*Your caveman is showing.*"

Quintus frowned and then spoke again. "Forgive me. I meant no disrespect to the hard-won equalities of women in this time. I simply believe it is unwise for an individual of any gender to travel to the past alone."

"*You* tried to," said DaVinci.

Quintus's face flushed. "It was a mistake, and I count it most fortunate that you accompanied me."

"Perhaps," said Dr. Littlewood, "taking into consideration the views and customs of the era, it would be wise if a man were to accompany you? I hope that doesn't make me, ah, *too caveman*."

DaVinci made a tiny snorting sound.

"I volunteer to go," said Everett.

Of course he would, thought Halley. Everett would always volunteer. It had led his other self to die in World War I. What might Everett do if he was sent back to 1918? Well, that was the other point of this endeavor, wasn't it? To figure out how to keep all of them—Edmund, Everett, and Quintus—safe.

"Actually," said Littlewood, "I suggest it should be Quintus. Everett and I should remain here so we can continue our work on the isotemporal return pocket theory, with a view to preventing, ah, further disappearances."

"Fine, fine," said DaVinci with a heavy sigh. "I'll go, too."

Everyone turned to DaVinci.

"Halley's going to need a lady-in-waiting or whatever to get her in and out of those corsets." She turned to Quintus with an impish grin. "Unless you were planning to help out?"

"Never," Quintus declared, stone-faced.

Halley smiled. For all the 21st century depictions of Roman Empire debauchery, Quintus came from the more conservative republican era, with morals to match.

"Me, Quintus, and DaVinci," Halley said. "Sounds perfect. Now let's get into these costumes and on our way to . . . when are we going to?"

"By my calculations," said Littlewood, "and taking into accounts variances in the calendars in use in our era and theirs . . ."

"February 9th, 1601," said Everett, finishing the professor's thought.

20

· *NEVIS* ·

February, Kansas City

Nevis could understand only a little of the files he'd stolen from Arthur Littlewood. He ran across something he hadn't thought of, however, in a discussion he read of potential alterations to he historical timeline. If Nevis was understanding correctly, there was a possible snag to his plans.

If he succeeded in putting Lewiston behind bars *in the past*, this would mean Nevis would never get the hack assignment to check out electrical grid anomalies in Florida. This in turn would mean he would never have learned about the time machine. Nevis queried Khan about this, but Khan didn't care to speculate whether, if an individual lived an entirely different life, such an individual would or would not retain memories from their original timeline. Khan had been evasive on the subject; probably he didn't want to admit ignorance. He'd said that they would cross that bridge after he'd figured how to make the machine work properly.

So, was Nevis willing to risk the chance of forgetting time travel was real? Or more importantly, was he willing to risk that the only individuals who knew about it were Khan and Littlewood?

He was back to the big red button scenario, with a narcissist and an absent-minded professor left at the controls.

There was a slim possibility that the government already knew about Littlewood's activities. Before his clearance had been pulled, Nevis had been able to confirm Littlewood's work was government-funded. But Nevis had found no ties to branches securing national secrets. When Nevis had asked Khan if the government knew anything, Khan had laughed, denying it. Unless Khan was lying, which Nevis doubted in this case, Nevis had to assume he was the only government official, or *ex*-official, who knew anything.

Another trail leading back to the red button. Was Khan to be trusted with this sort of technology? Was Littlewood? Of course not.

The more Nevis thought about it, the more he realized there were larger things at risk than the fate of his crooked former SAC Lewiston. The stakes were enormous for all of humankind, and for the sake of humanity, someone more trustworthy than Littlewood or Khan had to step forward. Fate or chance or whatever you wanted to call it had placed him, Benjamin Nevis, in the path of this technological juggernaut. He might have to come up with an alternative plan for apprehending Lewiston, instead of catching him in the past. There were times a man had to bow to the greater good.

What choice did he have? Humanity's future might hang in the balance.

# 21

## · EDMUND ·

### February 1601, London

Edmund spurred his horse along the familiar road to London. Geoffrey in trouble was, unfortunately, nothing new. Edmund was all too familiar with half-hour journeys on horseback into the great city to bail his brother out. He wondered how many times he'd done so in the years of life he'd missed. Probably ten or so; Geoffrey's antics generally coincided with the dispersal of his quarterly allowance.

Geoffrey had been imprisoned before, but never for treason. Edmund felt his stomach tighten at the word. It was bad. As bad as possible. But it didn't seem likely. Whatever Geoffrey had done to get himself arrested, Edmund felt certain it hadn't involved plots against the Crown. No, the most likely explanation was that his brother had fallen asleep drunk in the wrong company.

As Edmund joined the crowds flooding into London on foot, horseback, cart, and carriage, his progress slowed. He began to overhear the conversations of those traveling alongside him, indicating there had indeed been a plot of late against the Crown. Upon slowing to a near halt crossing London Bridge, he learned many arrests had been made.

A terrible thought crept in. What if Geoffrey had changed in the years since Edmund had known him? Was it possible his brother had turned seditious? It seemed unlikely, but then, the idea that his brother would end up a Puritanical priest had seemed equally unlikely when Halley had first told him this would be his brother's fate.

*Halley.*

Edmund's heart wrenched within him. What must she be thinking? Would she suspect he had left her? He *had* left her. Unintentionally, but assuredly. She would believe him to have left of his own free will. That thought cut Edmund to the quick, yet there was naught he could do. He could not contact anyone in the future. He could not build another time machine. He was trapped. Alas, poor Halley.

As quickly as the thought came, he chided himself for it. Had he not duties to which he must attend? He must endeavor to put his feelings for Halley aside.

As he crossed the Thames at mid-morning, the ordinarily crowded bridge was packed to its extreme capacity. It all seemed unreal, as if he were dressed in a costume and playing a part that was not his. But this *was* his part, and it was all too real, even if it had, from one perspective, happened four hundred years in the past. But had it? He shook his head to clear his mind. This was present, not past. Assuredly there would be consequences for failing to behave as the real Edmund ought to.

As he progressed into town, he inquired of passing Londoners for news of those committed to the Tower. Had there been executions yet? No one knew for certain, but everywhere there flew rumors of who would be hung, drawn, and quartered. Edmund's stomach roiled. *Merciful Father in Heaven, let Geoffrey be found among those falsely accused.*

The Tower loomed large and daunting before him. He caught glimpses of its white stone walls through gaps in the buildings that lined the narrow streets. What would he find there? Would he be denied admittance? He patted his doublet, within which he had concealed a purse of money. He hoped it would be enough to buy him entrance. The usual fee for this, he could only guess at, although it likely depended upon the temperament of the man who guarded the door. Or perhaps the *several* men who stood guard between the outside world and his brother, who was surely housed in some recess deep within the ancient edifice.

He ought to have brought warm clothing for Geoffrey. It was bitterly cold, even though the sun shone in a cloudless sky this day. That would be *why* it was cold, of course. The previous day's heat had escaped into the skies overnight. Dr. Littlewood had explained to him the phenomenon.

Littlewood . . .

Surely Halley would have informed the professor of Edmund's absence. Were they even now attempting to ascertain where he had fled? He knew not what to hope for. It seemed certain his second self had . . . *vanished* and that there was only one of him. And with

Geoffrey's life hanging in the balance, how could Edmund wish to be transported back to Halley? Not to mention, here he had a very pregnant wife and two sons, all of whom needed him.

But what of Halley? How could he live apart from her? Did she not need him as well? Had he not sworn an oath to be hers? Aye, the self-same oath he had doubtless sworn to Maria. He was being torn asunder, as surely as if he lay upon the rack.

Nay! He must put aside such thoughts. As Halley oft insisted: *one emergency at a time.* He dismounted, giving his reins into the hands of a waiting groom. Then he squared his shoulders and approached the men guarding the drawbridge leading to the famed and feared Tower of London.

The first guard extracted no fee, but the second and third were less scrupulous, and Edmund's purse was much lighter when he was finally admitted into Geoffrey's cell.

The chamber smelled of piss and vomit and mildew. Reflexively, Edmund reached for the nosegay that ought to have hung from his doublet, but of course it wasn't there. Having been for years without the need to protect himself from foul odors, he had not remembered to collect a nosegay before approaching the city.

Bearing the smell without remark, he greeted his brother as was his custom.

"Ho-la, brother."

"Ned? Is it thee, brother? Is it indeed?"

"As you can plainly see," replied Edmund.

"Nay, but I have had ill dreams. Very ill dreams." Geoffrey squinted and then nodded his head. "It is you."

Edmund noted the shift from *thou* to *you* and wondered whether Geoffrey intended to signify humility or to preserve a haughty distance. A raven landed on the ledge of the single window, which was without glass. An attempt had been made to hang a woolen curtain over the gaping hole, but whatever nail had held the left side was now missing.

The raven squawked and flew away.

"Tis well the window faceth not the opposite direction," said Edmund. "The wind bloweth bitterly this morning."

"I feel the cold."

Edmund had no doubt. As he watched, his brother's head seemed to loll slightly to one side.

"Art thou drunk?" demanded Edmund.

Geoffrey uttered a humorless laugh. "I wish I were."

"Art thou . . . *ill* then?"

"I slept very ill. Tis everywhere damp."

Edmund looked about and noticed the rime of moisture that clung to all the surfaces. It was very damp. Edmund shuddered inwardly at the thought of passing a February night in such cold.

"Brother, I must ask thee. What hast thou done?"

Another bitter laugh. "Not that of which I am accused." Geoffrey bent forward and picked a bit of candle wax from the mean table which was his only furniture apart from two crude stools and a bucket in the corner.

Edmund waited to see what else his brother would say. Geoffrey was never at a loss for words to proclaim that things weren't his fault, or that he was poorly used, or, that if Fortune would but favor him once, and suchlike things.

But when he spoke, Geoffrey did not bluster over his innocence.

"Know you of the rebellion that hath lately failed?"

"Undertaken by Lord Essex?" asked Edmund. "Aye. Tis all Londoners speak of in the streets."

Geoffrey grunted. "Of late, I was . . . *engaged* to speak to the Lord Chamberlain's Men—"

"Speak plainly. Were you paid?"

Geoffrey's face flushed, the color restoring a measure of youthful health to his appearance for all that it betokened shame.

"I vowed I would speak to them, to see if they would play *Richard II* upon the seventh of February."

"Which thou didst, doubtless from the kindness of thy heart," said Edmund. Though it was cruel of him to chide his brother in such circumstances, old habits were hard to break.

"If you would not have me seeking employment wheresoe'er I can find it, you should see to the raising of my allowance. Tis a pittance—"

"Cease thy complaining and continue thy tale."

"Though the play hath of late fallen from fashion, the players agreed to perform *Richard* for an additional forty shillings, to cover revenue lost from playing so unpopular a piece."

Edmund nodded. It was easy to tell why the play was not to the general taste; it spoke the tale of a monarch deposed. To produce it at a time when Elizabeth's charms were waning seemed foolish at the very least. As to the demand for an extra forty shillings, it seemed likely enough. Edmund had heard tell of the shrewdness of the Lord Chamberlain's men. Will Shakespeare and Augustine Phillips were said to have such a gift of haggling that even Charon the ferryman of Hades would take less than his accustomed fare from either gentleman.

"How came you to be lodged here?" asked Edmund, indicating the dank cell.

"At first I thought I was merely taken with such others as gathered at the Inn and suspected for playing part in the rebellion. Though they did place me in a cart with the truest offenders, gathered from I wot not where." At this, Geoffrey glanced to the doorway into his cell and leaned forward, lowering his voice. "But last night I overheard the Percys saying they would lay the blame for the performance at my feet and thus place themselves at a further remove from suspicion."

Edmund cursed. "So the players' fee was forty shillings. Was there some piece for thee?"

"Well . . . and the truth be told . . ." Geoffrey broke off.

"I prithee speak the truth, else why am I here?"

"I was given fifty shillings," said Geoffrey, "and gave but forty to the players."

"Keeping unto thyself *ten shillings*? Brother, this hath a bad appearance."

The sum was more than Geoffrey's quarterly allowance—almost as much as Edmund dispensed to him within the course of a year. "And didst thou not guess how this would look?" demanded Edmund. "That thou not only brokered the deal but profited from it?"

"I wished to act upon the stage," Geoffrey said.

"And that was why I undertook the negotiations. I meant at first to keep no money for myself, demanding only a role to act, but when they did set the fee at forty, which was fully ten shillings less than I was given . . ."

As he spoke, Edmund felt a sudden remembrance of those days when he and Geoffrey had been friends. He recalled his brother's youthful ambitions as an reciter of verse, his exuberance, his glee when performing. Edmund's heart sank as he recalled those happier times. Those nights when their grandfather demanded a sonnet or speech from Geoffrey. How proudly Geoffrey had recited, how the hall had rung with laughter and applause.

"I persuaded them to admit me as an actor among their number for the one play, in exchange for an extra five shillings."

"Ah, Geoffrey." Edmund sighed and pulled the empty stool toward his brother, sitting himself down beside Geoffrey.

"I have had ample cause to regret it," said his brother. His tone was despondent now, no shred of dignity or hope left. "I drank what else I kept, or rather, paid for others to drink with me."

Edmund felt a stirring of pity. Geoffrey, once such a merry youth, had become a young man without friends, except for those that could be bought with a tankard of ale.

"I shall do all I can to aid thee," Edmund said at last. "I thank thee for speaking to me honestly." In his periphery, Edmund saw a large tear fall from Geoffrey's eye. He reached for a handkerchief, but that, too, he had forgot. Shrugging off his fur-lined cloak, he bundled it around his brother's narrow shoulders.

He would not let Geoffrey perish as a traitor.

So. Who might aid him? Who had the ear of the Queen's Majesty? Sir Robert Cecil, perhaps? He was one of Elizabeth's chief councilors. Moreover, he had been a friend to Edmund's grandfather. Aye. He would ask for Sir Robert's aid.

Edmund now wished he had spent more time at court instead of in his beloved fields and forests. If he were more generally known among the queen's courtiers, he would be better able to help his brother.

At his side, Geoffrey hugged the cloak to himself and whispered, "Thank you, brother. For coming to see me. I . . . I did not know if thou wouldst. I know Maria's time comes apace . . ."

"So it doth," said Edmund. "But she hath been delivered safely before, and thou hast ne'er before stood accused of treason. I judged thine was the greater need."

"Thanks, good brother."

"Here," said Edmund. "This coin will keep thee in food and ale lest thou sicken from the bad water." He passed several coins into Geoffrey's hand, receiving thanks and promises Geoffrey no doubt intended to keep, however incapable time should prove him of so doing.

With a sigh, Edmund rose and left the small chamber, determined to treat with Sir Robert Cecil.

## 22

### · HALLEY ·

February, Wellesley

It took DaVinci and Quintus working together to hoist Halley's garment over her head. It weighed forty-six pounds and was sewn together as a single unit, something that wasn't correct for the era, but it would pass inspection by anyone who wasn't actually dressing or undressing her.

Quintus refused to look at Halley in her underwear, but Halley told him that if he didn't watch what he was doing, the gown was going to end up on *him* instead. After this, he was more helpful.

DaVinci's costume was simpler and constructed properly, with the skirt and sleeves put on separately from the bodice. For Quintus, DaVinci had chosen tights nearly the color of his skin and snug leather breeches.

"Where did his tunic and doublet get to?" asked Halley, suddenly frantic.

"Are you sure he needs them?" asked DaVinci.

Halley rolled her eyes and DaVinci produced the

missing garments.

By the time Halley had tied on the last ruff, choosing an albino peacock feather one for herself, Littlewood, Jillian, and Everett said things were ready on their end. Nervous energy coursed through Halley, sending shivers up her arms. Or maybe that was just an effect of wearing the heavy costume on a warm Floridian February day. She gave herself a final check in the mirror. She looked as Elizabethan as she was ever going to look. She could do this. She *would* do this. Edmund was depending on her, and she wasn't going to let him down, however badly she'd screwed things up before. She just hoped he would be in the mood to talk about their issues when they were reunited.

"Okay," she said. "Let's do this."

"We've arranged extended stays for you," said Everett, "giving you a better shot at locating the correct version of Edmund, assuming that there are two of them."

"We're sending Halley with Quintus first," said Littlewood. "Within minutes—well, as fast as we can re-ready the machine—we will then send DaVinci, calibrating her stay for only a shorter duration."

"So, *um*, I get to travel alone? Because . . . awesome." DaVinci didn't look like she thought it was awesome.

"You'll do fine." Everett grinned at her. "You're one tough cracker-jack."

"The shorter duration of your stay will allow you to report back on what you've found in the, ah, past," explained Littlewood. "In case we need to alter our plans."

"This is wise counsel," said Quintus, looking up. He'd been sharpening his Roman short sword, which Halley hadn't quite worked up the nerve to tell him was completely wrong for the Elizabethan era. "To form plans," he added, "intelligence is requisite."

"Babe, Littlewood's got a PhD," murmured DaVinci. Then she frowned. "*Oh.* You mean *intel.* Right. Never mind."

"Are we ready?" asked Littlewood.

Halley nodded grimly and strode to the platform. To Edmund, if everything worked out right. And if it didn't? Then they would just keep trying.

The time machine purred to life, gradually shifting to the roaring din that preceded a journey. Blue electricity hummed along the Tesla coils. Halley smelled ozone, or maybe just burning dust. On her next inhalation, her throat complained, aching a little worse than yesterday. She should have taken an Advil. Or at least packed one. Her mind was racing, bouncing all over the place. Was Edmund freaking out? Was he safe? Ugh! Her throat. She would have to get Edmund to make whatever soothing brews they used in his century for when you swallowed a tortilla chip the wrong way. Of course, the Elizabethans never swallowed chips the wrong way because they didn't know maize as a crop, much less tortilla chips—

*Focus,* she ordered herself.

The machine's roar grew to a nearly deafening decibel, until the moment Halley felt every muscle in her body lock in place. Her mind stilled. She couldn't move or breathe or see anything. And then, gasping for breath, she tumbled into the beginning of the 17th century.

## 23

### ·EDMUND·

### February 1601, London

Edmund knew Sir Robert Cecil to be a busy man. Just now, with Her Majesty's safety under threat, he would be an *extremely* busy man. Edmund wondered if the privy councilor had even slept for the past forty-eight hours, since Essex's rebellion had been quelled. The current circumstances conspired to make it near impossible that Edmund could gain an audience with Sir Robert simply by presenting himself at Court. Or perhaps he was just making excuses. Edmund hated court, even though he was an earl, and many would argue his place was there.

On the other hand, though it might be next to impossible to meet Sir Robert, the gentleman's habits were fastidious when it came to correspondence. Edmund need not waste hours at court when a letter would surely reach Sir Robert ahead a person, regardless of that person's rank. Having convinced himself of this, Edmund wrote a letter, paying the courier double his usual fee to ensure it reached Cecil before noon.

Sir Robert was not as quick to respond as Edmund hoped. By afternoon, Edmund had begun to grow fearful Sir Robert wouldn't respond at all, but that evening as he paced the Great Hall at Hensley, Edmund received a letter and an invitation.

Sir Robert remembered Edmund's grandfather well, and he emphasized that it was because of their previous friendship he was willing to make himself available to Edmund, in spite of his full schedule. Sir Robert would be pleased to receive Edmund in a fortnight's time, when the busy man expected to have his leisure somewhat restored.

Edmund groaned. "Two weeks?" he said aloud, leaning against the chimneypiece.

"Husband?" His wife paused her stitching. "What news?"

"Sir Robert will not see me for a fortnight. Alas, poor Geoffrey." Edmund kicked at one of the andirons, sending sparks swirling into the chimney.

"Thou needs must go to court, husband."

Edmund frowned. Maria might be right, but there were impediments beyond his distaste for court life.

"My habiliments are not suited—"

"Thou shalt have new garments."

"There is no time—"

"Nay, husband." She held up the length of fabric with which she had been at work. It was a sleeve. To the sleeve, she was stitching cream-colored poufs of fabric the size of pullet eggs, gathered and stuffed into small slashes in the fabric, so that they appeared to have been pulled through the slashes.

"I anticipated thou might'st require fresh garb.

Nan is broidering black to my best starched ruff, which thou mayst wear as thine own and no one be the wiser."

Edmund, unhappy Maria should give up her best ruff, was nonetheless sensible of how this solved his problem. She was always two steps ahead of him, he mused. It was another memory, but it felt so like his own memory. In any case, with new sleeves and a fresh ruff, Edmund would be the glass of fashion.

"I thank thee for the sacrifice of thy ruff," he said.

"I have no need to wear a ruff as a catch-lice," Maria replied proudly. "My household hath ever been louse-free."

"Best of wives," he murmured, grasping her hand from her needlework.

She slid her hand free. "*Busiest* of wives," she said, returning to her work. "Thou must go on the morrow, and see thou make haste. Do not, in considering thy wayward brother, forget thou hast a wife and family that need thee. This daughter will not wait many days more, I think."

Edmund's face grew grim. "To court, then. Tomorrow, and in haste."

Having said this, he recalled another memory: his wife, repeatedly advising that he not absent himself from Her Majesty's court forever. He even knew his usual response: to shrug and say he had no need of the Queen's smiles when the queen of his heart was ever at hand.

*The queen of his heart . . .*

He loved Maria.

He *loved* her. He felt new memories settling inside. Recollections of how he had fallen gradually in love their first year of marriage—a marriage arranged to settle his financial problems. It had been as wonderful as unexpected to find he loved her. Maria was clever, thrifty, generous, and beautiful. Even heavy with child, Edmund knew he preferred her beauty to that of any other woman in the realm.

In a motion at once sudden and familiar, Edmund removed Maria's needlework from her hands, caught her up in his arms, and kissed her. Her lips tasted of honeyed wine. Soft and yielding, she kissed him back, and he felt the need to take her to bed, or have her right here before the fire—

But then, overwhelmed by guilt and uncertainty, he broke off the kiss. Maria re-settled herself without comment, as if this were an everyday occurrence, and took up her needlework once more.

Edmund turned to gaze into the fire, to the ever-changing flicker of the embers. He felt as if he were awakening from a dream state. He inhaled. Exhaled. Repeated this, still staring into the fire. He was Edmund: one person. There was no other vanished Edmund, whose absence might cause him guilt. There was only . . . *himself.* He knew this with certainty: He had not merely stolen the memories of his other self; he had been fused—*rejoined*—to that other self. He was whole once again.

In one part of his memory he held his past years with Halley, and in another part of his mind, he held all of his memories of his life with Maria. They flooded through him now—along with memories of his sons, especially of Thomas, the eldest. Edmund recalled teaching Thomas the first declension of Latin, and how to bait a hook. How to brush a horse. How to ride upon a pony. How to pray and clean his teeth and clap his hands. On and on, the memories presented themselves, marching past in their hilarity and solemnity, joy and sorrow.

He was a sojourner from the future, happily and faithfully married to Halley. But he also belonged to Maria, and to this time and place.

Heavy with emotion, Edmund sank into the chair before the fire. Into *his* chair. He was Edmund, the Second Earl of Shaftesbury, and he had returned to Hensley Manor.

## 24

*·HALLEY·*

February 1601, London

Although Halley was a stickler for historical accuracy when building costumes from scratch, she had learned that actors were a lot happier when she made certain concessions. For the *As You Like It* costumes, this concession had been to add *pockets*, because Elizabethan pockets had been more like exterior purses. Unless you counted the codpiece, which men were known to have used as carry-alls, sewn-in pockets didn't exist. However, since you couldn't convince an actor it was okay to grab an energy bar from a codpiece (and really, it *so* wasn't okay), Halley had sewn twenty-first century pockets into several garments, including the one she wore to travel back to 1601.

Within her pockets, she had crammed a small treasure trove of items that might prove useful to grease any palms that needed greasing. She wasn't sure how hard it would be to gain admittance to Hensley Manor, where they hoped to find Edmund, but she knew better to expect they'd be welcomed with open arms. Hensley might not be the royal court, but it was reasonable to assume a manor so close to London could've picked up a few of the habits of courtiers, one of which was the practice of offering bribes—er, *gifts*—to obtain favors like, say, an audience with an earl.

She'd stuffed Quintus's doublet, too. In the late Elizabethan and early Jacobean period, men had adopted the interesting belief that a paunchy belly was attractive, so garments were constructed to bulge low at the waist. Gentlemen lacking the "attractive" beer belly would stuff their doublets to make it look like they had bigger bellies. Since Quintus's abs-o'-steel had zero pooch, Halley had been able to pack a few items inside his distended doublet. She wished backpacks or roller bags had been popular in the era, but even if they had been, people in Edmund's social class paid someone else to carry their stuff, and Quintus was traveling with Halley as her husband, not her servant.

Briefly, DaVinci had been *not okay* with the "husband" part, but once Halley had explained that only gentlemen were allowed to wear swords, DaVinci got onboard fast.

So what had Halley stuffed all the available pockets and pouches with? Her years with Edmund had taught her a thing or two about what inexpensive modern items would be valued most in Elizabethan England. Of all the modern luxuries Halley had introduced Edmund to, *coffee*, or caffeine anyway, had impressed him the most, but Everett, Jillian, and Littlewood had vetoed Halley introducing coffee beans three decades too early.

Instead, she'd grabbed measures of cinnamon, cloves, mace, and cardamom, in ground form, from Jillian's kitchen. Spices were compact, light, and extremely valuable, allowing them to pack the most punch per square inch of pocket space. Quintus's doublet held the spices, making him smell like Christmas. In her own pockets, Halley had placed the most expensive-to-her-era items, a few essential oils from Edmund's travel shave kit: rose, lemon, and frankincense. Rose oil had been popular in Elizabethan times for its scent, lemon for its rareness (lemon trees didn't do well in England), and frankincense for its anti-inflammatory properties.

The oils were in their original glass vials, since Halley hadn't had time to find Elizabethan-looking containers, but how much could vials have changed in four hundred years?

Now, as she hurtled through space-time and into 1601, Halley began panicking over how much she *didn't* know about this era. Sure, she was the best prepared of their group, but would it be enough? Or would she do something stupid and get herself locked up in the Tower of London as a witch or foreign spy?

Space-time released them into an icy morning just before dawn, as always leaving Halley feeling like she'd been punched in the gut. After recovering for a few seconds, Halley looked over to check on Quintus.

"Does it appear we have arrived where you expected?" he asked. He looked unaffected by their nauseating journey.

Taking a few deep breaths, Halley tried to orient herself. The cold burned her throat with each inhalation. Not seeing Hensley Manor at first, she began to panic, but then, turning she realized it was *behind* them, the familiar chimneys and turrets outlined against a lightening gray sky. A breeze, bitterly cold, blew across her hands and face. Courtesy of the same breeze, she caught a whiff from Quintus's doublet of spices and . . . cigarette smoke?

"This way," she said to her scented friend.

Actors being actors, Halley had not been able to prevent the highest-paid ones from smoking in their costumes when they thought they wouldn't get caught. Fortunately, tobacco was known in the Elizabethan era—Halley had heard the queen herself smoked after tobacco's introduction to court by the dashing Sir John Hawkins.

The smell reminded her they didn't belong here, that they were just playing dress-up and might be caught at any time. But what choice did she have? She had to rescue Edmund.

Taking a deep breath, she said, "Okay. This way."

The plan was to approach Hensley just as the household was stirring for the day. Halley hoped to catch Edmund alone, before his day really got going. Assuming he was here at all. Of course, he wasn't an early riser . . .

*One problem at a time.* They still had to get inside.

They reached the manor house just as the sky was turning a dull gray in the East. It wasn't all that early, because it was the dead of winter, but the Elizabethans had been in the habit of rising and sleeping with the sun. You burned fewer calories, candles, and logs in the winter that way. She remembered how Edmund had once explained this when he'd been trying to coax her into bed with him early. Her skin flushed at the thought.

*Oh God, please let him be here.*

As they approached the imposing edifice, Halley began to have second thoughts about their "landing." Maybe they should have had Littlewood insert them *inside* the Hall. It wasn't like there was a doorbell or intercom system to buzz them inside. Would anyone answer if they knocked on the substantial oak doors? They didn't look so much like doors as impenetrable Montecito-style gates.

"Here we go," said Halley, reaching out her hand to rap on the heavy door.

After she had knocked three times, Quintus released a deep laugh.

"That is no way to call the attention of the master of the house." Removing his sword from its sheath, he clutched the grip and used the pommel as a door-knock, delivered five resounding blows to the door—denting it in the process.

This, however, was enough to bring someone to the front door.

A very sleepy-looking someone with large pock-marks on one side of his face.

"Who calls so early?" demanded the under-rested individual. He eyed Halley's darker-than-English skin with curiosity. She swallowed. She and Quintus had concocted a quick story to explain her skin tone, if they needed it.

"And what make you here?" the porter added to his first question.

"It is I, Master Quintus Valerius, a friend of your master's," said Quintus.

117

Halley had wanted to be the one doing all the talking, but she also agreed it wasn't practical. At least not until they'd been received into the house. Your average woman of the era wouldn't go around making the introductions, despite the fact that a powerful woman sat on the English throne.

Just as Halley thought she was going to have to break out some rose oil or cinnamon to gain admittance, the pock-marked man swung the door wide to admit them. From the surly look on his face, Halley was guessing he'd decided there was more to be lost by turning away friends of his master than gained by demanding bribes. Or maybe Edmund's servants were honest.

"Come inside, come inside," the porter said, leading them into an impressive foyer, all paneled in polished walnut wainscoting.

Halley knew this wasn't the Great Hall, where she and Edmund had been hastily married. Instead, this front entrance was a part of the manor she'd never seen. Actually, most of the manor was a part she'd never seen. She'd really only been to the Great Hall, or rather, the musicians gallery overlooking the Great Hall.

The servant who had admitted them was now talking to a woman who had keys at her waist—the housekeeper, who would be a woman of great importance in the manor. She eyed them suspiciously, as if certain they were here to make off with the silver plate.

"I shall conduct you to the kitchens, where vittles may be had. It's naught but small beer and barley bread this time of year, and little enough of that," she said as they traipsed through passageways that varied from poorly lit to not-at-all lit. It almost felt colder inside than it had outside, although Halley had probably only felt warm outside because they'd been sweating in Florida just before.

They entered the kitchen where, frowning at each of them, the housekeeper invited them to rest on stools by the fire, after which she delivered the small beer and barley bread.

"And see you upset not the pottage," the woman said, indicating a huge iron pot held over the fire by a huge iron rod. "I shall ask after his lordship for you directly."

Drinking the room-temperature "small beer," Halley noticed her throat irritation again. Was she getting sick? A cold was the *last* thing she needed right now.

"That man is the steward," said Quintus, nodding toward a new man who was conversing with the housekeeper. Halley wasn't sure how Quintus would know this, but based on the man's garments, he was probably right. "I did once employ a steward," Quintus added.

Once? Halley felt her spine tingling. If they couldn't figure out how to stop space-time from pulling people back to their point of origin, Quintus might just end up back in Rome, employing a steward again.

Edmund's steward regarded them even more darkly than the dour housekeeper, if this was possible. After observing them for a full minute, he approached them at the fireplace.

"His Lordship is occupied with heavy matters,"

said the steward.

"He will wish to see us," said Halley.

Quintus raised an eyebrow at her, and she chided herself. A feisty female in this era wasn't going to last long.

The steward, however, replied in a way that seemed to take Halley's claim into account.

"Nevertheless, he is not at liberty today. Mistress Janet the housekeeper will see you installed in rooms, and if you wish for it, paper and ink can be provided for you to write his lordship."

Halley's heart sank. She needed to see Edmund. *Now.* She wanted to push right past this grumpy man and the grumpy housekeeper and shout for Edmund as loudly as possible, until he heard her and came running into her arms.

Quintus replied that they would greatly appreciate the generous offer of pen, paper, and lodging. After this, the steward departed, and the housekeeper conducted them along another of the seemingly endless dark passageways. It was from within one of these that Halley heard Edmund's voice. Heart pounding, Halley realized she knew where they were. They had to be traveling along a corridor parallel to the Great Hall. Halley recognized the high stone "windows" set atop the wall. The same decorative effect was visible from inside the Great Hall, where tapestries would be seen hanging beneath these same tracery windows.

She heard Edmund's voice again. He was here! In the Great Hall! She heard a woman's voice, too. With a sick feeling, Halley realized the woman was probably Maria Lavenham, Edmund's wife. Halley felt a sudden desperation to enter the Great Hall. The doors leading to it were just ahead of them, but the housekeeper was turning a corner that would take them away. Halley made her decision. She hung back from the group. She was going to bust into that hall and speak to her husband.

Just at that moment however, the second earl of Shaftesbury himself burst through the door and into her corridor, dressed head-to-toe as a true Elizabethan.

"Edmund!" cried Halley.

This was *not* the correct way for a stranger to address his lordship Edmund Aldwych, second earl of Shaftesbury, but she didn't care. Edmund was here. He was real and alive and . . . *bearded?* Or just unshaven, maybe.

His first glance at her was stern. A glare that said, "Who dares address me by my Christian name?" But seeing her, his gaze softened, and he mouthed the shape of her name.

Unmistakable. *Halley.* Just her name: *Halley.* It was enough.

She rushed toward him and, grasping his face in her hands, she stood on tip-toe and kissed him. At first he didn't kiss back, but then she felt his mouth melt into hers, warm and hungry. It was her Edmund! He deepened the kiss, and she shifted her hand to the back of his neck. Beard stubble prickled her chin, her cheeks, her lips. At her waist, she felt his hands settle and then grip, the tips of his thumbs grazing her breasts through far too many layers of cloth.

He was here. He knew her. She would apologize and say she shouldn't have hidden the truth about the pill from him, and then she would tell him they were expecting! It would all be okay.

Halley leaned in closer, pressing her body to his, but just at that moment Edmund pulled out of the embrace. He took a step back. He looked at her with an agonized expression. It took her back to their first week together—to a kiss stolen on Butterfly Beach when he'd told her that he couldn't remain with her, that duty called him home.

Why did he have that look on his face right now? Was he harboring some misplaced sense of duty to a earldom that wasn't even his? Or was he still angry at her? The elation she'd felt a moment earlier vanished, and then two things happened at the same time. The housekeeper began calling for her, and Edmund's wife—his *pretend* wife—pushed open the door from the Great Hall to join them in the corridor.

Attempting to smooth his features, Edmund addressed the woman.

"My lady wife, these are . . . cousins from Italy," he said, his voice pinched. He turned to the time travelers. "Alas, friends, I can offer you but little welcome. I must depart immediately. I am . . . I am . . ." He seemed unable to finish his thoughts.

Maria Lavenham spoke. "You are most welcome to our home." Her voice was low and resonant. A powerful voice belonging to a powerful woman.

Edmund stared at Halley, unable to tear his eyes from her.

"We thank you," said Quintus, bowing like Halley had taught him.

Half a second late, Halley dropped a curtsey. She didn't know what to say. Edmund had just met her, had just kissed her—kissed her like she was his world—and now he was leaving? She rose from her curtsey. She couldn't think. Her gown was too tight. She was going to faint. She forced herself to breathe from her abdomen, like she was always telling her actors, so they didn't get lightheaded wearing corsets.

Edmund's gaze finally broke from hers. As he turned to Maria, he looked even more distressed. What did that mean? Was it hopeful? Was it the look of a man about to tell his pretend wife he had to go now, because Halley was here? She prayed it was.

"Good wife," Edmund began, but he said it to the wrong woman.

Halley's veins seemed to fill with ice.

Edmund hesitated, casting his eyes on Maria, on Quintus, on his housekeeper—on anyone but Halley. Maria was his *good wife*. She was the lady to his lordship, heavy with his child in her belly.

Halley felt like she might be sick. Was it possible Edmund wouldn't want to return to their century? To her? She was carrying his child, too. What had she done to deserve this? As soon as she asked the question, she had an answer. If he knew her, he also knew how she'd lied to him. Day after day. Month after month. Her hand drifted to her abdomen, to the tiny heart beating inside her.

"Good my wife," Edmund began again, "thou wilt see these friends are housed and want for nothing we can provide." He shifted an anguished gaze to Halley. "I must depart on business most urgent."

There was yearning in his eyes as they locked with Halley's. She saw it. He wasn't rejecting her! She wanted to grab his hand and run away. She wanted to shout that he was *her* husband and to hear him say he would move heaven and earth to be with her again. She felt faint. The weight of the dress, the pressure of the corset. She could not get enough air. Quintus placed a supporting arm at her waist, taking her weight.

Edmund had already turned from her. He was speaking to Maria again. "Thou must inform these my friends of our present misfortunes. I know not how long I shall be."

Maria took his hands in hers and lifted them to her cheek, murmuring, "God go with thee and grant thee thy petition."

It was an intensely intimate moment. Halley felt her heart drop to the pit of her stomach. She knew the look in Maria's eyes. That look said, *You are mine.* Halley's eyes flew to read Edmund's face, but she was too late—his attention had shifted to his steward, who was striding toward them.

"All is in readiness, my lord," said the steward.

Edmund stepped forward, but then he turned and gazed on Halley.

"How long—" His voice cracked. He closed his eyes for the briefest of moments. Praying? Holding back tears? When he spoke again, his voice was low and rasping. "For how long shall we be favored with your presence?"

Halley couldn't speak.

"Two nights, my lord," said Quintus, "and as many more as are needed after that."

Edmund nodded curtly. "I must away. Farewell."

"Ed—*my lord*," said Halley, catching herself, "can we not speak?"

He threw a last glance over his shoulder. "Maria

will explain. I am in great haste." And then he spun on his heel and followed his steward.

She stood, paralyzed. She had lost him. He wasn't even pretending he wanted to talk to her. She had lost Edmund. Her husband. The father of her child. She felt the build-up leading to bitter, wracking sobs.

And then Quintus's voice, harsh in her ear. "Control yourself."

It was like having ice water poured over her head. Halley shivered, but did not cry. She wouldn't cry. She would to keep it together until she was alone, until she could face her empty future, her empty life.

"Master Valerius, Mistress Halley," said Maria, "the passageway is chill. Will not you join me at the fire in the Great Hall? There is much to discuss."

Halley followed, with Quintus's strong arm keeping her upright. Her body felt too light, as if pieces of her were breaking off and floating away. Or, no—as if her heart had detached itself to follow Edmund. The rest of her followed Maria Lavenham-Aldwych into the Great Hall.

## 25

### · HALLEY ·

### February 1601, London

"Our family sits in grave peril," said Maria.

At these words, Halley's attention was roused. The woman's "family" included Edmund.

"What's wrong?" asked Halley.

"It is Edmund's brother—"

"Geoffrey?" asked Halley.

Maria frowned. "You are acquainted with Master Geoffrey?"

"By reputation only," replied Halley.

"Please, continue," said Quintus.

"Though you be travelers from afar, you will have surely heard of the plot lately lain against Her Majesty the Queen?" asked Maria.

Quintus shook his head. Halley tried to remember what she knew about events in February of 1601. The date sounded familiar. Was there some rebellion, maybe?

"Lord Devereux, Earl of Essex," continued Maria, "formerly in the Queen's favor, has been for months waging a sort of war with Sir Robert Cecil, the Queen's secretary of state, because Essex disobeyed orders to fight in Ireland until its subjects bowed to the Queen. When Essex returned beaten, the Queen refused him admittance to court, even going so far as to detain him in his London house.

"Two days ago, he attempted to rouse the citizens of London into open rebellion, meaning to storm Whitehall Palace. It is not clear what Essex intended. Whether only to affright the Queen and gain admittance to her, or whether to overthrow her and set himself in her place. Either way, he is now held as traitor." Maria's eyes filled and she blinked several times, which Halley found unnerving. Did Maria sympathize with the rabble-rouser? History—and Halley—were on Elizabeth's side.

"Alas," continued Maria, "Edmund's brother is taken as one of those accused of rebellion. He is now housed as a traitor in the Tower of London."

Halley responded in shock. "A *traitor*?" Of all the things she'd planned for, *this* was not one of them. No wonder Edmund had taken off in such a hurry!

"Aye," said Maria. "Edmund has left but now to speak to the Queen's secretary. We are in hope Sir Robert Cecil will free Geoffrey on Edmund's avowal of his brother's innocence."

"Assuredly he will succeed," said Halley. Thanks to Wikipedia, she knew something Maria didn't. Geoffrey would end up as a puritanical priest, not a traitor executed for treason.

*Unless . . .*

Could Edmund's unexpected return have changed things? Halley still didn't even know how many

Edmunds were here in 1601. But whether it was one or two, could *her* Edmund's changed behavior after twenty-first century life somehow have goaded Geoffrey? What if Geoffrey was in jail because he'd made different choices than he would have made apart from her Edmund's unexpected arrival?

Halley's heart thumped in her chest.

"The Aldwych family staunchly supporteth the Crown," said Maria, "but things are topsy-turvy, and who knows what may follow?"

Halley glanced at Quintus. His brow was deeply furrowed and he seemed to be staring at his hands without seeing them—or anything else.

"All in all," replied Maria, "it is, methinks, not the best of times for those from papist lands to visit so near to London."

Was Maria going to ask them to leave, now that Edmund was gone?

"We are not, *uh*, Catholic," Halley said quickly. "We actually came to England to, you know, avoid persecution." She felt her face heating. What she'd come *here* for was to steal Maria's husband and take him back where he belonged.

"It is well you found us," said Maria, nodding thoughtfully. "We can shelter you from the inquisitive."

She *wasn't* kicking them out.

Smiling, Maria inquired, "Now then, tell me, how is't you are kin to my husband?"

Halley opened her mouth to spout more lies, but she was interrupted by the insistent shriek of a one-year-old.

"That is Johnny," Maria said. Then, with obvious

pride, she added, "I keep no wet-nurse."

She began loosening her bodice, and a servant carrying the howling child placed him at his mother's breast.

Quintus didn't look away, which Halley thought was strange at first, considering his extreme modesty. But then she realized he must have grown up watching women bare their breasts to feed their kids all the time.

Maria cooed to the baby, shushing him, whispering endearments. In spite of her discomfort with exposed boobs, Halley couldn't help looking. This was Edmund's child. With sudden certainty, she saw that no matter how many Edmunds were in this century, none of them would want to return with her. Edmund was a father here. His kids would inherit an earldom. How was Halley supposed to compete with that? She remembered the look on his face when he'd pulled out of their kiss. What if it wasn't anguish over missing her, or even anguish knowing he couldn't return with her? What if it had been guilt, for betraying his *real* wife. Maria, mother of his children.

It was the most likely explanation. The one that made the most sense. Halley's heart fractured. Edmund would never choose her over what he had here. How was she supposed to live her life without him? Her eyes were filling again when Quintus abruptly broke his long silence.

"I must aid Edmund in his endeavor to free his brother. I have assisted before in freeing those held by a strong enemy."

Halley's eyebrows rose. Her to-do list did not include explaining to DaVinci that Quintus had been executed for trying to jailbreak a traitor.

"No, Quintus," Halley said firmly. "You cannot."

Maria spoke. "Perhaps I have misled you as to my husband's intention. He does not storm the Tower. That would be madness indeed." The reprimand was implied and understated.

Quintus frowned but gave her his full attention.

"Edmund's reputation is untarnished, and upon that reputation are our hopes founded," she said. As she switched the child from one breast to the other, the baby woke and cried, unhappy at the sudden lack of food.

Under cover of those cries, Halley murmured to Quintus. "There will be absolutely no rescue attempts. The Tower is the most heavily guarded place you can imagine. You'll end up beheaded as a traitor yourself, and you'll bring Edmund's entire family down, now that they've offered us shelter. Do you understand?"

Quintus, his features stony, nodded. Was he going back to plotting? Halley sighed. DaVinci would know how to talk sense into him.

*DaVinci!*

Halley had nearly forgotten. DaVinci was due to arrive forty-five minutes after Halley and Quintus, to give them time to meet her outside and conduct her safely into Hensley Manor. It had all sounded much simpler before they'd encountered the reality of high stone walls, barred oaken doors, porters, stewards, and housekeepers. It seemed like a lifetime ago, almost a happy time, compared to what she was now facing. Why had it never occurred to her that Edmund might not want to be rescued?

Focus. She had to stick to what was happening

right now and worry about the future . . . some other time.

"Good my lady," said Halley, "my maid joins us shortly. I, *um*, sent her to make purchases for me." She hoped Maria wouldn't start asking questions about shopping when the sun was barely up.

"I shall see she is admitted." Lifting the baby from her breast, Maria turned to the servant who had brought the boy to her and spoke a few soft words.

The servant curtseyed and left with the child.

Maria rose. "I must about my day," she said. "The kitchens you have seen already, have you not?"

Quintus and Halley replied they had.

"My housekeeper is generally to be found thereby, if you cannot find me." She placed a hand to her belly. "I expect shortly to be at this one's command. But Mistress Janet will see you want for nothing in my absence."

Halley and Quintus rose and made their obeisance at the same time Maria did. After the door to the Great Hall had closed behind Maria, Quintus pulled out a wristwatch.

"It is past the time we were to meet with DaVinci," he said.

Halley nodded. "Let's go."

It was better than sitting here thinking of her bleak future.

They found DaVinci with her back to a wall offering shelter from the cold wind.

"Are you okay? How long have you been waiting? You must be freezing!" said Halley, running to her friend.

"I've been warmer," replied DaVinci.

"Can you walk? Shall I carry you?" asked Quintus.

"I'm fine. I can walk. I've only been here seven minutes, and honestly for the first five minutes or so it felt great to cool off."

Halley nodded, remembering her own initial relief feeling the cold. Florida heat and Elizabethan costumes didn't match well.

They walked the short distance to the manor, gaining admittance and, this time, a deferential bow from the porter. A servant awaited them inside the entryway and took them to their rooms.

DaVinci couldn't stop whispering to Quintus about the leaded glass windows, the carved wainscoting, the tapestries. She was so absorbed she hadn't even picked up on Halley's mood.

When they arrived in their room, a servant was there, building a fire.

"It will catch presently," said the young woman, "and burn as bright and hot as ever you might wish."

Quintus ushered the servant from the room.

Halley felt suddenly exhausted. She sank into a chair at the hearth, but after only a minute, she realized the seat was uncomfortably close to the heat of the fire. Half-heartedly, she fanned herself with one hand.

DaVinci spoke first. "You look awful, Halley. And where's Edmund? Did you not find him?"

Halley blinked back tears. What was there to say?

"He is gone," said Quintus, "but he will return when he is able." He then explained about the Essex rebellion, Geoffrey's imprisonment, and Edmund's preoccupation with freeing his brother.

"Oh, wow," said DaVinci. "Who would have seen

that coming?"

"Who, indeed?" said Quintus gravely.

"Oh. I was supposed to show you this right away," said DaVinci, withdrawing a piece of paper from one of Halley's "modern concession" pockets.

"What is it?" asked Quintus.

"Everett had this idea. You're looking at a printout of the Wikipedia page on Edmund Aldwych, second earl of Shaftesbury." She held it out for Halley. "You're supposed to check and see if anything looks . . . *altered*. You know, to indicate either Edmund or you guys did something that changed history."

Quintus frowned. "Could you not check it yourself?"

"Well," said DaVinci, "in the time between your arrival here and my departure from Florida, history could have rewritten itself, changing the things I, *uh*, knew about Edmund. This sheet would look right to me no matter what, but Halley might notice things that aren't right. Make sense?"

"Quintus and I wouldn't have had our memories altered," Halley said to DaVinci. "It would be like when you went back to save your house, and you returned with all these memories of going to college that none of the rest of us had, because, well, in the timeline all of us knew, you didn't go to college."

Feeling anxiety creeping in, Halley began to read, trying to recall the things she remembered reading about Edmund on several visits to his Wikipedia page. It had been at least six months since the last time she looked, but everything looked right to her. Ten children by Maria Lavenham, a wealthy woolen-trade heiress. Six of the kids survived infancy, the oldest inherited the title. The earl was nearly implicated in a treasonous plot, but he managed to extricate both his brother and himself . . .

Halley frowned.

Was this new? Or had she just forgotten about Edmund's having been "nearly implicated"? It sounded vaguely familiar, she decided, but it just hadn't mattered to her the other times she'd read it—not like it mattered now.

"Everything checks out," she said.

"Good," said DaVinci.

"It does not follow that everything will continue as it ought," said Quintus. "We may yet cause damage we do not intend. In a very real sense, neither this paper nor Wikipedia exist yet. This record of Edmund's life has not yet been made."

DaVinci nodded. "Littlewood did mention that because of the length of time between now and our own time, most changes will have smoothed out, with any damage occurring closest to where we, *er*, interrupt things today."

"Khan's law of . . . something," murmured Halley.

"Yup. So, was Edmund happy to see you?" asked DaVinci.

Halley felt all the previous emotions returning to attack her, full force.

"Did he not recognize you?" DaVinci asked gently.

"He knew who I was," Halley said in a choked voice.

"That's huge. Everett was so worried—well, it's great he was worried for nothing. So I guess when Edmund comes back from rescuing his brother, we can all go home?"

Halley wondered if it would've been better if Edmund hadn't recognized her. Her eyes dropped to the Wikipedia printout describing his life. His *good* life, full of children and grandchildren, a title he could pass to his son—all things the twenty-first century couldn't give him. All things *Halley* couldn't give him. It was the life for which he was meant. And it didn't include her.

At last she raised her eyes, meeting DaVinci's. "I guess it all depends on Edmund," she said at last. "On what he wants out of life."

# 26

## · *KHAN* ·

### February, Kansas City

During Khan's meeting with Arthur Littlewood, Khan made a split-second decision to withhold information. Littlewood had handed him a hypothesis (on the proverbial silver platter, no less) to describe what was creating the isotemporal return pockets and making objects disappear. It had come in the form of a simple question: "Where could the energy necessary for such return pockets be coming from?" Khan knew the answer to that.

He might not know *why* his machine was drawing extra power, and he certainly didn't know how to fix it—yet—but he knew where the energy for the return pockets was coming from. It was his machine. As for the chaotic nature of the disappearances, Littlewood had agreed with him that nonlinearity could account for those. And thank goodness for that. If the disappearances followed chronology, Khan would have been one of the first to go.

On the flight back to Kansas City, Khan scribbled

formulae on the back of his drink napkin and then when he ran out of room, the air sickness bag. Should he share the information with Littlewood? If he kept it to himself, it might come in handy in the future as leverage . . .

That decided it. Khan was a fan of keeping an ace in his pocket.

Leverage had served him well with Nevis, recently. After complaining for weeks that Nevis's presence kept him from working at his best, Khan had apparently convinced Nevis it was true. A classic exchange: I can only give you what you want if you give me something I need.

No, Khan wasn't giving away the information to Littlewood when he didn't have anything to gain by doing so. Yet.

Back in his own lab, Khan set to work. What error of construction had introduced the extra power his machine was drawing? If he could eliminate that, he could stop space-time from snatching duplicated items out of the present, sending them who-knew-where. Khan shuddered, distracted at the thought of being sent *who-knew-where*. He returned yet again to his derivations and calculations. He had gone over every line, but could spot no error. He had reviewed every aspect of his process control program but could see no mistake. It was intensely aggravating.

More and more, his drive to get the machine functional was centered on the desire to send Nevis on a one-way trip. He had not, of course, told Nevis of the potential hazard of return voyages made without the machine turned on. It was the beauty of working with someone so ignorant of Khan's first and second laws of temporal conservation. Nevis couldn't formulate the right questions, or *any* question more specific than, "Is it safe?" to which Khan would of course reply, "Yes." He might even throw in a little reassurance: "The laws that govern time travel are inexorable. You and I could no more make them 'unsafe' than we could make gravity unsafe."

Khan hadn't yet worked out what it was Nevis wanted from the past, other than vague hints about "righting an egregious wrong." Fine. Let him right his wrong. But Khan wasn't having Nevis sticking around, no doubt continuing to blackmail him, after that. A scientist needed freedom.

If getting rid of Nevis was high on his list of tasks, getting out of this hellhole came next. It was his second February in Kansas City, and the place hadn't improved on acquaintance. He was going somewhere warm. Venezuela, or an island nearby. Or maybe the Maldives. Just as soon as he could to figure out where he'd introduced the error governing the power draw . . .

It was with these pleasant thoughts in mind that Khan first noticed Benjamin Nevis had set up surveillance on the lab. There was a hidden camera, a tiny black one of only one-and-a-half centimeters square, hidden in Khan's own mini-speakers, which he'd purchased to listen to opera. Not because he enjoyed opera, but because it annoyed the hell out of Nevis.

Khan's nostrils flared as he looked straight into the camera.

*Uh-oh.* He was *staring* into the camera. And looking angry. He couldn't have Nevis realizing he'd caught on.

"You stupid speaker!" he thundered. "Why aren't you working?" After this, he set the speaker back down and began muttering to himself about blasted faulty electronics made in Canada. After a decent interval, he looked back to the speaker, and said, "I guess it would help if I plugged you in." Rolling his eyes at himself, he pretended to do just this, and then continued business as normal, with only slightly more dislike for the man who'd insinuated his way into the lab.

What did it matter if Nevis wanted to spy on him? The man was a complete ignoramus who wouldn't understand space-time if it bit him in the ass. Between bouts of anger and grudging admiration, however, Khan questioned for the first time the wisdom of sticking with Nevis as a colleague rather than Arthur Littlewood.

## 27

### *· EDMUND ·*

### February 1601, London

Edmund rode his horse hard, trusting the poor beast was glad of the exercise on so cold a morning. Over and over, his thoughts returned to Halley—to her kiss. Her lips had seared his, and he burned still with the heat of her mouth.

He chided himself a fifth or sixth time: *he must not think on her.*

He must think of his duty. Think of Geoffrey, languishing, imprisoned. Think of the consequences for his family—for his sons—should Geoffrey be found a traitor. Pressing his heels to his horse's flanks again, Edmund felt sudden remorse for having let himself be delayed by the appearance of Halley and Quintus. What if he should find himself at the bottom of an endless line of suitors to Sir Robert? The Presence Chamber was surely more crowded than ever, just now. All those nobles who could, would attend at court, whether to show their loyalty to the Crown or from a desire to be kept abreast of news regarding treasonous Essex. Could Edmund hope to be heard?

He *had* to be.

He should have returned to court last night and taken rooms. His grandfather had lived at court briefly and often admonished Edmund that he must do the same if he wished to get ahead in life. Since becoming Earl, however, Edmund's ambitions had been confined to his own manor and his own household. Now that there were children, his desire to remain at home was doubled. What pleasure could compare to the sunshine of his son's smile?

At the question, meant to be rhetorical, Halley's visage appeared in his mind's eye, and his memories seemed to slide sideways. Halley's love could compare . . .

He wanted a life with her. Halley had come here, presumably to return him to that life. But was this even possible? And would she—or Littlewood—know what was possible? Whether one Edmund might return while another remained, as had happened originally? Or were all the Edmunds irrevocably fused together by whatever hand had brought him hither? What if Halley and Quintus had no answers? Or what if the answer lay not in science but in divine ordination? In either case, how could Littlewood be expected to know about something that had never before happened—this translation from his single self into a self that recalled two lives.

*And two loves.*

Good God! Surely he could not be expected to make choice betwixt them! Merciful heaven, let this pass . . .

He began to pray, chanting his way through those parts of the *Book of Common Prayer* he had committed to memory. But here, too, was confusion. *Lead us not into temptation*: what did that mean in his circumstance? Had not Christ declared the Father intended a man to cleave to one wife?

Abandoning the prayer book, Edmund forced his thoughts back to his brother's peril. It was almost a relief to return to that problem. There was a solution for Geoffrey: obtain his brother's release. What solution was there for a man with two homes, two loves, two sets of conflicting vows?

He spurred his horse forward, trying to rid his mind of all thoughts but those pertaining to the present moment. His brother's life lay in question. He must gain admittance to the Presence Chamber, find Sir Robert Cecil—or perhaps the Queen herself—and plead for his brother's release.

As a peer of the realm, Edmund's admittance into court was assured—a privilege granted to the noble born. It was for the denial of this privilege that Essex, once so favored by the Crown, had mounted his rebellion, attempting to force his way into court.

The palace, at last, loomed before Edmund. Within minutes, he was admitted to Whitehall, giving his name and title to a tall man who looked under-rested, underpaid, and woefully under-dressed compared to the brightly costumed nobility he admitted. Edmund thanked the man, who paid him no heed, having already moved on to the next finely clothed aristocrat in line.

Edmund had donned the new sleeves and the ruff Maria had made for him, and even he could admit he cut a more dashing figure dressed thus. But would it help? His aim was to clear his brother, not to strut peacock-like among fellow aristocrats. Yet it seemed the one could not be had without the other . . .

Although Edmund had arrived early, the Presence Chamber was far from empty. From the look of some of his fellow-petitioners, they had not bothered going to bed. He knew well of the Queen's ability to out-dance her courtiers, sometimes until dawn. What if she and her privy councilors had but recently gone abed? Edmund's hopefulness faltered. Until he reminded himself such a thing was beyond his control and was therefore not worth wasting his thoughts on. How long was he willing to wait? For as long as it took.

He searched the milling crowd for someone he might know. Names came to him: Camden, Carlisle, de Montfort, and many others. Men whose company his father and grandfather had encouraged him to pursue, back in the days when Edmund's heart had been for the sea. Before his elder brother had died, leaving the peerage to Edmund. Those dreams of maritime adventure seemed now a lifetime ago. He recollected how deeply he had longed to venture across the ocean, but now he had seen what lay on the far side of the Atlantic; it could not enchant with the same siren-call as before. He had seen the New World, from one ocean to the other, and he loved none of it so well as the wife who lived therein, his Halley. Nay! What thoughts were these? His mind was like a stone cast over still water, skipping hither and yon. It must cease! He was here, in the Old World. Here, where *Maria* was his wife. Here, where dwelt Thomas and John, and soon baby Charles, whose futures hung on

143

what he accomplished today at court.

But even as he reminded himself of these things, he remembered Halley's face. The severe arch of her dark brow at those times when she informed him that his sixteenth century was showing. The heady peal of her laughter when she told him she loved him the more for it. The warmth of her light brown skin as they lay unclothed beneath crisp hotel sheets. The memories assaulted him, hard and fast. How could he have thought it possible to resume his life here, to forget Halley? And yet . . . he must. Here he was a father. His children, so beloved that his heart ached to think on them—these same depended on his success today.

And yet . . . *what if?* What if he could travel forward again with Halley and also remain behind? If he could multiply himself once again, as had happened before? But could he willingly leave this life? He shook his head. He knew not the answer. His situation was impossible.

He looked about for a flagon of wine with which to steady himself. Finding some, he poured it and drank slowly, gazing about the Presence Chamber, where eventually Her Majesty Elizabeth Regina must venture forth to greet her knights and ladies.

At the top of the room, from whence the Queen would issue, stood a cluster of men dressed with more flamboyance than Edmund would have thought possible. None wore orange—a color reserved for the Crown alone—but they had clothed themselves in every other color of the rainbow. Yellow-y golds seemed especially popular, although one young man with long blond hair wore a deep emerald green doublet and brown breeches over ivory hose. These colors, in combination with the bright jewels sewn to his doublet, put Edmund in mind of a Christmas tree.

It was the intrusion of yet another twenty-first century recollection.

He must endeavor to keep his seventeenth century wits about him.

He approached the gaudy group, composed of earls like himself and one duke. But if he had hoped to be recognized and admitted to their number, he was disappointed. Those around the outskirts closed rank at his approach, showing him the backs of their flamboyant cloaks. Irritated and uncertain, Edmund looked about for another group to which he might attach himself. Beside a table with flagons of ale and wine, he saw an overdressed young man about his own age. Under pretense of refilling his goblet, Edmund approached the young man.

The two conversed pleasantly enough until Edmund brought forth his purpose: to seek the release of his brother, lately imprisoned following Lord Essex's failed coup. Upon hearing this, the young man with whom Edmund conversed turned pale and remembered himself of urgent business he must conduct at the opposite side of the hall.

"Pray you forgive me," the young man said, with a bow not quite as deep as Edmund's rank deserved.

Scowling, Edmund found himself once more alone. Two more times, he attempted to attach himself to lone courtiers, only to find himself rebuffed as soon as he mentioned his purpose.

By late afternoon, the Queen had still not made an appearance, nor had Sir Robert Cecil. They were presumably engaged in the business of the Crown, along with others of her privy council, none of whom were presently in the hall.

As the day came to a close—early because it was winter—Edmund gained the attention of a very talkative, very finely dressed man some fifteen years his senior. The man did not introduce himself, as though Edmund must naturally know his name.

"I am told," the man said, "that your brother hath been unfortunately detained at Her Majesty's pleasure."

"He hath," replied Edmund.

"You have my deepest sympathy."

Edmund grunted. "I would rather have the ear of my lord Sir Robert Cecil."

"As would many gathered hereby." The man was silent for a moment before adding, "Such things can be procured, you understand."

Edmund did not understand. He indicated this with a single raised brow.

The man began toying with a bright pendant he wore, encrusted with rubies, emeralds, and dull uncut diamonds. When Edmund said nothing, the man removed the glove of his right hand, the fingers of which held each a ring whose value Edmund could not begin to calculate, having never purchased anything so fine.

The man tucked his glove into his doublet and began admiring his rings. "Every introduction has a price, you see."

With that, Edmund *did* see. His disgust must have displayed itself on his face, for the man with whom he had been conversing assumed a haughtier expression.

"I wish you the favor of Lady Fortuna," said the man, bowing exactly to the level due an earl. "You will need it."

Almost as soon as the man departed to entreat a bribe from some other courtier, Edmund heard a commotion at the top of the room. He turned in hopeful expectation. It was one of the queen's ladies in waiting. Kat—or Katherine. Edmund remembered having danced with her when they were children. Would she remember him?

He pushed forward along with the rest of those gathered in the hall, but Kat or Katherine or whatever her name was merely whispered into the ear of the duke in the cliquish group at the top of the room and then returned from whence she had come. The duke detached himself from the group, departing the chamber on some errand unknown, presumably at the behest of the Queen.

Briefly Edmund considered pursuing the man and stating his need of assistance, but no—if the man were engaged on an errand by the Queen, it would be unwise for Edmund to detain him.

Squaring his shoulders, Edmund returned to the alcove he had claimed as his own for the past several hours. Just one more courtier lounging in hopes of a favor, a redress, a promotion—who knew. He was bored and hungry and altogether wretched.

But then he remembered Geoffrey, who was *actually* wretched, and he berated himself for indulging in self-pity. He could surely await, posturing with the best of them for the sake of his imprisoned brother.

As it grew late, Edmund grew weary. His mind began to wander between the centuries he knew. At moments he saw his fellow courtiers as elegantly dressed men and women representative of the finest members of a noble realm, but then his perspective would shift to that of a twenty-first century observer, and the men and women surrounding him looked like nothing so much as a collection of gaudy throw pillows, decorated to within an inch of their lives with tassels, poufs, slashes, and jewels.

Just when he was beginning to despair of speaking to anyone, there was a hubbub at the top of the room. Edmund looked up to see musicians following a train of courtiers dressed more soberly than the peacocks in the hall, and at the head of all walked Her Majesty, Elizabeth, crowned and resplendent in virginal whites and golds. Her face paint was so thick it resembled a mask, but there was no mistaking her for anything but one of the world's most powerful sovereigns. This was a woman who knew her place, and that place was at the very apex of humanity.

Those in the room swelled forward, attempting to move elegantly so as not to appear to rush the queen and her attendants, but within a minute the bottom half of the room emptied of all but those servants engaged to refill platters and flagons.

Edmund, who at six feet stood taller than most of the others in the room, glanced eagerly from face to face of Her Majesty's attendants, searching for Sir Robert. Alas, he did not see the man anywhere.

A moment later the musicians struck up an energetic *galliard*, which Her Majesty led with Thomas Egerton, Keeper of the Seal, who looked very much as if he would have preferred a warm bed and a cold beer. Edmund shook his head at himself. No one in this century preferred their beer *cold*.

For another two hours, Edmund waited to see if Sir Robert Cecil would put in an appearance. As he himself grew more and more weary, Edmund observed that the Queen seemed to be getting her second wind. She danced with more enthusiasm and leapt with more vigor than anyone else in the room, despite being twice the age of many of them.

Watching the Queen as she flirted, accepting elaborate compliments the givers must have spent all day composing, Edmund grew more and more despondent. He pressed forward at every opportunity, but he began to admit he had no chance of reaching her inner circle this night. Nor did Sir Robert Cecil appear. At last, Edmund admitted defeat. Having no heart for dancing or merriment, it were better he departed until the morrow.

There were no rooms to be had at court, and so, dejected, Edmund gave up and rode to the Tower, to offer his brother what small comfort he could.

# 28

## · HALLEY ·

### February 1601, London

Halley didn't know the first thing about how to get someone out of jail in 1601, but she knew enough about her husband to be certain he wouldn't rest until he'd done it. Maria, who'd been impossible to avoid even though Halley wanted to avoid her, told her the Earl had sent word he would return that evening rather than hire rooms at court. Midnight arrived, and still he wasn't back. Maria bid Halley, Quintus, and DaVinci goodnight, saying she would rather await her lord in bed. Halley wanted to shout that she'd rather do that, too.

"We still don't know what's going on with Edmund," she complained to her friends as soon as Maria was out of earshot. "How is it fair he wouldn't even take five minutes to let us know that?"

Quintus replied. "He is an honorable man. Since he chose to leave as he did, we must assume he had no time to spare."

Halley wanted to snap back that she deserved

better, but her throat was so sore that speaking wasn't worth the effort.

"Hal's got a point, though," said DaVinci. "We don't know what's happened to Edmund. I mean, is there another Edmund hiding out somewhere, or is he the only one? And are we even sure he recognized you guys?"

"It appeared so to me," said Quintus.

"He knew me," said Halley.

Of course Edmund had known her. He'd whispered her name under his breath. He'd kissed her. He definitely knew who she was. The problem was that it looked like he *also* knew who Maria was.

Maria. The woman was everything a generous hostess should be, but it would have been a lot easier if Maria had been stingy, grumpy, and honestly, quite a bit uglier. In fact, it would've been great if the kids were all brats, too.

Halley allowed herself a painful glance at the musicians gallery.

DaVinci, noticing, took her hand. "How are you doing?"

Halley returned her gaze to the fireplace. "I've been better."

Quintus withdrew his sword and began sharpening it or honing it or polishing it—Halley couldn't tell which. She reached for a goblet of spiced wine and swallowed, the burn of the alcohol numbing her throat enough that she could ask the question that haunted her.

"What if space-time decrees there's only going to be one Edmund, forever and ever, amen?" she asked.

DaVinci replied, "There's not a shred of evidence

suggesting—"

Halley cut her off. "There's no evidence either way. *No. Evidence.* We can't even run an experiment."

"This *is* the experiment," said Quintus.

"That's right," said DaVinci. "We are running the experiment. Which means we are doing exactly what we should be doing to keep everyone in this room happy."

Halley looked at her friend. Fire sparked in DaVinci's eyes. Halley wasn't the only one who stood to lose everything if space-time wasn't in a generous mood. They all stood to lose exactly the same thing: the love of their lives.

"It's not fair," she said softly. "How are we supposed to figure this out?"

"I pray," said Quintus. "To Venus and to the Virgin Mary."

"Wow, babe," said DaVinci. "Aren't you resourceful."

Halley felt a tired smile creep onto her face. It was so Quintus to hedge his bets. And if Halley had known any prayers to the goddess of love . . .

"Well, there's no sense borrowing trouble," murmured DaVinci.

"The wisdom of Grandma Shaughnessy, I presume?" asked Halley.

"If so, she had it of the Christus," said Quintus. "Father Joe often quotes something much like that."

"You never cease to amaze, babe," said DaVinci. Her eyes then drifted back to Halley. Frowning, DaVinci placed a hand on Halley's forehead. "You're face is weirdly red. I think you might be running a fever."

"I'm just too close to the fire." Halley tried scooting her heavy chair over the flagstones and away from the flames.

"No. I'm closer to the fire than you are," said DaVinci, testing her own forehead, "and I'm not as hot. Quintus, check her forehead."

"There's no need—" began Halley, but Quintus had already risen.

He placed a hand to her forehead, to her wrist, and to the back of her neck.

"Assuredly, you are fevered," he said at last. "You require rest, garlic, and cucumber. I shall ask the housekeeper."

Before Halley could protest, Quintus rose to exit the Great Hall.

"I'm putting her to bed," DaVinci called to Quintus. Then, to Halley she said, "Did you say your throat's been bothering you?"

"Yeah. I thought it was all those chips we ate, but maybe I'm getting a cold."

"Your nose isn't running. How many days since this started?"

Halley shrugged. "Two? No. Three? Or maybe four."

DaVinci stood. "Come on. Let's get you in bed, and then I'm using my phone flashlight on your throat."

Halley rose and went with DaVinci to their bedchamber. She did feel a little achy and feverish. Actually, a lot achy and feverish.

Once DaVinci got Halley's outer layers off, Halley crawled gratefully into bed. DaVinci pulled her cell phone out. Halley didn't have the energy to scold her for bringing it.

"Don't look at me with that judge-y face," said DaVinci. "Littlewood made me bring it for the timer, because I'm going back before you guys, remember?"

"Oh. Right." Halley had been so focused on Edmund that she'd forgotten about DaVinci's imminent departure.

"Open your mouth as wide as you can."

Halley did, and it made her throat feel even worse.

"Oh my gosh," said DaVinci. "You can close your mouth. You have strep throat."

"It's just a little sore throat—"

"—covered in white splotches," said DaVinci. "Strep. I had it last winter."

Halley sighed and closed her eyes. "Great. That's just perfect."

DaVinci pocketed her phone. "Okay. When I leave to report on things, I am getting you some antibiotics."

"When Quintus is already bringing cukes and garlic?" asked Halley, trying to inject a little levity.

"Very funny. I'm sure Quintus means well—he was the go-to first aid guy for his legion—but you are getting on antibiotics, stat. Strep is highly contagious and can lead to scarlet fever, which would *not* be good for the pregnant lady."

Halley's breath caught. *She* was pregnant, too. "Would it be dangerous for . . . the baby?" she asked.

"Honestly? I don't know. But it can't be good to have a newborn—"

"DaVinci, I'm pregnant." Tears spilled from her eyes as soon as the words were out.

"You're what? You are? Pregnant? Oh my gosh!

Congratulations! I mean, are congratulations in order or not?"

Halley squeezed her eyes shut to clear them of tears. "I don't know. I have . . . no idea . . ." Her throat was too tight to talk.

"Okay," said DaVinci. "As soon as I get back to Florida, I am researching the hell out of strep and pregnancy, *and* I'm getting you antibiotics, *and* I'm bringing you prenatal vitamins. And don't even go there with the 'there weren't prenatals in the blah-blah-blah century,' or I swear I will bring a pregnant doctor with me. Pregnancy doctor. Whatever."

"OB GYN," whispered Halley, smiling halfheartedly.

"That's the one." DaVinci pulled Halley's covers higher and then asked softly, "Does Edmund know?"

Halley shook her head. "We had that fight, and I didn't get the chance to tell him before he . . . disappeared." As soon as the final word was out, Halley began sobbing.

"Okay, *shush-shush-shush*," murmured DaVinci. "You need to rest. You need to rest for *both* your sakes. And I will give Edmund a talking to as soon as . . . " She broke off just as Quintus entered the room bearing a tray.

Halley brought a finger to her lips, and DaVinci nodded vigorously.

"Have you shared food or drink with anyone?" Quintus asked as he set down the tray. Something strong-smelling was steaming in a small clay vessel.

Halley shook her head. Then she remembered kissing Edmund. Did that count?

"I . . . I kissed Edmund. This Edmund. Just this

155

morning."

"Hmm . . ." DaVinci arched a single eyebrow. "So . . . what kind of kiss was this? A quick little peck on the cheek?"

"*No,*" whispered Halley. Her skin seemed to burn with the memory of his mouth melting into hers this morning.

"Okay," said DaVinci. "Antibiotics for Edmund, too. And we'd probably better warn him not to, *um,* kiss Maria or the kids."

Halley wanted to feel happy at the thought of Edmund not able to kiss Maria, but what did kissing matter when she didn't even know if he wanted to be with her anymore?

He'd pushed away from their kiss.

"Drink this," said Quintus.

She swallowed the warm liquid, vaguely spicy and salty and alcoholic, all at the same time. It eased her throat.

"She will sleep well," was the last thing she heard before she sank into oblivion.

## 29

## · *EDMUND* ·

### February 1601, London

When Edmund was re-admitted into Geoffrey's cell, he noticed that an improved table had replaced the rickety one from earlier. A candle burned brightly on the table. Better still, the window had been covered, keeping some of the cold out.

Geoffrey was curled into a tight ball and wrapped inside Edmund's fur-lined cloak. Edmund had missed the cloak just now when he rode over from Whitehall, but seeing his brother thus miserable, he could not regret the sacrifice. Tomorrow he would bring blankets. Food from home. Flagons of wine.

Ye gods, but he was thirsty.

Edmund reached for a jar of beer—also new—and drank deeply. Then, reflecting Geoffrey might be thirsty when he woke, Edmund set the vessel down.

"Brother," he said quietly.

Geoffrey startled, scrambling backward on all fours.

"Tis I, Edmund."

His brother stopped scrambling and rose unsteadily. "Thou dost not drink, surely," he said, noting the jar in Edmund's hand.

"I left some for thee," replied Edmund, attempting to hand it to his brother.

"It may be poisoned!" Geoffrey's face crinkled as though he was going to cry. "And if it be poisoned, brother, and thou diest? Who then will see I am given justice?"

Edmund sighed. Geoffrey's paranoia was infamous.

"None mean to poison you. Nor am I poisoned, as you can see plainly," said Edmund.

Geoffrey rose and stepped closer, taking the candle from the table in order to examine Edmund's eyes.

"You see? I am whole and well."

Grunting, Geoffrey took the jar of ale and consumed it.

"Hast thou had food as well?" asked Edmund.

"Aye. But I feared to eat it." He indicated a wrapped bundle on the table, containing stale bread and some sort of meat or vegetable pie.

Edmund extended his hand. "Let me be thy taster," he said, knowing Geoffrey might well starve himself otherwise. After a bite of each, Edmund returned them to his brother, who devoured the food. He must ask Maria what foods else he could bring, such as would nourish best, whilst providing the least temptation for a hungry jailor. His wife would know this sort of thing.

His wife. Great God in heaven. *One* of his two wives. He had to return home to speak with each tonight . . .

"I cannot stay," said Edmund.

"Aye," said Geoffrey. "I did not expect thou wouldst bed down here with me." He said it in a slightly accusing tone, as if to imply a good brother would do just that.

"I visited court today," said Edmund, "and shall do so again on the morrow and so on, till I have secured thy release." He felt suddenly exhausted and wished only to be home. "I must leave. I pray you pardon the shortness of my visit."

He turned for the door.

"Brother," cried Geoffrey.

Edmund turned back.

"Thanks. Much thanks. Thou art a good brother. And a good man. And better to me than I have deserved."

"Goodnight, brother," said Edmund.

As he rode home to the confusion of his two wives, his double life, the opening lines of one of Shakespeare's sonnet repeated to the thud of his horse's hooves:

*Two loves have I*
*Two loves have I*
*Two loves have I . . .*

## 30

### · *HALLEY* ·

### February 1601, London

Although Halley had fully intended to wait up for Edmund, she slept hard and woke to a darkened room, with only the flicker of fire for light.

"Ed-*mund*," she rasped.

DaVinci was at her side in an instant. "Quintus, reheat that drink for her," Then she turned to Halley. "How are you feeling?"

Halley struggled to keep her eyes open. "I . . . want . . . Edmund."

"Here, swallow this," said DaVinci, holding up what looked like brown jam. It had a strong smell. Tangy and sweet and vaguely familiar.

Halley didn't have the strength to protest. She swallowed whatever it was—watermelon pickles? No, pickled *jam*, maybe? The slippery substance seemed to burn its way down to her stomach.

"Quintus is reheating some willow-bark-infused mead that the housekeeper gave him earlier. It helps you sleep."

"Ed-*mund?*" She'd meant to say, *And what about Edmund? Is he okay? Is his brother okay? Why isn't he here?* Instead, her eyes closed and she drifted. Beside her, DaVinci and Quintus were speaking softly, but a throbbing headache made it seem like they were shouting.

"The willow will bring her relief," Quintus murmured.

"And the mead knocks her out cold," replied DaVinci. "Win-win!"

Halley groaned, trying to indicate she wanted them to stop shouting—or was it whispering? Mercifully, they fell silent, and she slept again, not waking until the following morning.

~ ~ ~

"Halley?"

It was DaVinci. Halley's head still ached, and her throat burned, but her joints no longer felt like they were on fire.

"Your fever's down," said DaVinci. "We got you to take some meds earlier, but I don't think you were very awake."

Halley rubbed her eyes. DaVinci was right about the fever. She didn't feel hot. In fact, she felt a little cold.

"Do you think you could eat a little something?" asked DaVinci.

Halley propped herself up a little and noticed someone sleeping in a chair by the fire. Edmund?

"Ed-*mund*," she rasped.

But it was only Quintus, who stirred and rose, crossing to Halley. He placed a cool hand to her forehead.

"I need to see Edmund," Halley said.

"*Shh*, let's get a little something inside you." said DaVinci. "Drink this."

Halley swallowed the warm beverage.

"It's an herbal tea," said DaVinci. "With willow bark for pain. Last night you got mead with the same bark. And before you ask, mead is honey fermented with water and beer-yeast." She smiled proudly.

"The fever is reduced," said Quintus. Then he smiled, his gaze drifting to DaVinci. "Caesar accepted mead once as pay from a Gallic tribe that kept bees."

DaVinci smiled back at him.

"Super cool, babe."

"Where's Edmund?" Halley asked again. The drink was definitely helping her throat.

DaVinci and Quintus exchanged glances.

"You're . . . *quarantined*, Hal. And Edmund didn't get Geoffrey free yesterday, so he went back to try again this morning. He left before dawn."

Halley felt tears burning in the back of her eyes. He'd left before dawn? Without even stopping to see how she was doing?

"Does he know I'm sick?" she asked, her voice cracking. There was no one as comforting as Edmund when she was sick. How could he have left?

"*Um*, yeah. Everyone knows you're sick. Hence the quarantine. Speaking of which, let's get that second antibiotic down you."

"Second?" asked Halley. "But you . . . did you already leave and come back?"

"Had to," said DaVinci. "They were fresh out of amoxicillin at the local apothecary."

Halley finished the cup of warm willow bark tea.

"You slept through it all," said DaVinci. "I visited our century for about six hours and ran errands like a crazy person."

"Oh." Halley's brain felt like a mud-slide had passed through—and possibly set up residence. "I missed that."

"Well," said DaVinci, "Littlewood was able to insert me back into this timeline only ten minutes after I left. So it was almost like I never left."

Quintus raised one brow. "It was assuredly *not* like you never left."

Halley heard his concern; Quintus was worried about the woman he loved—unlike *some* men. It was so unfair! Edmund might at least have kissed her goodbye. He'd already been exposed.

"Here." DaVinci was holding out another cup. "Drink this now. You'll like it."

Halley eyed the drinking vessel with suspicion. "Is this more of that . . . *jam*? That tasted like sweet pickles or something?"

"Oh," said DaVinci, eyebrows lifting. "I'm impressed you remember that. You were pretty out of it."

"What was that?"

"Some kind of chutney with preserved cucumber. A guarded family remedy for fevers, I guess," said DaVinci. "Cucumbers. Who knew, right? But, no, this isn't the chutney. I promise you'll like this."

Halley accepted the cup with some lingering misgivings. Lifting it to her mouth was a challenge; her muscles responded sluggishly. Catching a glimpse of the contents, she looked back up at DaVinci. "Orange juice? But . . . how—"

"Before you ask, yes it's modern. I brought a juice box. And, yes, I already burned the box. I wanted to bring you a complete breakfast from Chick-fil-A, but Everett vetoed that idea."

The juice was unexpectedly delicious, although that could have been because of the weird aftertaste left by the willow-bark tea.

"Thank you," murmured Halley, returning the empty cup.

"Someone was thirsty," said DaVinci. "Now: antibiotics round two."

"I think I missed round one," said Halley.

"Yeah. I slipped it in the cucumber stuff. You're supposed to take the meds with actual food, though, so we definitely want you to eat this time."

"Understood," said Halley. "Bring on the grainy bread and hard cheese." Her throat felt enough better that she thought she could manage crusty Elizabethan bread.

"Actually," said DaVinci, "I managed to get you eggs and ham, Hensley Manor-style."

"Oh?"

"We've been keeping it warm over here," she said, walking to the fireplace. As she brought the food to Halley, DaVinci described some sort of custard-egg dish she was totally teaching Branson the next time she saw him.

First Halley tried the ham, which was pretty much . . . *bacon*. After that, she picked at the egg dish, which was oddly sweet, like a fluffy, sugared crêpe. But when DaVinci handed her the antibiotics, she frowned.

"I'm feeling so much better," she said. "Maybe we should save the drugs for Edmund and . . . and, you know, Maria." She couldn't say "his wife."

"Nope. Edmund, Quintus, and I discussed this already. Edmund's a carrier. You're a carrier. Twenty-four hours after antibiotics, you two won't be contagious. Well, technically your fever has to be gone, too. But since you and Edmund are the carriers, you're the ones we have to heal, to prevent the sickness from spreading."

Halley nodded at what her friend said, but she was hung up on the fact that Quintus and DaVinci had spoken with Edmund, and she still hadn't. It wasn't fair. Was Edmund avoiding her now? Didn't he care how sick she was? How did he not understand how badly she needed his reassurance that things would be okay? That he would go home with her, and damn the consequences? She knew it was selfish, but she didn't care. She was tired and she was sick and her husband had been sleeping in someone else's bed.

"It's really the last straw, you know? Getting sick now," Halley said.

"Oh, Hal . . ." DaVinci sighed and took the empty plate from her friend. "There's something we need to talk about. A couple things, actually. You being sick is . . . well, it's not the only bad thing going on right now, okay?"

"What is it?" asked Halley.

DaVinci looked to Quintus, whose face had darkened.

"What?" Halley repeated.

It was Quintus who answered. "Everett has vanished."

# 31

## ·NEVIS·

### February, Kansas City

Back in January, Benjamin Nevis had decided on a course of action he wasn't crazy about, but which had to be pursued. If he was going to be the man to bring time travel into "custody," it would first be necessary to render any machine he didn't control—such as Littlewood's—inoperative. Nevis knew a little about explosives, and he set out to learn more.

He wasn't crazy about returning to Florida to blow up Littlewood's machine, and that meant that with each passing week, he found another reason to put it off. But then one day Khan, in arguing against asking for help from Arthur Littlewood, had let slip there was yet *another* time machine in Montecito, California. This machine, Khan claimed to have built on his own, using nothing but the information on the thumb drive. Khan wasn't sure where the other machine was now, for which he blamed Littlewood.

By engaging in some investigative research, Nevis had determined where the third machine was being stored, and he even made inquiries about purchasing it. The owners seemed to think it was an art installation of some kind, and they were *not* selling. So now he had two machines to destroy. Only then would his monopoly on time travel be absolute. Well, always assuming Khan could get the machine in Kansas City to work. That in itself was reason enough to put off destroying the others. But he had two addresses, and he had a materials and supplies list for his little foray into the world of controlled explosives. One of these days, he was going to have to hop a couple of planes and take care of things.

## 32

### · *HALLEY* ·

### February 1601, London

Halley's eyes flew wide. "Everett vanished? You mean . . . he disappeared like Edmund?"

DaVinci nodded solemnly. "Littlewood saw it happen. He says that now he's sure some sort of power flux within space-time is causing the disappearances. He doesn't understand where the energy is coming from. But he stressed that, *um* . . . Crap. Help me out here with the science-speak, babe?"

Quintus obliged. "Littlewood feels that because Edmund and Everett vanished due to an instability, and not a planned journey, it is impossible to predict the consequences of returning them to the twenty-first century. Littlewood has attempted to communicate further with Jules Khan on the matter, but Khan has not responded."

"But Littlewood told us to ask Edmund a few questions," said DaVinci. "Like, whether Edmund knew the fate of the, *um*, other Edmund. The one who was here in 1601 *first*, which we did this morning

168

before he left."

"What did he say?" Halley's heart pounded.

"He is no more," said Quintus.

"*What?*" said Halley.

"Babe! Seriously?" DaVinci turned to Halley. "1601 Edmund *does* still exist. It seems that he merged back together with our Edmund. So now there's only one single Edmund."

"Oh no," murmured Halley. Only one Edmund, who contained both his two selves? This wasn't good, but it sure explained a lot . . .

"But . . . but he can be split in half again, can't he?" asked Halley. "Multiplied by space-time or whatever when we take him home?"

"Littlewood says we can't be sure until we try it," said DaVinci.

"We are running the experiment right now," said Quintus.

"There's something else," said DaVinci. "Another hiccup that Edmund and Quintus noticed." DaVinci unfolded a piece of paper. "Everett had me make another printout from Wikipedia, on Edmund and his family."

As Halley's eyes flew down the page, DaVinci spoke to her softly. "Everett and Dr. Littlewood didn't catch it because it's not a change, to them. I didn't catch it either because I was so caught up with prescriptions and everything—"

"Oh," whispered Halley, seeing the change. "Oh *no!*"

She looked up at DaVinci.

"According to this, Geoffrey dies at the Tower of London."

## 33

### · *EDMUND* ·

### February 1601, London

The Wikipedia pronouncement was at the forefront of Edmund's mind: somehow, he must reverse Geoffrey's doom. Beyond the terrible loss of his brother, that doom would cast a pall over the Aldwych reputation and his sons' futures. Edmund needed no Wikipedia page to tell him that.

Quintus had delivered the news as soon as Edmund had returned to Hensley, shortly after one in the morning. They had spoken of many things, but of none more urgent than Geoffrey's fate. Edmund had been grateful Quintus did not ask him to speak of Halley, or of Maria, or of his plans for the future. Edmund didn't know what his plans were.

There had been the news of Everett's disappearance, too, but there was nothing Edmund could do about Everett. He did not even know what he could do concerning his own "disappearance."

One thing had come to him, though, as he tossed and turned the four hours he tried to sleep. Yesterday,

DaVinci had brought the *first* printout, which said Geoffrey lived to become a priest. Today, it read differently. Something had changed between yesterday morning and last night, and because of it, Geoffrey would die a traitor.

Edmund knew of only one thing that had changed between yesterday and today.

He had become distracted.

He had kissed Halley, whom he had thought lost to him forever. Then he had experienced horrifying guilt when his wife Maria, *heavy with his child*, had nearly walked in on the kiss. Since then, his love for Halley and his love for Maria—and his uncertainty what to do—had colored his every thought. It had kept him from being able to focus single-mindedly on freeing Geoffrey. Edmund needed to look no further than his own distracted heart to find the cause of his brother's death in the Tower.

Edmund slid from his bed and dressed in the dark.

He could not let this happen. He could not allow his personal conflict to cost Geoffrey his life. This had been the change to the timeline: Edmund had lost focus. This distraction, unchecked, would lead to his brother's being executed as a traitor. He vowed it would not happen.

His own wreck of a life, he could deal with after. For now, it must be his brother alone he thought of. By half past five, he was admitted to the Presence Chamber and strode to the top of the near-empty room. Here we would await the arrival of those peers with the most influence in the realm, other than the Crown's privy council, at least. He reasoned the gentlemen would arrive singly, which would make it more difficult for them to close ranks against him. But even if they arrived together, Edmund was in no mood to brook a rebuff today. He would be heard. He would see Geoffrey cleared of the appellation *traitor*.

The room was quiet but for servants cleaning and the snores of a few gentlemen who had fallen asleep drunk. All about him, Edmund saw evidence of a night of festivities that had lasted well past his departure at eleven. Servants now scurried to retrieve goblets, replace flagons, and mop up spills. The goblet of one slumbering gentleman clattered from his lap to the ground, but the gentleman was too inebriated to waken.

Edmund's mind returned to the Wikipedia pronouncement.

To his brother, executed. Tried and found guilty.

Edmund swore under his breath. "By God's wounds, it shall not be."

He would not betray his brother's trust in him.

The idea of betrayal stirred that other hornet's nest of thought: that he must either betray one of his wives by remaining, or the other by departing. But nay—he must not tread along that path: he had sworn off it.

A man was approaching him. It was Lord Camden. Swiftly Edmund bowed and gave greeting.

"Good morrow, sirrah."

"You are up betimes," murmured Camden.

"I might say the same of your lordship," said Edmund.

Camden laughed. "I am country-bred. I care not to sleep past the crewing of the cockerel."

"Crewing" echoed strangely in one part of Edmund's brain, while another part of his brain assured him the word could be spoken thus, here.

Edmund commanded himself to stay focused. "I am no friend to late nights," he replied.

Camden eyed Edmund in silence before speaking.

"I hear tell you have need of friends."

Edmund squared his shoulders and prepared to swallow his pride.

"I have, my lord. My brother is wrongly caught up in the net alongside those who attempted harm to the Queen. In very truth, though, my brother hath no wish except for Her Majesty's health and happiness."

"I am sure she will be glad to hear it," Camden said dryly. "Have you applied to those who might help you?"

"My lord," said Edmund, with a half bow, "I do so now."

"I hold no sway among the privy councilors."

"Nor do I. Worse still, I am ignorant as to who does," said Edmund. "Through my love of hearth and home, I have neglected court life."

"Hmmph," grunted Camden. "They say you have as many brats as years in your good lady's bed."

Edmund smiled. "God hath seen fit to bless us with three children."

"Much to your brother's disappointment, no doubt."

"Nay, my lord. Geoffrey is not a man to disregard the right of rule in his own case any more than in the case of the throne."

"Much good may it do him," said Camden, signaling a servant for ale.

173

"To whom should you apply yourself, my lord, were you in my place, with such a brother?"

"Why, to Heaven," said Camden. He quaffed his ale swiftly. "But also to Sir Roger de Beaumont."

"I know him not."

"You may recognize him by the great quantity of rings upon his fingers."

Edmund recalled the man who yesterday had suggested a bribe was in order.

"I see. And is there no other way forward?"

"Sir, I will speak plainly on two matters, as one country-loving gentleman to another. First, there is no other way in this present climate of Essex's treachery. Second, when once my friends do join me, I must ask that you depart. You do surely recognize that though your brother may be guiltless, he is nonetheless held for the gravest of crimes. Treason is an offense none at court can afford to appear careless of."

It was true. Camden had risked much simply to address him.

Edmund bowed deeply. "I thank you, sir, for your candor."

"If you wish to forward your plea, navigate along those channels which will deliver you thence."

Edmund departed to a quieter place from which he could reflect on Camden's advice. That it was sound and well-meant, he had no doubt. That he could bring himself to act on it was . . . *less* certain. It grated against his sense of what was right. To offer money or jewels to one he could neither respect nor like? It was a filthy and low business, as hateful to his Elizabethan self as to his twenty-first century self.

But his brother . . .

Was it this pride that would stand in the way of securing Geoffrey's release? It must not. Edmund's conscience might shrink from it, but in action he must not shrink. His course was plain. He must ride home and raid his meager treasury, not returning without a substantial gift with which to bribe his way to the ear of one of Her Majesty's privy councilors.

It was nearly three miles from Whitehall Palace to the environs of the bridge across the Thames. London Bridge would put him within half a mile of his brother's lodging at the Tower. Thus it would be but an additional mile to go there and back to the river crossing. Edmund determined he would visit Geoffrey and apprise him of how things stood.

When he was admitted to his brother's cell, Edmund found Geoffrey hunched over the single table in the room, evidently at prayer.

"How dost my brother?" asked Edmund.

"Hungry," replied Geoffrey. "Ill-rested. Thirsty. Ill-companioned, apart from thy visits." He looked up at Edmund with baleful eyes.

"I have brought thee this woolen coverlet, and with it Maria's love."

"Thy wife hath no love for me," said Geoffrey.

Edmund did not attempt to contradict him. He set the blanket on the dry straw upon which Geoffrey had been sleeping.

"Nay, here, here," said Geoffrey. "Bring it here. I do freeze without a proper fire." Geoffrey wrapped himself in the length of wool, shivering—possibly for effect only. It was hard to know with Geoffrey. "Dost thou see how my hands do quaver?" Geoffrey held out one hand. "Thinkest thou my nails are blue?"

175

Edmund frowned and examined Geoffrey's hands. "Thy fingers are well enough. Tis only dirt that discolors them."

Geoffrey grunted, almost as if in disappointment. "Yet my head doth ache with the cold. My legs can scarce bear me up for want of food. And I have an ague coming apace . . ."

While Geoffrey continued to catalog his numerous woes, Edmund set a flask of broth, another of wine, and a packet of dried fish alongside a considerable wedge of cheese. Eventually Geoffrey seemed to decide he would prefer eating and drinking to complaining, and he consumed the whole lot of it, without asking Edmund if he were hungry. He was not. He was consumed by fear for Geoffrey, anxiety over his wives, and uncertainty as to his success in any endeavor.

"Brother, I fear you must prepare yourself to stand trial for treason."

His brother made no response, except to finish the last of the wine. After this, he took himself to the corner lined in straw and lay himself upon it.

"I am afraid, Ned," Geoffrey confessed at last. "I did never conspire against the Crown, yet I know not how to prove it."

"I shall plead for thee," said Edmund.

"Aye."

Neither spoke for several minutes.

Eventually, Geoffrey threw back his new blanket and opened his cloak somewhat.

"I grow heated from the food in my belly," he said. "I thank thee, Ned." He hesitated and then added. "A better brother would have left some food for thee."

"Thou art as good a brother as I desire to know," Edmund said softly.

"I will be better. By God's wounds, I will devote myself to acts of mercy and charity."

Edmund smiled, imagining where Geoffrey would apply for funds for these acts of charity. Aloud, he said only, "I doubt it not. Rest thou for now, brother. I return to the palace this afternoon, where I shall speak for thee to all who will listen."

Geoffrey responded with a soft snore, his eyes having closed already.

Edmund crossed over to him, to resettle the blanket lest Geoffrey should grow cold while sleeping. He passed a hand over his brother's forehead, smoothing back his hair, and then frowned. Geoffrey was warm. Using the sensitive skin of his wrist, Edmund checked first Geoffrey's forehead and then his own. They felt much the same.

Exhaling heavily, Edmund pulled his gloves back on in preparation for the ride home. He throat felt dry, and he wondered if the jailer or porter might sell him a pot of ale, but by the time he was conducted from his brother's cell, he had forgotten to ask.

Back home in half an hour, Edmund went at once to his dressing chamber to seek out the chest wherein he kept the jewels he had inherited from his mother. He settled upon his mother's necklace, the finest piece of all. As he examined it, an odd prickling ran along his spine. Here it was, the necklace Khan had duplicated after Geoffrey had pawned it at a goldsmith. The goldsmith of course retained the necklace when Khan had departed, thus Edmund had been able to recover it in both centuries.

He turned over the clasp and fingered the ruby he'd removed for Halley's wedding ring. He then recalled how Maria had declared she would not wear so fine a necklace, disdaining it as much as Halley treasured it. Well, it would not be missed here at least. His decision made, Edmund deposited the necklace in his coin purse, tied at his waist. It was at this point he recalled the drugs Quintus had ordered him to take, lest he contract Halley's illness. He had dropped the medicine into his coin purse and then forgotten all about it.

Edmund frowned at the small pills. Halley had shown him articles on the Internet detailing the ills of overprescribing such curatives, and he had refused antibiotics on the only occasion a physician had offered them. He'd gotten well just fine on his own.

Briefly, Edmund wondered if his own dry throat might indeed be a sign he was ill, but then he decided it was natural to be hot and thirsty from much riding. He shook his head at the colorful pills and dropped them back into his purse.

Before he'd entered his dressing closet, Maria had not been in the bedchamber. He checked again before exiting to be sure she was absent still. He longed to go to her, to ask if she felt any of the signs indicating her time had come, but he knew that attention to one wife would only increase his guilt over the other. He must not increase his distraction.

"Nay, sirrah," he said to himself. He had a task to complete. He must aid his brother. After that, there would be plenty of time to decide what was to be done with his divided heart. And so, avoiding both the women he loved, Edmund rode back to Whitehall.

Late in the afternoon, Sir Roger de Beaumont reappeared, and Edmund approached him, cutting off another gentleman with the same goal. In less time than it took to reheat coffee in a microwave, Edmund had succeeded in bribing a court official. Sir Roger promised that if Edmund should deign to present himself at eleven of the clock that evening, he should, for his generous gift, have introduction to not one but *two* members of the privy council. What he did with the introduction was entirely up to him: no refunds, no complaints.

Heartily sick of all of it—court, bribes, and officials—Edmund determined he would spend the interval with Geoffrey. He arrived at the Tower just as the weary sun sank below the horizon. Here new troubles greeted him. Geoffrey, sprawled on cold stone and not his straw bedding, was fevered and wandering in his speech.

# 34

*· KHAN ·*

February, Kansas City

"It's been forty-eight hours since you consulted with Arthur Littlewood," Nevis said to Khan.

Khan, tinkering with a sensitive instrument, didn't respond.

"I want you to bring Littlewood here," Nevis announced.

Why would Nevis want that? Khan had been thinking about it—a lot—but he'd decided to try a few more things. If Nevis would just get out of the lab, Khan might even fire up the machine. After propping something in front of the surveillance camera, of course. No, this wasn't the time to invite Arthur Littlewood over for tea.

"There's no way," said Khan.

"Can he fix whatever's not working?"

Yes, but he wasn't telling Nevis that.

"Can he?"

"Maybe," snapped Khan. "Can you stop interrupting me? I'm trying to get some work done."

"If Littlewood can help, invite him here."

Khan had already decided that he didn't want Littlewood here. He wanted to maintain the secrecy of his location. He was so close. If he could just get the machine working, he could promise to send Nevis wherever he wanted to go, and then: *Oops!* Turn off the power.

"That wasn't a request," said Nevis. "I'm ordering you to get him here, whatever it takes to make that happen."

Khan barked out a laugh. "Order me all you want. Call him yourself if you want."

This was a bit risky, but the fact that Nevis hadn't threatened to do it already gave Khan just enough confidence to try calling the bluff. As Khan had hoped, Nevis did *not* threaten to call Littlewood. Had he figured out there was no way Littlewood would help if he knew Nevis and Khan were working together? Khan had certainly figured it out.

"Listen," said Khan. "I know you're tired of waiting, but I'm nearly there. Besides, I'm the last person in the world Littlewood wants to talk to. Well, other than you."

"He just met with you in Florida."

"I know," said Khan. "But I didn't tell you everything about that visit. Littlewood and I . . ." He broke off, trying to look upset. "Well, he and I had a huge fight at the end of our meeting. We parted on very bad terms. The worst terms."

"You didn't mention that before."

"You're not my mother."

"I am *not* your mother," said Nevis, "I'm the man telling you that you'd better make up with Littlewood.

I'm tired of waiting for this machine to be operational."

"And you think I'm not?" Khan threw his hands up. "Thanks for trying to help, but there is no circumstance under which Arthur Littlewood would agree to come here. Understand? I'd have to be literally his last hope for solving . . . some *unsolvable* problem."

Nevis drummed his fingers on the desk four times and then stood.

"I'm going to give you twenty-four hours to get this thing up and running. If it's not working by this time tomorrow, I'm calling Littlewood myself." With that, he exited the building.

Khan swore.

## 35

## · NEVIS ·

### February, Kansas City

Nevis had come to a decision. Ironically, Khan had just provided the push Nevis needed. It was time to destroy the other two time machines. Khan didn't think Littlewood would come help him unless he was desperate? Fine. Let's make him desperate. It stood to reason that the destruction of Littlewood's machine would make Littlewood much more interested in assisting Khan with his.

Nevis placed a call to United Airlines.

Forty-five minutes later, he had a flight booked to Santa Barbara, California followed five hours later by a red-eye from Los Angeles to West Palm Beach, Florida, followed by a third flight which would return him to Kansas City darned close to the twenty-four hour deadline he'd given Khan. The next twenty-six hours would be grueling, but very soon, all of Nevis's worries would be behind him.

Besides wanting Littlewood on-premise to get the machine working, Nevis had another reason for wanting the professor in Kansas City. One he'd been trying to find a way around. Unfortunately, there was no way around. The problem was that taking out the machines was only a partial solution. As long as the men capable of building them were still alive, they posed a threat to humankind. Bringing Littlewood to Kansas City would . . . *simplify* the one final step Nevis had to take.

Nevis didn't like what he was planning. Not one little bit. He wasn't a cold-blooded killer, but there was only one course open to him, he told himself, delivering one helluva pep talk on his drive to the airport.

The two scientists had to be eliminated. Nevis didn't want to do it. It was wrong, but if ever there was a time to think beyond his own moral comfort, this was it. Sometimes the stakes were too high for a man to ask himself what he did or did not want to do. Sometimes there was no good choice. Or rather, there was a bad choice, and there was a worse choice. Eliminating Littlewood and Khan would be bad. Allowing them to continue unchecked would be worse.

It was the only choice possible. Littlewood and Khan had to go. Nevis didn't like it, but he liked the alternative less.

# 36

## · *EDMUND* ·

### February 1601, London

Edmund could see Geoffrey was very ill. Illness was common during imprisonment where neither exercise, fresh air, nor wholesome food and drink were to be had, but Edmund had been hopeful his brother, ever hale and robust, would escape sickness.

He woke Geoffrey, bidding him drink.

His brother protested weakly but eventually swallowed a mouthful of small beer.

"How long have you been thus?" Edmund asked without much expectation of a response, nor did his brother answer him.

His own throat was afire, and Edmund finished the small beer in the vessel, reasoning that his brother could do with something more fortifying than weak beer. Into the now-empty vessel, Edmund poured first some wine and then some water. He took a sip to test it, feeling the wine burn its way down his throat. He was less than hale and hearty himself, if truth were told. He even felt overly warm, especially considering the chill of the now fireless cell.

He called for the jailor and offered coin for a roaring blaze. Then, alone with Geoffrey once more, Edmund raised the cup to his brother's lips.

As he did so, he made an important connection.

"Angels and ministers of grace," he whispered. "This is my fault. I've infected my brother."

His Elizabethan-trained mind might never have made the connection, but his twenty-first century mind had been warned against sharing cups when sick. Or . . . kissing.

*Gracious Father on high!*

He turned the exclamation into a prayer and reached for the nearly forgotten medicinal capsules hidden within his coin purse. In his haste, he spilled two, one of which bounced and nearly rolled into the fire. Swiftly, he retrieved it and turned to his brother.

"Geoffrey," he said softly. "Thou must swallow this . . . *curative*. Here, ope' thy mouth, brother."

Geoffrey groaned and twisted away. It took five anguishing minutes for Edmund to persuade his brother to drink and swallow the antibiotic. After this, he debated whether he ought also to consume one of the pills, but he decided against it. Quintus had mentioned the total amount of medicine DaVinci had acquired was only meant to cure one person. Quintus had insisted Edmund take half of the capsules, lest he place others at risk.

Others like Geoffrey.

Edmund upbraided himself for not having paid more heed to Quintus's caution. Here as well, he had been too distracted by his troubles to do what he ought to have done. Had he begun the treatment,

Geoffrey would not now lay ill. He glanced at his brother to see if warmth from the fire or the wine might have restored color to his Geoffrey's pallid face. In truth, Geoffrey looked much as one at Death's own doorstep might.

Edmund swore in silence. This—*this*—might explain why Geoffrey's fate had changed: because Edmund had brought disease. And why was he diseased? Because in his weakness, he had kissed one wife while the other stood only steps away!

A curse was on his tongue, but as his eyes rested on Geoffrey's pale cheeks, Edmund decided prayer might be of more lasting benefit. He spoke aloud all the prayers he knew, adding silently, *please, please, let this cup pass Geoffrey by.*

One thing was certain. Regarding the curative pills, Geoffrey should have them all. Even if Edmund's throat were to turn putrid, he had not spent two nights in an unheated, filthy cell. Geoffrey's case was the more dire. If proof were required, did not the Wikipedia printout prove it?

It was also plain that someone must remain with Geoffrey. Someone who could be trusted to feed Geoffrey his medicine on schedule. Edmund could not do it; he had the appointment with the two privy councilors late this night. Perhaps Silas, a stable hand whose wife had delivered Maria's children. Silas himself had treated minor injuries when Edmund had been small. Or—better still would be Quintus, with his soldier's experience of fevers and nursing.

Or why not send both?

Yes. Silas should guide Quintus here, and be messenger between the Tower and Hensley while

Quintus remained with Geoffrey. Edmund himself must return to court. He must hire rooms close by and haunt the Presence Chamber by day and night until Geoffrey was safely removed from prison to his home.

He leaned low to whisper to his brother.

"I must leave thee, but I shall send others to aid thee."

He removed his woolen cloak and piled it upon Geoffrey's other layers. Seeing Geoffrey was in no state to respond, Edmund then departed and rode hard for Hensley.

~ ~ ~

When Edmund arrived home just after sunset, he found Quintus waiting for him in the Great Hall.

"You do not return with your brother," said Quintus. "I grieve for you."

Edmund recounted his day, ending with a request Quintus would ride with Silas to the Tower, where he would remain and care for Geoffrey.

"I trust your abilities," Edmund concluded.

Quintus frowned. "I have only such training as is common to a soldier of Rome."

"Which is more than the training had by any barber, surgeon, or leech in London."

"Very well. I will go."

While Quintus communicated the new plans to DaVinci, Edmund roused Silas. Half an hour later, Quintus and Silas joined Edmund in the Great Hall. Edmund had fallen asleep in his chair before the fire and had to be roused.

"You are not well," said Quintus.

Edmund stirred.

"Remain seated," said Quintus.

"You must give these to my brother," said Edmund, retrieving the medicine.

Quintus frowned. "You mean for him to have all?"

"Aye. He dies otherwise," snapped Edmund.

The frown on Quintus's brow deepened. "DaVinci returns again to Florida very soon. Already she has determined to tell her physician that her medicine was consumed by her dog, so that she might obtain more. But whether her deception succeeds or not, my belief is that you should take two of these pills, along with two more of those by Halley's bedside."

At the mention of Halley's name, Edmund wished to take her in his arms, to ask her forgiveness for having been angry at her, for having left her. It had been petty of him, to storm out like a child when he ought to have sat and listened like a man.

"How does my love?" Edmund asked, his voice cracking on the last word.

"Halley or Maria?" asked Quintus.

Edmund hung his head in his hands, curling over on himself.

"They are both as well as can be expected. Halley recovers, while Maria prepares for birth."

Edmund nodded. "I must return to Whitehall," he said, attempting to rise.

"You must sleep," Quintus said sharply. "And begin your course of antibiotics."

"I will not take them," he said. "Geoffrey's need is greater."

"You will take one now or I will not aid your brother."

Edmund's features hardened, but then he nodded and swallowed one capsule. He could always get Silas to take the rest to Geoffrey later . . .

"My lords," said Silas, interrupting his thoughts, "the horses await. They will catch an ague standing still out of doors in this cold."

"Pray you depart," said Edmund. He felt his own legs beginning to shiver as with cold. "And God go with you."

Quintus nodded and strode from the room with Silas in his wake.

When they had gone, Edmund stepped closer to the blaze in the great hearth, silently thanking his grandfather for his foresight in installing fireplaces and chimneys.

He was tired. So, so weary. He tried to remember when he'd last slept a full night, but the days blurred together. Blurred, also, were the faces of Halley and Maria. Halley, smiling and pregnant, her belly swollen like a billowing sail—but no—that was Maria, was it not? Halley had foresworn pregnancy—

Edmund startled, having slumped semi-conscious to the floor before the fire. One knee stung sharply where it had struck the edge of an andiron. He needed to rest before returning to court. Just a few hours . . . or even a handful of minutes . . . sleep, blessed Lethe . . .

When next he awoke, the blazing fire had burned low. He attempted to sit up, but his limbs seemed made of gelatin. God's wounds, but he was thirsty. Tired and hungry and so horridly thirsty . . .

"My lord?"

Edmund opened his eyes, which had fluttered

shut again. It was Joan, Nan's younger sister. "Is it daybreak?" he asked. "Have you come to make up the new day's fire?"

"My lord, you are unwell," she said, reaching to feel his forehead. "You are fevered."

"I am fine," said Edmund, willing himself to sit upright. As he did so, his head spun and throbbed. Good God in Heaven! He had slept through his promised introduction to the privy councilors. He must return to court. He must gather an additional bribe and speak to Sir Roger. *Now.* Shuddering, he forced himself upright.

"My lord!" Joan reached for him as he fell. She broke the fall and succeeded in helping him into his fireside chair. "I shall call for Mistress Janet," said Joan.

Edmund began to shiver. He was so very, very cold. Again he tried to rise, but his shuddering legs would not lift him. He sank weakly back into the chair.

He did not remember falling asleep, but he when next he awoke, the sun was bright. He had missed his appointment with the privy councilors. He had failed Geoffrey.

## 37

### ·NEVIS·

#### February, Southern California

Nevis's carefully constructed plan to destroy two time machines and return to Kansas City within twenty-six hours began to unravel shortly after his act of arson in Montecito.

He'd planned to drive from Santa Barbara to catch his red-eye flight from LA to Florida, but he hadn't reckoned on traffic. Southbound Highway 101 was down to only one lane just north of Ventura. At some point while he was still stuck on Highway 101, his red-eye flight departed without him.

When he arrived at LAX, he was informed the next flight available would depart at 5:15 in the morning. In the time it took him to try and argue his way onto an earlier flight, the 5:15 flight sold out, which meant he had to catch a flight departing at 7:25 instead. Exhausted by his ordeal, Nevis crashed on the floor beside a wall outlet so that he could recharge his phone.

Unfortunately, Nevis inadvertently set his wake-up alarm for PM and not AM, which meant another missed flight and another negotiation for a new ticket. By 9:45 AM, however, he was on a flight that would, irony of ironies, require him to change planes in Kansas City before depositing him in Orlando, which was two and a half hours from Wellesley instead of West Palm Beach airport's two hours. Well, at least he was on his way.

He texted Khan, telling him he would be in closer to midnight than noon, and asking if he'd managed to get Arthur Littlewood to agree to a visit?

Nevis was unsurprised when Khan didn't acknowledge the text.

A surly flight attendant forced Nevis to put his phone in airplane mode while informing him he could purchase Wi-Fi once the plane was above ten thousand feet. He did this just in time to discover he'd run out of battery and had left his charger plugged into the wall at LAX. His day just kept getting better. On top of it all, he wasn't looking forward to another round of arson. It had been too many years since he'd trained with explosives, and that training had been aimed at preventing explosions, not causing them.

He rolled his sweater into a ball which he cradled between neck , shoulder, and airplane window, before attempting to catch another few hours of sleep.

# 38

## · *KHAN* ·

### February, Kansas City

It was time to fast-forward operation *Get the Hell Outta Here*, thought Jules Khan. As soon as Nevis left the building, Khan conveniently tipped over the speaker with the surveillance camera.

"Oops."

Fueled by a new determination, he commenced experimenting with his partially working machine. Twelve hours later, however, Khan was exhausted and no closer to his goal. His whiteboard pen had run out of ink. The floor was littered with piles of crumpled paper, and his lab book was a mess. He simply couldn't find the nonlinear solution he wanted. His machine was still drawing too much power, which meant that every experiment he ran brought him one step closer to vanishing who-knew-where. To some hell populated solely with objects stolen from other centuries.

"Really?" he asked himself, rubbing his eyes.

He was being ridiculous. He didn't believe in hell,

dammit.

Maybe he *should* ask for Littlewood's help.

He felt himself twitch and realized his eyes had drooped shut. He was exhausted. Too tired to solve problems. He needed rest. After a quick snooze, he would tackle the problem anew. An hour of sleep. Two at most. The last thing he needed right now was to make an error in his work. He sure as hell didn't want to miscalculate and send himself to the Antarctic instead of the Czar's summer palace.

He slept hard, missing a call. A second call served to wake him up, though. After letting it go to voicemail, he sat up, yawned, and reached for his mug of cold coffee. His phone reported he had two messages, both from Nevis. Khan played them back. The first message was merely another extension of Nevis's projected time away.

"I'll expect an update bright and early. Do I make myself clear?"

Nevis sounded even more exhausted than Khan.

"If you want to make yourself clear," muttered Khan, "you should try yawning less in the middle of sentences."

Khan then listened to the second message.

"Forgot to tell you—" Nevis's sentence was interrupted by yet another enormous yawn, rendering a few words unintelligible. The part Khan could understand continued thus: "—should give Dr. Littlewood a call. I think you'll find he's very amenable to meeting with you. You and I now possess the only functional time machine on the planet." Another huge yawn. "We'll discuss our next steps when I return."

The only "functional" time machine? What did

that mean? It did not sound good. It sounded horrible, in fact. With a terrible knot in his stomach, Khan searched the Internet for anything out-of-the-ordinary in Wellesley, Florida.

After barely one minute, he found it.

"Oh no," whispered Khan. "Nevis, you *idiot!*"

There had been a warehouse fire on the edge of town, at an address Khan knew very well. Nevis had just burned Littlewood's lab to the ground.

# 39

## · *HALLEY* ·

### February 1601, London

Halley awoke to probably the last thing she expected to hear: DaVinci in earnest conversation with Jillian Applegate. She opened her eyes thinking she'd been dreaming and that she would find only DaVinci and Quintus in the room, but no—it was *Jillian*, alive and wearing a seventeenth century gown that was several inches too long for her.

"Halley! You're awake," said DaVinci, rushing to Halley's side. "You'll never guess what happened."

"*Uh*, Jillian's here."

"Oh," said DaVinci. "Yes, that happened too. But that's not what *happened*-happened. I mean—*ack!* You tell her Jillian."

Jillian climbed onto the bed beside her, looking more somber than DaVinci, but what else was new?

"I'm sick," warned Halley.

"You've been on antibiotics for thirty-one hours," said DaVinci, "so you're not contagious anymore."

She did feel better. In fact, she felt mostly normal,

with only the barest of scratchiness in her throat.

"Is this about Geoffrey? Has his Wikipedia page changed?" asked Halley.

"Oh. No. Not that." DaVinci's face fell as she pulled yet another Wikipedia printout from her pocket. "Jillian brought this, and it's all same-same."

Halley glanced down the sheet. Sure enough, Geoffrey was still scheduled to die in the Tower.

"Does Edmund know?" she asked. "I need to talk to him—"

"Wait, Hal," said DaVinci. "You need to hear Jillian's news first. Then we'll talk about you, *um*, talking to Edmund."

"What's wrong?" asked Halley. It had to be serious if Jillian had traveled all the way here. And then she thought of something. Her voice softened. "Is this about . . . Everett?"

"Yes," said Jillian. She took a deep breath. Folded her hands in her lap. And then she began to explain how, after Everett had vanished, she'd traveled back to find him.

"We knew the results with the, *er*, 'Edmund experiment' were still uncertain," said Jillian. "Plus, Everett had planned ahead—"

"He's a planner," murmured DaVinci.

"—and written down where he could be found," continued Jillian, "day by day starting in April 1905—"

"Which," said DaVinci, "would be fourteen months forward of when Jillian grabbed him from the past—"

Jillian interrupted. "I did *not* grab him!"

DaVinci rolled her eyes.

Halley said, "She didn't."

"Fine," said DaVinci. "Fourteen months forward of the moment Everett impulsively kissed Jillian right as space-time grabbed her."

This brought a tiny smile to Jillian's solemn face. "Anyway," she continued, "Littlewood sent me to the Wright brother's little bicycle shop in Dayton, Ohio, and Everett was there—right where he'd predicted he would be, working as a shop boy for the Wright brothers. I guess April was when bicycle sales would pick up every year—"

"Did he know you?" Halley asked breathlessly. "Did he return home with you?"

DaVinci grinned.

A grin could only mean one thing, right? But why was Jillian looking so serious? Had something gone wrong?

"Tell me," Halley said.

"He knew me," said Jillian. "And just like DaVinci told us about Edmund, Everett had two sets of memories. He says it's pretty confusing, by the way—"

"Did he return with you?" asked Halley.

"Yes," said Jillian. She was biting her lower lip.

"And?" demanded Halley.

"He also . . . he still died in 1918." Jillian's eyes were fixed on the floor.

Even DaVinci's expression sobered at this. Halley understood this was hard news for Jillian to take. But for her and Edmund? It was the best outcome she could have hoped for.

"This means Edmund can come home," she said. She was trying, for Jillian's sake, not to appear too jubilant.

Jillian spoke softly. "I would have liked to have saved them both," she explained, her eyes filling with tears. "But for Everett, the choice would have been agonizing. If there had only been one of him . . . if he had returned with me only to find that his Wikipedia page no longer reported him dying while fighting the Germans . . ." Jillian shrugged helplessly. "I don't know where he would have chosen to live the rest of his life."

"He would have chosen *you*, Jillian," said DaVinci. "Death at age twenty-eight without you or a long happy life in the twenty-first century with you? Come on."

Jillian shook her head ever so slightly. "So many lives were saved by his courage in 1918. You know what he's like. I couldn't have asked him to choose me over that."

DaVinci murmured, "Whatever. I would've read him the Riot Act."

Jillian released a tiny laugh. "I'm sure you would have."

Halley was working hard to contain her own bliss. For her, the entire point was this: *Everett hadn't had to choose.* Everett had been able to live both lives, and this meant, *so could Edmund!*

She sank back into her pillows. She couldn't help the soft smile forming on her face. Two Edmunds! She would still have a husband. Her child would have a father. Maria would have a husband, and those screaming, laughing hellions running up and down the halls at all hours would have their dad. It was almost too good to be true.

And then, in the middle of her excitement, she

thought of something.

"Jillian? Did you say whether Everett still remembered everything when you guys got back to the twenty-first century?"

"He's got all of his memories of those fourteen months and seven days. He told these funny stories of following the Wright brothers around until they had pity on him and hired him."

"I see," said Halley quietly. She nodded. "I see."

"See what?" demanded DaVinci. "Why's your face all squinchy?"

Halley could feel tears forming, burning behind her eyes. Everett's choice had been simple. All he had to let go of was of a few months selling bike tires. But Edmund? For Edmund, it would mean losing his family. Sure, one of him would get to stay behind in the seventeenth century, but the one who traveled forward to the twenty-first?

"This means Edmund would be saying goodbye to his wife and kids forever, if he came back with me."

She managed to choke the words out just before tears began to stream down her cheeks. It was so unfair. It was horrible. How could she ask him to choose? What was worse, she thought she already knew what he would choose. How could he leave nearly three years of his life behind him, when those three years had included the births of his children? How could he leave his sons, never to see them grow into men? And what kind of monster would ask him to?

The tears became sobs.

Jillian murmured softly at Halley's side. "I'm so sorry. Here I've been sad about a past I already *knew* had happened, and you've got . . . *this*."

"We didn't think about the consequences for Edmund," murmured DaVinci.

Halley's throat was so tight that she didn't think she could speak.

"He'll choose you, Halley," said DaVinci. "He has to. It wouldn't be fair—"

"No!" said Halley. "What . . . wouldn't be . . . fair—" She paused to catch her breath between sobs. "I couldn't . . . *ask* . . . *him* . . . *to* . . ." She couldn't finish the sentence.

"Well, let me tell you, *I* could ask him," said DaVinci.

"You'd ask him to leave his children?" murmured Jillian.

DaVinci had nothing to say to this. Instead, she crawled into bed on the other side of Halley, passing clean handkerchief after clean handkerchief to her, while Jillian stroked her hair, until Halley had finally cried it all out. At least, for the time being.

The three women were silent for a long while after that, but eventually their quiet was broken by the entry of Joan, the young serving girl who kept their fire stoked.

"Begging pardon, my lady—" She broke off, frowning at Jillian. "My *ladies*, that is," she added, as if hoping for a little clarification.

"This is Lady Jillian," said DaVinci. "She's Sir Quintus's, *um*, cousin, and she stopped in to visit. Visiteth." She looked to Halley and Jillian as if to suggest they continue the introductions.

"Good morrow," said Jillian.

"My lady," said Joan, dropping a curtsey to Jillian.

Then she turned to address Halley. "Master Quintus did charge me before he left to provide news to you."

"Quintus *left?*" asked Halley.

"He went to, *uh*, doctor up Geoffrey," said DaVinci. "It happened last night. You know, Lady Halley," she said pointedly, "he took the special potions he carries around from *you-know-where*."

"I understand thee," said Halley. Geoffrey must have caught strep, too. Was this why the second Wikipedia printout had reported him dying in the Tower? It would make sense. But if Geoffrey had strep . . . Did he get it from Edmund? Was Edmund sick? She felt her stomach sinking.

"Prithee, Joan, how does his lordship the earl?" Halley asked, slipping right into Elizabethan English.

The serving girl shook her head sadly. "He is very unwell, I am sorry to report."

Halley's throat caught. Edmund *was* sick. Why hadn't her friends told her? She shot accusing looks at DaVinci and Jillian.

DaVinci's eyes dropped, and she murmured, "We were getting there."

"You needed to know about Everett before talking to Edmund," said Jillian.

Halley took a slow breath. Of course. That was true. But to not tell her Edmund was sick? Was his life in danger? Would he recover? Was there a new ending to his Wikipedia entry now as well?

"*Calm down*," murmured DaVinci between her teeth. "*We'll talk in a minute*."

Halley met her friend's eyes. DaVinci gestured with her head to the serving girl, raising her brow pointedly. Halley understood and tried to calm down.

Edmund was on antibiotics. Joan the serving girl didn't know this and couldn't know it. If Edmund's life had been in danger, Jillian and DaVinci would have told her up front. She was letting her imagination run away with her.

Joan spoke up again. "The housekeeper hath taken charge of his care. She says that if his fever will but break, we may hope for the best."

Halley threw back her covers. "I have to see him," she said. She addressed Joan. "You may go. My ladies will dress me."

Joan curtseyed and departed.

As soon as the servant was gone, DaVinci spoke. "Okay, Hal, you are like, totally 'Master of Being Elizabethan.'"

Halley ignored the compliment, her focus back on Edmund. "I'm stopping my antibiotics. Edmund and Geoffrey need them more than I do."

"No!" said Jillian.

"Actually, that's not a terrible idea," said DaVinci. "I mean, we can get Halley more as soon as she gets pulled back to our century. But when it comes to Edmund, well, one version of him is staying here no matter what—I'm sorry Hal—and that Edmund is going to need to make sure he shakes this, before it becomes scarlet fever or whatever."

"Oh. True," said Jillian. "Geoffrey and Edmund should be the ones taking the meds we have available right now."

"When did Edmund start taking them?" asked Halley.

DaVinci frowned. "Well, Quintus and I counted some out for him in the wee hours the other morning, but last night around seven he admitted to Quintus he hadn't taken any. At that point, Quintus basically shoved one down his throat. Hmm. He's due for one, like, now."

"We have to assume he'll continue to be contagious until at least nine tonight," said Jillian. "Maybe midnight, to play it safe."

"Okay, said DaVinci, "so trust me when I say I hate this idea, but Quintus and I agreed. When space-time pulls me back to the future, I'll get one more round of antibiotics for the Aldwych family and bring them back here. Just to make sure Edmund and Geoffrey recover completely."

"Oh, DaVinci," said Halley. "Will you?"

"Yeah. As long as you guys agree to address me as 'DaVinci, Master of Space-time' from now on."

In spite of everything that wasn't right, Halley guffawed. "You got it. Right now, though, I need to see Edmund. Can you guys help dress me?"

"Are you sure you're feeling up to getting out of bed?" asked Jillian.

"Yes. I just need some help getting my forty-two pound costume back on."

Now that she had a plan of action, Halley's tears no longer threatened. Finally, she was having it out with Edmund.

DaVinci and Jillian settled the heavy dress at Halley's waist and began snugging the ties in back. "Not gonna lie," said DaVinci. "I won't miss wearing the whole farthingale, bum-roll combo when I get back."

"You'll have to change out of it to get more antibiotics," said Jillian, "and then put it back on to come here."

"Ugh. You had to remind me."

"Remind me," said Halley, "when do each of us get pulled out of this century?"

"I've got four more hours," said DaVinci. "But I'll come right back. By your reckoning, I mean. Obviously it will take me time to get more meds. But after that, unless there are any objections, I would like to go home and stay home."

"Of course," said Halley. "I'm really grateful for everything you're doing."

"Aw, don't make me cry," said DaVinci. "My mascara's not waterproof."

"You and I," Jillian said to Halley, "will be here another twenty hours. I leave at a quarter to six in the morning, and you'll go fifteen minutes after, since we're not in the same temporal pockets."

"Or using the same 'harmonics,'" said DaVinci, putting air quotes around Littlewood's scientific term.

Twenty hours, thought Halley. Tears threatened again at the thought he might not want to go with her. *Stop it*, she told herself. She needed to be strong now, more strong than she'd ever been. Her mind went back into planning mode.

"Okay," said Halley. "I'm going to see Edmund."

She had less than a day here with the love of her life, and she had a decision to make: was she telling him she was pregnant or not?

# 40

*· HALLEY ·*

## February 1601, London

Halley found Edmund in the Great Hall before the fireplace. He was slumbering in some kind of makeshift bed. It looked like they'd shoved a low table, or maybe an Elizabethan ottoman, up against his chair to make a "chaise lounge" out of the two pieces of furniture.

He stirred as she approached. It was impossible to be silent when you had skirts dragging on the ground.

"Edmund?" she said softly.

"My love," he murmured, eyes still closed.

Who did he think was there?

When his eyes opened, they were dull. There was a faint sheen of sweat on his face. Automatically she touched his forehead. He was hot.

"Halley," he said softly. "Are we alone?"

She nodded. "Yeah. For now, anyway."

He reached for her face, and for a minute she thought he was going to pull her closer for a kiss, but his hand fell back to his side. The gesture, the *almost* of it, filled her with a sense of loss, of what saying goodbye would feel like. She shoved his blankets over so she could sit close.

"Is there news of Geoffrey?" he asked.

Halley shook her head. "Nothing's changed. I mean, there could be news at any time, but the printout hasn't changed."

"Alas." Edmund's gaze shifted to the fire. "I bade Quintus take all the medicine that remained to my brother, but he would not. I shall command Silas to do so when he returns with news."

"Oh Edmund, you stupid, honorable man." She allowed a few tears to squeeze out. Then she reached into her pocket for her half of the pills. "Listen, you have to take mine—"

"Nay—"

"*Yes*, you do. DaVinci's getting more in a couple hours, and you need to get back on schedule before you infect your entire household."

Edmund seemed to consider what she'd said. "I see the wisdom of what you suggest."

She helped him sit up enough to take the pill. He flinched as he swallowed, still in pain, no doubt, because he hadn't kept up on his meds. Mistress Janet the housekeeper appeared just then, with a decanter of willow bark infused mead. Halley recognized it by the smell. The decanter was swaddled in woolen cloth, like a tea cozy.

"My lord, my lady." The housekeeper bowed. "Does your ladyship desire I should attend my lord?"

"I will nurse Edmund. Thou mayst continue to . . . to go about thy accustomed duties."

"Aye, my lady," said the housekeeper, setting

down the mead. "Cook will brew more, an' if you should require it."

"I thank thee." Once the servant had gone, Halley spoke softly to Edmund. "We have a lot to discuss."

It was the understatement of the past four days.

"And you have a choice to make," she added.

She took one of his hands in hers and outlined what had happened with Everett. How Jillian had retrieved him. How space-time had, once again, multiplied him so that he'd been able to return to the twenty-first century while also remaining behind in 1905.

"Then my course is plain," said Edmund. The lack of enthusiasm in his voice wounded Halley, but she reminded herself he was exhausted. Even speaking was hard for him right now. Besides, probably the less enthusiasm the better, considering what she still had to tell him.

"There's more."

She continued, explaining that whether he stayed in 1601 or returned to the future, he would retain all of his memories. "*All* of them, Edmund."

She gave him a minute to let it sink in.

His eyes gained a more alert expression. "This means I would be able to remember still my children and my . . . and Maria. That I might—" He broke off. His alert expression shifted to one of dismay. He must've realized that no matter how much he wanted to remember them, ultimately, remembering a family he couldn't be with would be terrible. Returning with Halley would mean a lifetime of loss.

"Yeah," Halley said softly. "You wouldn't just go back to who you used to be in my century."

His eyes pinched shut his as his face settled into a deeply anguished expression.

"Alas, my wife," he murmured.

Halley didn't know if he was talking about Maria or addressing herself. She didn't know what to say. There was nothing that would make this better.

They were silent for a minute. And another. But then the silence was broken by a howling cry. Halley looked to the door where the sound was coming from. It was one of Edmund's sons, protesting in the passageway outside that he wanted his papa, *now*, and he didn't care if he fell ill.

Edmund's eyes opened. His lips drew tight.

"The antibiotics haven't done their job yet," said Halley. "You're still contagious until you've taken three more doses."

"I understand," said Edmund, sinking back against his pillows. "I will not risk James's health."

A second cry broke the silence that followed his statement, but this wasn't a child's cry. It was a woman's cry: sharp, brief, and guttural.

"Maria's labor is begun," Edmund murmured. He kicked at his blankets. At first Halley didn't understand what he was doing, but when he started to get up, she figured it out.

"No!" She grasped his shoulders. Fever heat radiated from his skin. "Absolutely not."

"Maria calls for me." He was resisting Halley, and she was shocked how little strength he had left. Normally, she wouldn't have been able to hold him down.

"She can call all she wants," said Halley. "But you're not going in there and giving her strep throat."

"I was to attend her—"

"I'm sure she's perfectly capable of giving birth without you there." Her voice faltered as she thought of having to do the same thing herself in nine months.

Edmund opened his mouth to protest, but Halley cut him off.

"Another three doses. This one, one more in six hours, and another around nine. Midnight is the soonest you should visit them."

He stopped resisting her. A shudder ran through his frame, and he sank back against his cushions.

"I've never attended her births," said Edmund. "This was to have been the first time." He exhaled heavily. "Fear me not. I shall not visit sickness upon her."

After that, they were both silent, listening to Maria at one end of the manor and Edmund's boys at the other. Both children were now howling for him.

Very softly, he released a single laugh.

Halley stared at him, brows raised. But then she realized it was funny, in an awful sort of way. It was a contest between members of the Aldwych family, to see who could make the most noise.

Edmund's face pinched as he tried to swallow, and Halley recalled the willow bark infused mead.

"Here," she said, pouring him some. "Drink this. It really does help with the sore throat."

Edmund took several sips and then handed the mug back to Halley. "Thou and I have much of which we must speak."

Had he already made up his mind? Fear gripped her. He was going to tell her he had to stay. And really, how had she hoped to compete with an entire houseful of family members, all of whom were literally screaming for Edmund? She couldn't compete on this level. She wanted to shout that this wasn't her fault, that it wasn't fair, that she needed him, and couldn't he see that? But at the same time . . . how could she ask Edmund to leave his family behind? Permanently. If she loved him, how could she ask? Did she want her marriage if the cost was Edmund's happiness? How "fairytale" did she think her life was going to be, with her husband miserable for the rest of his life, haunted by what he'd lost?

Her breath came in short gasps. The situation was impossible. She couldn't control him. She couldn't force him to choose her. She felt light-headed. She couldn't get enough air—

"Halley," said Edmund. He placed a hand on her chest. "Breathe, beloved. Breathe."

"I can't!"

"Breathe."

He placed one of her hands over his. She felt the warmth of his skin. He was here. She was here. Hope wasn't lost. She forced herself to take a long, slow breath. She exhaled slowly. A minute passed, and then another one. She focused on Edmund's hand over her heart, on his presence next to her.

There was so much she had to tell him. If this was goodbye, there were so many things she wanted him to know. She slowed her breathing, slower, slower, until finally she was calm enough to speak.

"I have to tell you . . . I have to apologize, Edmund. I hurt you. I hid things from you. I lied to you. I'm so sorry. I . . . I wasn't ready for kids, even though I knew you wanted them. I should have told you I was taking the pill. I should have made you a part of the decision. I owed you that."

"Nay, Halley." Edmund sighed. "I failed you. I should have asked if you wanted children. I did not consider carefully what you told me of how women in your age had options . . ." He shook his head. "I did not consider it because I did not *wish* to consider it. My behavior in this regard was . . . it was the most egregious example of, well, of allowing my 'sixteenth century' to show."

Halley managed half a smile. "I think it's *seventeenth* now, but who's counting?"

Edmund matched her sad smile with one of his own. Then he grimaced in pain and lifted the mug of mead to his lips.

Setting the cup down again, he continued. "I must also beg thee to forgive how I departed from thee."

"It's okay. I understand."

"I behaved like a child, storming from thy presence as I did." He smiled wryly. "These past days I have had ample opportunity to compare my behavior to that of a child in tantrum." He paused and then met her eyes. "Canst thou forgive me?"

She murmured, "Of course."

At some point he had slipped back into the more intimate *thou* form of address. She felt a nostalgia that almost overpowered her, recalling their first months together in Los Angeles when she'd had to work so hard to cure him of *thee*s and *thou*s. Their life had been good then, crammed into a tiny studio over someone's garage, with iffy electricity and no privacy. She looked up at the Great Hall's thirty-foot ceiling. How had Edmund managed life in a studio after this? Her eyes scanned the room with its massive chimneypiece, its tapestries and clerestory traceries, its musicians gallery.

Her throat caught, remembering the vows they'd exchange there. How was she supposed to let all of that go? She forced her gaze back from the gallery. Back to her hands in her lap. And there, like a tiny ray of hope, was the thought of the child she was carrying. A piece of Edmund. Tears filled her eyes, and she couldn't blink them back.

Edmund took her hand. "My love."

She shook her head. "I'm being stupid. Most people never get to experience the kind of love we had—"

"Halley, how canst thou speak of it as if 'twere past?"

More tears. She couldn't get words out.

In the hall, there was a new sound.

"Tis Silas," murmured Edmund. "He will have news of Geoffrey. Wilt thou admit him?"

Halley rose to let the manservant in.

He crossed to Edmund, bowed, and spoke.

"My lord, thy brother doth improve, but he is still weak. Master Quintus says we are to keep him warm and requested I return with more foodstuffs."

"Of course," said Edmund. "Tell Mistress Janet to provide all that you need. I thank you for your pains, Silas."

"No pains, my lord. Tis a rare beautiful morn for riding. But I'll quit your lordship now to visit the larder, that I may speed my return to your brother."

"Go," said Edmund. He sighed and closed his eyes. The brief interchange seemed to have left him too exhausted to speak anymore. At first Halley thought he was drifting off to sleep, but then he opened his eyes again and addressed her.

"For that Geoffrey doth improve, I am grateful, but according to thy report, he is still to die in the Tower."

"Yeah," said Halley. "I'm so sorry, Edmund."

"I must return to court," he said. "Now that it seemeth illness will not end my brother's life, I must plead for his innocence." His eyes drooped and fluttered shut.

There was no way he was going *anywhere*. But she had a pretty good guess how her husband would respond if she told him that. Especially with his judgment affected by alcohol. His sixteenth century notions of manliness would be showing all over the place.

His eyes flickered open, and he struggled, trying to wake himself back up. "I must . . . I must . . ."

Quickly, Halley refilled his mug with the willow-infused mead. "Drink, my love. You need to, *um*, fortify your strength." Not her finest moment in marital transparency, but she wasn't about to let him stagger out of bed.

In the end, Halley got three mugs of the willow-infused mead inside Edmund. He was barely conscious enough to swallow the last one. Now she had a decision to make because what Edmund said about Geoffrey's illness not killing him was probably true. With antibiotics a-plenty and Quintus doctoring him, Geoffrey would recover just fine. They were back to the charge of treason doing him in. Or possibly torture . . . Halley shivered. So was Geoffrey's neck worth saving? Edmund thought so, and in the unlikely event he chose to return with her, he wouldn't leave this century with his brother's life hanging in the balance.

She felt herself inching toward a decision, although it wasn't easy to commit to it with Edmund looking flushed and in need of help and somehow still handsome enough to make her want to rip his doublet off right then and there. Leaning over him, she kissed his forehead softly and resettled his blankets.

Then, forcing herself to look away, she left the Great Hall in search of the serving girl Joan.

Joan was sitting before the fire in the kitchen, but she jumped to attention when she saw Halley.

"I require that thou keepest watch over his lordship," said Halley. "He must not rise. Dost thou understand?"

"Aye, my lady."

"Should he attempt to leave his bed, prevent him. Tie him thence if need be, but he must not leave his bed this day. My, *um*, cousin shall help thee to attend him."

Joan nodded and raced from the kitchen.

That was step one taken care of. Halley's stomach rumbled. After grabbing a hunk of cheese from a table, she sank onto the stool where Joan had been and broke off a piece of cheese. She couldn't remember the last time she'd eaten anything.

She stared into the flames, absently resting a hand on her abdomen. What was her next step? As she chewed, a tiny thought began to form, growing just like the baby in her belly. She could tell Edmund he was going to be a father. That he didn't have to give up being a dad. That they could share it together. That

216

she needed him. Because she did, didn't she? Didn't she deserve Edmund? Didn't her unborn child deserve a dad? It was the perfect way to force Edmund's hand. And who would blame her? Why should they both be miserable, after all? She could make him choose her, if she told him.

But then her throat tightened. Another round of tears threatened.

The whole point of choice was *choosing freely*. If she told him about the baby, and that she needed him, he would go with her. He would be a good father, too. But there was a dark side to this option: if she told him, she would always have to live with the knowledge that his choice had been coerced, and that *she* was the coercer.

She stood and poured herself a mug of fizzy small beer.

She had vowed to love Edmund, that day in the musicians gallery. Love wasn't coercive. *She* wasn't coercive. At least, she didn't want to be. Although . . . she'd just forced him to drink enough mead to basically pass out. Wasn't that coercive? She thought about it, but then she decided it wasn't the same thing. Dosing him with mead was a strategy she wouldn't be ashamed to tell him about later. Once he was well, he would thank her for it.

*He might thank her for telling him he was going to be a dad with her, too . . .*

But there was still a difference, and it had to do with her. She couldn't live with herself if she did this. Her eyes filled with bitter tears. This was the truth: she couldn't live with herself if she forced his hand with the pregnancy card. Some guys might have been

capable of making a free choice after hearing that kind
of news, but Edmund wasn't one of them. He would
pick duty every time. And that meant not telling him.
Loving Edmund meant keeping this from him so that
he could choose freely. So did she love him? Her eyes
brimmed with tears. She loved him more than she'd
known it was possible to love anyone. She would do
anything for him. And today, that meant letting him
make the choice he needed to make, even if it didn't
include her. He might never know what she was
willing to lose out of the depth of her love for him,
but she would always know.

And there it was again, that seed of a plan that
had begun forming in the Great Hall. There was a way
to let Edmund know how much she loved him. A way
to demonstrate that his concerns were her concerns.
That she would shoulder and share his burdens.
Wasn't that what love was all about?

She would nab that royal pardon for Geoffrey,
whether he deserved one or not. She laughed out loud.
This wasn't about Geoffrey. It was about Edmund. It
was about richer and poorer, sickness and health. His
concerns belonged to her. This was about being
married partners.

Swiping her eyes dry, Halley began to attack the
problem of freeing Geoffrey in the same way she
would've attacked a costume emergency. How much
time did she have to solve the problem? What were
her financial resources? What assets could she employ?
It was always a matter of time, money, and laborers.
To solve most problems, you only needed two out of
three. Well, she had herself for labor, and possibly a
servant or two. She had items from the twenty-first

century for currency. And as for time? Heck, she had almost nineteen whole hours.

"*Huh*. What do you know? Three out of three," she said, smiling to herself as she strode back to her room. Now all she had to do was tell her friends.

DaVinci was the first to speak when Halley entered the bedchamber. "How's Edmund?"

Jillian looked up. "And how are you?"

"He's good. I'm good, too. Or . . ." Her throat tightened just a little. She swallowed and smiled. "I'm as good as I can be in the circumstances. So here's the thing. I need you to keep an eye on Edmund. Joan is there too, but I need to know you guys will make sure he stays in bed and takes those antibiotics."

"Where do you think you're going?" asked DaVinci, her arms folding over her chest.

"Some place called Whitehall Palace. I'm securing a pardon for Geoffrey from the most formidable queen the world has ever known. Wish me luck."

# 41

## ·*HALLEY*·

### February 1601, London

It had been a long time since Halley had ridden a horse. After enduring stern looks from the steward when she explained she needed a ride to court, she'd been assigned a horse and a groom to see she got there safely. Halley might have employed a little deception, letting the steward believe Edmund had *ordered* her to go plead for Geoffrey. But hey, it had gotten the steward moving.

The housekeeper had gotten in on things, too. Halley looked down at the basket jostling in her lap as she rode to London. Probably influenced by one too many press junkets, Halley had decided to pack up a Hollywood-style goody bag to take to court. It would be a "two-fer" gift. In exchange for an introduction to Her Majesty, Halley would allow the person making the intro to give the Queen the goodies as if they'd come from the, *er*, introducer.

The housekeeper, hearing Halley was pleading for Geoffrey, donated more gifts than Halley could carry.

She'd sorted through the offerings, keeping the wheel of *Parmigiano* cheese (unbelievably expensive in this era), and the jar of scented water decocted from the manor's lavender garden. To these she had added her standing collar made of albino peacock feathers and Edmund's essential oil of frankincense, a curative gift likely to appeal to the aging Queen. Jillian had tossed in a pair of uncut diamond earrings, because of course Jillian just happened to be wearing uncut diamonds. The entire assortment was nested in a length of purple cloth shot with gold thread Halley had found in her bedchamber.

So. She was ready. Or as ready as she was ever going to be. Ride to court, bribe someone into an introduction by allowing *them* to present the gift basket to the woman wearing the crown, convince Good Queen Bess of Geoffrey's innocence, and bring Edmund's brother home. No problem.

The sun had broken through a thick layer of midwinter clouds. Halley was grateful; it made the ride slightly less miserable. She'd gotten used to Florida's sunshine pretty fast, and she had missed it, cooped up inside for the past few days. Well, by tomorrow morning she would have all the Florida sunshine she wanted. With or without Edmund.

Since getting on her horse, she'd nearly talked herself into informing Edmund he was a dad. Didn't he have a right to know? The kid was as much his as hers. And if knowing she was pregnant was going to influence his decision, did that mean it was a bad thing? Who was she to make that decision for him?

Oh, the irony. She was the same person who'd already made other reproductive decisions without consulting him. So maybe she should turn a new leaf and *tell him*. Her motivations weren't pure, but the thought of leaving Edmund—of never seeing him again? He'd been the bright center of her life for almost three years. It would be like never seeing the sun again. How could she move forward without Edmund? She squeezed her eyes shut.

How? By sticking with the decisions she'd already made, that was how.

*No crying*. It would ruin her makeup—a hasty attempt to shift her light brown skin paler, in a court where everyone was expected to aspire to the Queen's ceruse-whitened skin tone. So: *no crying*. Halley needed to keep thoughts of Edmund as far away as possible.

She'd survived loss before, and she could do it again. For over a decade, she'd thought she had met her father, only to find out later that the man had been an actor hired by her mom so Halley would stop asking to meet him. She'd had to give up the dream of knowing her father. Who better to help her own child through that heartache? Ugh! She was choking up again.

At least her baby wouldn't lack for love and family. She'd made one decision. As soon as her current position ended, Halley was settling down in Wellesley. She would start an online site for custom cos-play and raise her daughter—or son—with Auntie Jillian and Uncle Everett and Auntie DaVinci and Uncle Quintus. Her eyes threatened to fill again, but this time it was in gratitude for her incredible friends. They were her family, and they would be a good family for her child, too.

The groom spoke, interrupting her thoughts. "My

lady, yon is the palace."

Nothing like a royal residence to focus her thoughts! It was time to start behaving like a peer of the realm, or a peer's wife, at any rate. It helped that she made her living watching actors, who routinely transformed themselves from slouching millenials into the crowned heads of nations. She was dressed the part, and this was an era where only those who *were* wealthy could afford to dress like the wealthy. Halley had once read that clothing themselves in very basic wool or linen consumed sixty-five percent of the earnings of people in this era. In any case, dressed and coiffed as she was, no one questioned her entrance into the chamber of presence.

She drew her shoulders back, raised her chin, and joined the throng.

It was unnervingly like being on a set. In fact, the room looked a lot like the court setting that opened the *As You Like It* she was currently costuming. It was almost eerie, and she found herself slipping into a strange state of unreality. She was playing a part. She was not making costumes, she was wearing one. Living in one. Living a confusing alternate reality—and this matched the state of her mind, perplexed and uncertain.

At least it was giving her something to focus on besides what tomorrow would bring. Swallowing, she banished all thoughts of her own century from her mind. She examined the crowd to locate the best-dressed group adorning the Presence Chamber. This was the group she had to infiltrate. Halley was totally qualified to make judgments like: *who was the most powerful person in the room?* Every fiber, every color, every choice of trim told a tale of rank, right down to the metal of a courtier's aiglettes—those hollow cord-finishes which would someday give rise to plastic shoelace tips. Sumptuary laws, the rules of who could wear what, were strictly enforced under Elizabeth I. The men wearing purple, gold or silver embroidery, or sable fur were either dukes or earls. A glimpse of orange would indicate the Queen was in the room. Halley felt a frisson of anticipation jolt through her. She was attempting to meet Queen Elizabeth the First. The actual Virgin Queen. Good Queen Bess. Arbiter of fashion, wearer of enough lead paint to literally kill a person. *That* Elizabeth. Halley swallowed again.

Yeah, she could tell who wielded power in this room. There they were: clustered at the opposite end of the chamber. But how was she going to get herself introduced to them? Even if she knew what was hinted, implied, or stated by every bit of clothing in the room, she did not know how to claw her way to the front of the room. Not to mention, she wasn't sure what she was going to say to convince a highly suspicious group of men to release someone from prison, on her say-so. She'd been trying not to worry about this, but she was a nobody. A nobody who maybe ought to have grabbed a few extra gift baskets.

Within her first hour at court, though, Halley parted with her one and only basket. She surrendered it to someone wearing a ridiculous number of rings, who promised she should have an introduction to the Queen. An hour later, Halley noticed the same guy was *wearing* one of Jillian's uncut diamond earrings.

She swore under her breath. She should have held on to the basket to deliver it herself. But it had been huge and in her way, and she'd grown aware an actual lady would have had a servant carrying it for her. So, bye-bye basket, and hello to managing on her wits alone, as a complete unknown.

She spent the next hour wandering the room, trying to keep from looking desperate for company, trying to learn who was whom, and who might get her where she needed to go. Unfortunately, she wasn't making much progress. She should have kept that basket. How else was she going to get the attention of people that mattered? By her third hour in the room, she was close to despairing. She still hadn't made friends with a single person wearing purple. She was going to fail and have to go home to tell Edmund that his brother's life was still in peril.

Maybe she should just call it and head back now. The sun would be down soon. Why had she thought this was something she could do, just by putting on a little makeup and a velvet gown?

Around sunset, though, there seemed to be a shift in the attitude of those examining her. There was, it turned out, an unexpected upside to being unknown. It meant she was an object of curiosity, something the dude wearing Jillian's diamond earring was apparently promoting as he circulated. Maybe he *would* get her that introduction after all. The next time he smiled and inclined his head to her, she returned a small smile. Gradually, people started introducing themselves, having been told, they informed her, that she was cousin to an earl. *Yes,* she told those who asked, *she was sure his lordship was hereabouts—she could hardly have come on her own, could she?*

Diamond-earring dude had evidently let drop she

was a countess from Sardinia whose bloodline might have once included a converted Moorish prince. He reported that Halley herself had, of course, fled the oppressive Catholicism of her homeland to become versed in the true Christian religion, as defended by the Queen of England.

These details were further embellished by others in the next two hours, while she circulated and was admired; Lady Halley the Sardinian was someone new to meet, someone new to gossip over. She was sure her clothing and manners were being discussed and dissected, down to the polish on her shoes and the tilt of her neck as she performed a curtsey. Hopefully being "Sardinian" would explain any lapses in etiquette.

Before long, she heard it rumored she was fabulously wealthy—*unmarried or was it widowed?*—and the granddaughter of a Sultan. One of these rumors, or possibly both, got her the attention of the younger son of Lord Pembroke. After he greeted her, she brought up Geoffrey's unfortunate imprisonment. There was no sense hiding what she was here for, after all. As soon as the friendly younger son heard Halley's tale of falsely accused Geoffrey—also a younger son—he brought Halley to the top of the room, to meet a few of his dad's closest friends, every last one of whom wore gold or silver embroidery and a splash of purple in their outfits.

Halley's target group was here, where the secondary power brokers hung out. The first circle, of course, was composed of Her Majesty's Privy Council—whose duties included investigating treason. Anyone they felt was guilty would proceed to trial and probable execution.

As for these men dressed in gold, silver, and purple, they were probably all related to privy councilors or to the Queen herself. This got Halley one step closer to her slam-dunk.

After Pembroke's son finished the introductions, Halley explained Geoffrey's situation. At this point, several members of the group quietly detached themselves. Now Halley was left arguing with only five men, who were insisting that where there was smoke, there was fire.

"It's not logical," Halley said. It felt like this was all she'd been saying for the past twenty minutes. "If Geoffrey meant to rise up against the Crown and good people of London, wherefore was he sleeping in a drunken stupor on the morning the rebels drove through town? Employ the simplest logic and you can see—"

She was cut off.

"My lady, you cannot be expected to understand logic."

It was one of her chief opponents. Lord Dempsey? Lord Darnsey? Their names were blurring together. She was so tired. Sickness and riding seven miles and milling around for hours on end was taking its toll. She'd made it to the group she needed to convince, but she wasn't convincing anyone of anything. Instead, they were lecturing her on how little she, as a woman, could understand about real life and the legal system of England.

"Spare thy pretty head, thou wert better," said Lord Something or Other.

"She cannot be expected to understand," said

another lord.

"Logic lies not within a woman's natural gifts," said a third.

At this point Halley was so close to boiling over that she nearly missed what was happening. Across from her, two men had dropped into deep obeisance. This caused the others in the circle to turn, and Halley decided she'd better check out who was standing behind her.

It was the Queen.

Elizabeth Regina.

Protector of the Realm.

Victor over the Spanish Armada and Catholicism.

She radiated power, dressed in a splendid gown of golden-orange silk with a diaphanous ruff encircling one of her famous red wigs. Halley knew in that moment that she would never again be intimidated by an Oscar award-winning actor or director. Not after seeing the Virgin Queen herself.

Half a second behind everyone else, Halley joined those bowing before their sovereign.

The Queen, above the need to acknowledge bowing and scraping, had already turned her attention to a gentleman at her side dressed in red and white.

"What think you, Howard?" asked the Queen. "Doth Logic sit within the garden of gifts God hath cultivated in women?"

"I know of no man," replied Howard, "better able to argue for this than Your Majesty."

"It would seem my Lord Admiral disagrees with you, Dempsey," said the Queen. She returned her gaze to Howard. "And a good thing, too." She then turned to Halley, who was still holding her best curtsey. "Rise child. Who art thou?"

Halley rose. She saw Lord Dempsey glaring at her, his face red with humiliation.

"I am called Halley Mikkelsen, your majesty, cousin to your servant Edmund Aldwych, who hath sent me in his stead to argue . . . logic."

"Thou shalt find little enough of it here," the queen said dryly. "But what, pray, does your cousin mean in sending you alone? I see not the man hereabouts, nor have seen him these many years."

"He is much occupied in caring for such of your subjects as fall under his care," Halley answered carefully. "He fell heir to his father's debts."

"Do not we all," murmured the queen. Her courtiers tittered at the jesting remark. "But for what reason come you hither?"

Halley noted the change from a familiar address back to a more formal one and figured it was time to fish or cut bait.

"Your Majesty, with your permission, I crave to bring before your mercy the fate of Geoffrey, younger brother to the Earl of Shaftesbury. Geoffrey hath been wrongly accused as a traitor and is now imprisoned for it."

"So might many a traitor argue," said the Queen.

"Indeed, Your Majesty. I have been seeking to persuade these your courtiers with logic, by asking how it might be that one who intended treachery should drink himself into oblivion the night before it was to be attempted?"

The Queen turned again to Howard, her Lord Admiral. "Was this Geoffrey Aldwych apprehended among those who marched on Whitehall against Our

Royal Person?"

"No your majesty."

"Hath he been a companion to Essex?"

"No your majesty."

The queen frowned gravely. "Howard, see you do speak with the man. Judge you how much danger he poseth, and see you let *logic* prevail."

Her courtiers tittered as Howard bowed deeply and departed, presumably to free Geoffrey from the Tower.

Halley opened her mouth to thank the Queen, but Elizabeth had evidently had enough politics for one day.

"Do you dance, child?" she asked Halley.

Without awaiting an answer, the Queen turned to someone she addressed as Hunsdon, and ordered him to summon the musicians.

Just like that, it was over. Halley was left standing alone with the younger son of Lord Pembroke, watching Queen Elizabeth as she progressed among her subjects, a greeting here, a sharp word there, every inch a powerhouse.

And a believer in the use of logic, apparently.

How had it happened? How had she managed to gain the ear of the Crown? How had she managed to speak, much less to put words in the right order? Halley had met some famous people, but none of them measured up to Queen Bess. It had been almost *easy* to speak with Her Majesty, thanks to the Queen's style of interaction. Sure, Elizabeth was powerful, but she had made herself instantly relatable, too. She'd taken the one thing they shared in common—womanhood—and used it to build a bridge, which she then crossed so she could hang out with Halley. No wonder everyone worshipped her. What was not to like about power clothed in that kind of charisma? Well, charisma and fifty to sixty pounds of velvets, silks, and jewels.

Suddenly Halley felt as if her legs were going to collapse from under her. She wasn't sure how long she'd been awake, but she was pretty sure if she'd been Cinderella's carriage, she would've turned back into a pumpkin. She realized that like Cinderella, she'd completely lost track of time. Her heart started pounding.

"What time is it?" she begged of a servant passing by. "Is it late?"

"The Queen did quit her councilors early this e'en, at 7:00," replied the servant. "Judge you how much time hath passed since then."

It was still early! She could make it back in plenty of time to tell Edmund the good news about Geoffrey before space-time snatched her away. Struggling to conceal a yawn, Halley strode out of the Presence Chamber.

When she was reunited with the groom and their horses, she asked him to take her to the Tower. She really wanted to get home to Edmund, but it would be cruel to keep the good news from Geoffrey, if for some reason the Lord Admiral decided to put off his visit.

The groom, however, flat out refused to bring a woman of her station to the Tower in the middle of the night. Apparently there were some things a lady *couldn't* do, even under the reign of Good Queen Bess.

# 42

## · DAVINCI ·

### February, Wellesley

DaVinci really, really hated time travel. Of course, she wouldn't have chosen to stay stuck in the Elizabethan era, either. She stumbled off of the time machine platform, her arm muscles still in spasm from the journey. The machine groaned as it shut itself down.

"Can someone get me a glass of water?" DaVinci croaked. "All I've had the past two days is warm beer." She turned to Everett. "And you. Help get me out of this thing. No going all modest on me. I'm an artist. I draw nudes for fun and profit."

Everett, blushing bright pink, gave DaVinci a hand until she was down to her chemise, at which point she admitted she could manage on her own.

After the disrobing was finished, DaVinci caught Everett and Littlewood up on life in the seventeenth century.

"We seriously need more drugs for strep, which means, *oh joy*, I get to lie my way into another batch of antibiotics, and then put this stupid dress back on and get sent back to 1601 all over again." Distracted by a repeated sound, she turned to face the table behind her. A phone—Jillian's—was vibrating as text after text came in. "Okay. Seriously? What is up with Jillian's phone? It's like, blowing up with messages."

Everett crossed to retrieve Jillian's phone. "She did not wish to carry it with her to 1601." He frowned. "Well, I'll be . . ." He looked up. "I think we had best respond to these text messages."

"What is it?" asked DaVinci.

"It's her mother. There's been a fire in the west wing." He looked up. "Her mother says to tell DaVinci they are so sorry to report her performance art sculpture is 'toast,' in her words."

"Um, guys?" said DaVinci. "She means the time machine. That's our backup time machine that's toast."

At this, Littlewood's brow contracted. "What suspicious timing . . ."

"It is surely a coincidence," said Everett. "Jillian's mother reports the fire department is blaming it on wiring the family knew they should have repaired."

"It's very odd, though," said Littlewood. "We meet with Jules Khan for the first time in over a year, and the time machine is destroyed within days."

"He seemed in a really friendly mood, to me," said Everett.

DaVinci grunted a small laugh, but then conceded. "True. Even I can admit he was the nicest version of himself I've ever seen."

They discussed the situation for another few minutes, but eventually decided it had probably been an accident, like the fire department was saying.

"Okay, so now that we're done with that," said DaVinci, "who's going to drive me to the clinic so I can lie about the antibiotics I didn't actually take for my terrible, terrible earache that I don't actually have?"

Everett offered to drive her, with Littlewood remaining in the lab to prepare for DaVinci's re-insertion into 1601.

"Oh. And Littlewood? Make it a quick layover this time, will you?" DaVinci winked and departed with Everett.

~ ~ ~

Dr. Arthur Littlewood sighed with relief as DaVinci departed the twenty-first century, a fresh bottle of antibiotic pills in hand. There was nothing to do now but await her return, which was calibrated to occur in ten minutes time.

Everett had been quiet all day, and Littlewood wondered if he should ask if anything was the matter. He thought he could guess the answer. It was to do with the young man's recent journeys through time. How troubling it would be to return to one's life, only to abandon it again, with new memories remaining in one's mind.

Littlewood sighed. Jillian would be back in sixteen hours. Much better to have her ask Everett how he was doing. Still, he ought to make some sort of effort to rouse his friend's spirits.

"I don't suppose you might be hungry," said Littlewood.

"What? Oh. Yes. I believe I am."

"Once DaVinci returns, what do you say we all get Cubanos for lunch?" Littlewood knew Everett loved a good Cuban sandwich.

The young man smiled. "An excellent suggestion. It will be nice to get out. We've been spending too much time down here. Can't have us turning into underground moles, now can we?"

Littlewood agreed and then, while the two waited for DaVinci's return, Everett recounted how he'd helped the Wright brothers level a pasture of every last molehill to allow for safe takeoff and landing.

By the time Everett was finishing his tale, the great Tesla coils began to hum with electricity, and then in a flash of blue light, DaVinci reappeared, landing as she always did, on her backside.

"Get me out of this thing," she said, referring to her gown. "And then we burn it."

"Perhaps I might suggest lunch before the incinerating?" asked Everett.

"Yes. Modern food." DaVinci grinned in approval.

Their lunch break extended to more than two hours, because DaVinci had insisted she couldn't eat a Cuban sandwich without an Iron Beer, and the sandwich vendor had been sold out. Fortunately they found the soda without having to drive all the way to Miami for it, which Littlewood had begun to fear DaVinci might insist on.

They still had another thirteen hours before first Jillian and then Halley would reappear. Littlewood was rather wondering if he could talk Everett into doing the honors of staying awake to greet the pair. He wanted nothing so badly as a nice, long nap.

Unfortunately, a nap was not in the cards.

"Good heavens," said Littlewood, as they drove around a corner.

A line of fire engines blocked the drive that led to Littlewood's warehouse.

"What could possibly take three fire trucks . . ." DaVinci didn't finish the question.

"That," said Everett, pointing to a column of smoke that had been hidden by the other buildings.

"It's the laboratory," said Littlewood.

"*Impossible*," whispered Everett.

DaVinci blanched. "Is the time machine safe?"

The three exited the car and sped on foot toward the lab, staring in disbelief. Smoke was billowing from the lab's single stairwell. Littlewood gazed in horror and then pulled out his phone and dialed Jules Khan's number.

# 43

## · HALLEY ·

### February 1601, London

When Halley returned to Hensley Manor, she made a beeline to the Great Hall to tell Edmund about Geoffrey. She was exhausted. Her sit bones ached from the unaccustomed riding, and her fingers had grown numb holding the reins. Even with constant hand-switching, she hadn't been able to keep her fingers warm in the night air.

But then she saw Edmund, asleep in his chair, and nothing else mattered. The sheen of fever had vanished, and his color looked normal. A little pale, but Elizabethan-era Edmund had been pale. To Halley, he'd never looked more handsome. Firelight danced across the angles and planes of his face, and she leaned forward to kiss him. When he didn't stir, she hesitated. Maybe he needed sleep more than news. She would sit here with him, and tell him as soon as he woke up. She pulled the other chair—Maria's, presumably—across the flagstones until she was close enough to share the cushion Edmund's feet rested on.

A yawn escaped her, followed by another, and another. She should build up the fire. In a moment she would. Just as soon as her fingers and toes had thawed. She yawned again.

When Halley woke up, the first thing she noticed was a pallet set up where Maria's chair had been before she moved it. On the pallet lay Geoffrey, home at last. Halley smiled with relief. How had she slept through his arrival? She could only imagine how happy Edmund would be. Turning to see if he was awake, she realized Edmund wasn't here anymore. The blankets were piled in a vaguely human-sized lump so that she hadn't noticed at first, but his chair was definitely empty.

She grabbed for her wristwatch, suddenly afraid of how much time had elapsed. 4:30 AM. She breathed a sigh of relief. An hour and a half still left. Ninety minutes to tell Edmund . . . whatever she was going to tell him.

She rose to find him, and then her heart seemed to contract. She knew where he would be. If it was 4:30 in the morning, his medical quarantine was past, and he would be with Maria, checking on her and their newborn son. Of course he would want to be with them. He loved them. But her fears whispered another reason why he'd left her sleeping in the hall. He didn't just love Maria and his kids; he loved them *best*.

Down the passageway, her skirts trailed behind her, heavy like her heart. She needed to hear his choice from his own lips, just as he needed to hear that she loved him and would always love him, even if . . .

She couldn't finish the thought.

Just walk. Just breathe. Just find Edmund.

His bedchamber loomed ahead and down the hall from hers. The door was thrown wide and stoppered open. An icy breeze wafted past her. They must be cleansing the room of "unwholesome vapors," or something.

She shouldn't be here. She was an intruder. She didn't belong here. But then she heard a voice. *His* voice. A soft laugh. *His* laugh. And then a woman's voice: *Maria's*. He and Maria were whispering. They were in bed. Edmund's bed. Together.

She shut her eyes tightly. Another breeze carried the icy cold of night past her.

There was no place for her here.

Slowly, Halley turned. She let the tears fall. She shuffled across the passageway. Pushed open the door to her own room. There was nothing to make this better, no words to make things different.

"Halley?"

It was Jillian, curled up in bed, but she threw back the bedcovers as soon as she saw Halley.

"DaVinci left hours ago," said Jillian, giving Halley a hug. "I was sleeping when you returned, and then when they brought Geoffrey, you were asleep, and I didn't want to wake you. DaVinci brought the antibiotics—oh, Halley . . . you're crying."

Halley couldn't speak.

"Oh, oh, oh," murmured Jillian. "Come here. Your hands are like ice. Here. We'll sit together."

Jillian led her to the wide chair before the dying fire, and they sat side by side, while Halley sobbed and tried to answer Jillian's questions about Geoffrey, about Queen Elizabeth's court, about how her throat was doing. Jillian asked about everything except

Edmund, as if she knew to avoid that wound. As if she understood. After a while, they fell silent, Jillian smoothing Halley's hair, holding her, rubbing small circles on her shoulder.

Eventually though, a beeping alarm interrupted their quiet. Jillian removed the watch from one of her pockets and silenced it.

"I'll be leaving in a few minutes," she said.

Halley nodded. "Yeah. Me too I guess."

"Littlewood set my return fifteen minutes ahead of yours, in case, you know, you needed . . . some time for . . . a private goodbye."

Halley's eyes ached from crying, but another tear slipped out at the word "goodbye."

"You and Quintus are traveling at the same time, but you don't have to be in the same place to leave together, in case you weren't sure. And . . . I hate to say it, but I have to step away from you," said Jillian. "Dr. Littlewood warned me severely about not touching anyone when it was time."

Halley nodded and stepped several feet back. It wouldn't be long now. In a few minutes, she would rejoin her friends. She would begin her new life. Just her and the tiny baby growing inside her.

Jillian's form seemed to shimmer for a moment, and then she was gone.

Halley was alone.

Looking around the room, she remembered her arrival here, how she'd come full of confidence that Edmund would return with her. That she would "rescue" him. Now that those hopes had been shattered, she couldn't bear staying in the room another minute. Her skirts swirling, she fled the room, heading for the Great Hall.

Geoffrey was still fast asleep before the fire. Halley could trace his resemblance to Edmund, and her throat contracted again, thinking of how this would be the last time she'd see those high cheekbones, or their echo, anyway. Turning from Geoffrey, Halley approached the chair Edmund had slept in. *His* chair, here in his Great Hall. With a sudden impulse, she grabbed one of the blankets. It smelled like Edmund. Earthy, with something clean and astringent—chamomile, maybe? She could take it with her, but just as quickly as the impulse had come, it disappeared. She didn't want a blanket. She wanted her husband. Her eyes drifted to the musicians gallery, and she realized that was where she wanted to spend her final minutes in the seventeenth century.

Up, up, up the narrow stairs. Memories returned as she climbed. The gown she'd worn for her wedding day . . . meeting nine-year-old Edmund so unexpectedly . . . the roast peacock . . . DaVinci's fascination with the tapestries . . . Halley smiled. She placed a hand on her abdomen and made a promise. "I swear you will know everything I can tell you about your father, little one."

And then, inhaling, she realized she wasn't alone.

Chamomile. Earth. The scent of Edmund, second earl of Shaftesbury, her husband. It was Edmund, looking grief-stricken and pale and heartbreakingly beautiful.

"My love," he said softly.

Halley heard the goodbye before it left his lips.

## 44

### ·*EDMUND*·

### February 1601, London

When Edmund awoke on his makeshift bed in the Great Hall, he felt at once how his health had been restored by sleep and the antibiotics. It was night. Quite late, judging by how low the fire burned. In a chair beside him slept Halley and, beside her, two men were placing Geoffrey on a pallet. Geoffrey moaned in his sleep and then fell silent.

In hushed whispers, the men—Quintus and Silas—explained to Edmund what Halley had done, and how Geoffrey had been released after a few questions. Edmund could hardly believe it. He wanted to rouse Halley to offer his thanks, but Quintus cautioned against it, saying that if she had slept through all their noise, she must require rest badly. When Edmund inquired as to the time, Quintus stealthily checked his watch and reported it was three in the morning.

After that, Silas and Quintus departed. Edmund could hardly believe it was true—that Geoffrey's doom had been lifted. His brother would not die in the Tower. Halley had freed him. Yet again, she filled him with wonder. And humility, too. She had done what he had not been able to. Edmund couldn't wait to hear it all, from Halley's own lips.

He gazed at her, willing her to awaken right now.

But that was selfish. She needed rest. She, too, was but newly recovered from sickness. He would let her rest. Space-time would not call her back for nigh on three hours, and before then, he would return to have speech with her. There was so much to say.

For now, his quarantine period ended, he must visit Maria. He needed to speak with her, too.

The housekeeper had thrown wide his bedroom doors, allowing air from outside the house to pass through the room to cleanse it of impure spirits or vapors—Mistress Janet had no problem holding both beliefs. Edmund slipped into bed beside Maria.

She was awake, and kissed him, and then he asked her to listen to a tale most strange.

Edmund told her everything, from the day he'd first met Halley, the day on which his life had been sundered in twain.

Maria listened, asking but a few questions, her pale brows knotting in hurt and confusion and astonishment, but never in disbelief. She thanked him for his honesty, and for trusting her with so great a secret. And then she told him in no uncertain terms what she expected of him.

With only twenty minutes before Halley's scheduled departure, Edmund left Maria to find Halley and to bid her a lasting farewell.

When he saw she was no longer slumbering in the

Great Hall, he felt a moment's terror that he had mistaken the time, but then he recollected she would not have risked vanishing in sight of Geoffrey. That would explain why she had departed the hall. Edmund raced to her bedchamber, calling softly for her. Seeing her not, he checked the bed, but she was not there either. Her seat before the fire was empty as well, but it was still warm. From her? Or from the dying fire?

Where was she? Had he, after all, missed her? Where might she be? He closed his eyes in concentration. If he were Halley, where would he go? From whence would she wish to cast her last glance upon Hensley Manor?

And just like that, Edmund knew.

He turned, running for dear life to the musicians gallery.

~ ~ ~

It was Edmund. He'd come. He'd found her. Halley's tears prevented her from speaking. Edmund clasped her at the waist, pulling her into a kiss that broke her heart, so warm, so tender, so full of love for her.

"I had to say goodbye, my love," Edmund whispered into her hair.

She nodded, her head cradled against his broad chest.

"I will love you unto my dying breath," he said. And then he kissed her again, his soft, warm lips tasting of mead, and for that brief moment, belonging to her alone.

She would never forget this kiss. Any of his kisses. She would remember him always.

"I understand," she managed to say. Her chest ached, as if she could feel her heart breaking into small

244

pieces, and on each piece was Edmund's name. "I know you have to stay. I understand, and I love you. I will remember you and love you till I die, too, Edmund."

He stepped back, holding her by the shoulders at arms length. His eyes pierced hers. "Halley, beloved—you cannot think . . . Halley, I am not *only* remaining here."

Her heart seemed to stop beating.

"I am also going with you."

"But you said . . . you told me you were here to say goodbye."

His eyes filled with tears. "So I am, my love. One of me must live here, never to look upon your beloved face again. Tis he that saith his goodbye."

She shook her head, not believing what she was hearing. A part of her wanted to scream for joy, but another part felt sudden, crushing pain at the thought of what this would cost her husband.

"You . . . *can't* . . . Edmund!"

"Mistress Halley," he said softly.

Halley's heart ached with the memory of all the times he'd called her that, a thousand moments of shared intimacy.

Edmund spoke, his voice low and tender. "I could no more leave you to grieve without me than I could have left Geoffrey to rot in the Tower. Either way, love, I bear great loss. But I must go with thee, that thy loss will be the lesser."

She was sobbing so hard she could barely speak. "But . . . how will you . . . bear it?"

His arms encircled her. "My love, I made vows. Two sets of vows. I will not break either. How could I claim to love you if I did not cleave to you, in suffering as in health? Our lives are knit together, Halley. I could not live with myself if I sundered our bond."

Edmund bent to kiss her again, and with this kiss, Halley felt the tug of space-time, calling them both back home. Back to her home—no, back to *their* home. And for once, she didn't mind that her body was irrevocably frozen in position.

# 45

## · KHAN ·

### February, Kansas City

"Dammit!" Khan crossed his arms and began pacing the length of his laboratory, empty but for him.

So it was true. Nevis had just destroyed not one but *two* time machines. Khan had, on a hunch, Googled Montecito, California for structural fires, only to discover there had been a similar conflagration at the home of that girl from the meeting in the Sunday School classroom—the girl who'd looked like money. Her home in Montecito was obviously where Littlewood had stashed the machine taken from the *other*, dead, Jules Khan.

So that was it. Khan had no back-up machines. Not only that, but Khan was sure Littlewood would blame him for everything.

Khan's hands shook with fury as he dialed Nevis's cell.

Nevis didn't pick up. Khan called a second time. And a third.

The third time, Nevis answered.

"Yes?"

"Where are you?"

"Tailing a car in Florida."

In Florida? Nevis wasn't even trying to hide he'd done it. Khan gritted his teeth.

"Do you have *any idea what you've just done?*" The question exploded out of Khan.

He knew Nevis responded poorly to shouting. He suspected that in person, Nevis might draw a firearm on him for it—but they were in separate states at the moment, and if shouting at Nevis had ever been called for, it was now.

"What I did is to our mutual advantage," Nevis replied coolly.

Their mutual advantage? There was no such thing! No *them* or *theirs* or *they*. It was Khan, alone, and now Nevis had gone and blown up any chance Khan had of getting Arthur Littlewood to talk to him about the objects disappearing and his own all-too-likely disappearance.

"You'll thank me for it when you've calmed down," said Nevis.

"I'll thank you for destroying the only fully functional machines in existence? Sure I will. If only I'd thought of it first," sneered Khan.

"Sarcasm is the basest form of rhetoric," Nevis said. "Now that Arthur Littlewood has lost his ability to travel at will, don't you think he might be in a better mood to speak with you, since you just happen to have the only machine?"

Khan's mouth fell open. "*That* is why you did this? To get Littlewood to help me?"

"You said he would only agree to assist you if he

was at the end of his rope. Or something like that. Well, now he is." Nevis yawned. "So are we done?"

Khan tried to control his voice when he replied. He needed to sound serious. And powerful. And possibly dangerous.

"I don't want to see you here again," he said softly.

For a moment, Nevis was silent. Then he chuckled. "I miss you too."

"I mean it. You are no longer welcome here."

Nevis exhaled heavily. "Do you really need me to list all the reasons you don't want to fight me?"

Khan shivered. He knew the choice of the word "fight" was purposeful. He didn't reply. Nevis had already called his bluff, anyway.

"Here's what's happening," said Nevis. "I need you to contact Littlewood and ask for his help. That's not a request."

"Did Littlewood see you at his lab when you blew it up?"

"Of course not. I waited until everyone was out of the building."

"I refuse to have Littlewood connecting your actions with me," said Khan. "He can't know you and I are working together."

Nevis seemed to consider this. "I'll take your suggestion under advisement. But one way or another, Arthur Littlewood is helping you get that damn machine up and running."

"When will you be back?" Khan asked tersely. He needed to know how much time he had left.

"Didn't I say? Hmm. Let's just leave it at, expect me when you see me."

The line went dead.

Khan swore so loudly his voice reverberated in the warehouse. And then his phone rang.

It wasn't Nevis. This time it was Arthur Littlewood. Khan let the call go to voicemail, so he could evaluate how safe it might be for him to speak to his former colleague.

The message was short.

"Jules, this is Arthur. There's been a terrible accident. I need your help. Lives are at stake. People will die. Please, *please*, call me as soon as you get this message."

# 46

## · *KHAN* ·

### February, Kansas City

Khan tried not to think about all the reasons returning Littlewood's call was a bad idea. How Littlewood might call the cops on him out of a need for revenge, or justice, or simply so he could steal the only remaining time machine. But if Khan was scared of Arthur Littlewood, he was now more afraid of Benjamin Nevis. Nevis had just committed arson—twice!—and must have had pretty good reasons for thinking he was going to get away with it. The man was insane. That decided it.

Khan raised his phone and dialed Littlewood's number.

The professor answered at once. Gone was his awkward hesitation and stuttering.

"Jules? Jules Khan? Is it you?"

Khan barely grunted out a response before Littlewood began speaking again, at three times his usual measured pace.

"Listen to me carefully. There's been a terrible

disaster."

"It wasn't me!"

A brief pause followed. "Are you willing to prove that to me?"

"Or what? You'll turn me in for operating a singularity device without a license?"

Littlewood exhaled noisily. "That wasn't what I meant to imply. I need your assistance, and I would consider your assistance as proof you do not wish me harm."

Khan massaged his forehead. "I wish you no harm." The one wishing Littlewood harm would be *Nevis*.

"Good. Does your time machine work?"

Khan frowned at the sudden change of subject. "*Um*, yes. Almost. Sort of. I've been having trouble with it—"

"I will help you get it operational. I need your help. I need you to trust me."

Khan could hear the desperation in Littlewood's voice.

"Please," said Littlewood. Tell me where I can find you."

Khan frowned. And told him.

# 47

## ·DAVINCI·

### February, Florida

For DaVinci, there had been no question of not joining Littlewood and Everett as they traveled from Wellesley to Kansas City. Quintus's life was at stake, along with Jillian's and Halley's and possibly Edmund's. Littlewood had explained that if he could get Khan's machine up and running, they could focus space-time from Khan's lab—Jules Khan was literally their last hope.

There had been a frenzied search for the quickest way to get to Kansas City, and it had turned out that a three-stage journey where the middle stage involved Everett flying them to Tampa was their best hope.

It wouldn't be the first time DaVinci had flown with Everett at the helm. Everett had a twenty-five percent ownership of a four-seater, twin-engine Cessna 310 that he took out as often as he could afford to fuel it. The airplane was kept at a regional airport in Fort Pierce, Florida, on the Atlantic coast, forty-seven miles from Wellesley. DaVinci was in charge of stage one of their trip: driving them all to Fort Pierce, while Littlewood and Everett did some troubleshooting with Khan by phone.

It would have been pointless for her to try to follow their conversation, so she spent the drive in private, silent conversation with Christ, the apostles, and Mary the Mother of God. For Quintus's sake, she then added brief requests to Venus Venetrix, defender of Rome, and Hermes, god of travelers, trying not to think of what her grandmother Shaughnessy would have to say about this.

By driving to Fort Pierce and then flying to Tampa, they would be able to catch a commercial flight out of Tampa that would get them into Kansas City six hours ahead of the next available flight from any other Florida airport. DaVinci had been all for Everett flying them the whole way to Khan's lab, but he'd explained the Cessna couldn't fly as high and fast as a commercial jet.

With lives literally depending on her driving them safely to Fort Pierce, DaVinci managed to hold back the tears on the way to the regional airport, but once they were airborne, she gave up all pretence of being okay. Mercifully, the noise of the two propeller engines drowned out the sound of her crying for the fifty-three minute flight.

In Tampa, Littlewood paid Southwest Airlines an extra forty dollars a passenger to get them to the front of the A-boarding group, so that they could grab seats by the door and be the first off the plane in Kansas City. DaVinci had pulled herself together and kept it together through security and right up until the moment they were seated with their tray tables locked and seatbacks in their full upright positions, at which points she lost it all over again.

Everett squeezed DaVinci's shoulder. "We're getting there six hours before Halley and the others are due back. That's plenty of time."

"But what if it's not?" sobbed DaVinci. "What if there's something so wrong with Khan's machine that you and Dr. Littlewood can't fix it?"

"No sense borrowing trouble," Everett replied grimly.

In most circumstances, DaVinci would be the one quoting this bit of Grandma Shaughnessy wisdom. But this wasn't "most circumstances." This was a race against time *and* space-time, and if they didn't win the race, Quintus, her two best friends, and possibly Edmund would only return as mummies.

## 48

### · *NEVIS* ·

### February, Florida

Nevis's next course of action was uncertain. It depended on Arthur Littlewood, and to a lesser extent, on Jules Khan. Nevis was confident Khan would contact Littlewood. He felt less certain he could rely on Littlewood to cooperate, and so he'd waited at Littlewood's Florida lab, planning to tail him. Curiously, Littlewood and the two young people with him didn't seem interested in sticking around the smoldering laboratory. In Nevis's experience, people who'd just suffered a catastrophic loss were likely to remain glued to the spot, staring as if they could undo the damage by looking at it hard enough. Either that, or they entered into lengthy discussions with emergency personnel, trying to get an answer to the question: *how could this have happened?*

Littlewood, however, did neither. After initially running toward the remains of the building, Littlewood had stopped short, pulled out his phone, and either placed or answered a call. Nevis hoped it was a conversation with Khan. He needed Littlewood to troubleshoot Khan's machine *onsite*. He needed both scientists in one place.

Nevis's conscience was still bothering him over this one. He reminded himself of the consequences of doing nothing. Of how humanity's fate hung in the balance. At least one of the two scientists was unbalanced, and the other was, well, inept, and naïve. Not a combination you wanted in men poised over the big red button.

No, he would do what had to be done, in accordance with the oath he had taken fourteen years earlier. The FBI may have fired Nevis, but that didn't exonerate him from upholding his oath.

After Littlewood concluded his phone call, he and the two young people got back in their car. Nevis tailed them all the way to Florida's eastern coast, calling Khan and ordering him to contact Littlewood and bring him to Kansas City. Nevis was hopeful this was underway. Littlewood was headed to West Palm Beach airport. From there, Nevis could follow the scientist back to Khan. He should probably buy a baseball cap to make hiding his face on the flight a little easier.

However, Littlewood and his companions turned for Fort Pierce's regional airport instead of the airport in West Palm Beach. Nevis swore. The possibility Littlewood had alternate air transport simply hadn't occurred to him. Nevis certainly didn't happen to have a personal craft sitting around in Fort Pierce.

At the small airport, following the movements of the group became trickier, but with the help of binoculars Nevis managed to identify the craft they departed in. Now he just needed a heading. If they were flying all the way in *that* thing, he would probably get to Kansas City first. The twin engine plane left the runway.

Nevis exhaled noisily. To acquire intel, he was going to have to use the fake badge he'd acquired after turning his real one in. So far, he'd avoided this. He hadn't pulled a badge on anyone since the day he'd located Jules Khan. If the wrong person made inquiries, the fake badge could get Nevis in a lot of hot water. But this was a regional airport, not the kind of place swarming with US Marshals, and he needed to know where that plane was going. Besides, considering what was on his to-do list for the day, this was hardly the time for squeamishness. Exiting his vehicle, Nevis pulled on his suit jacket, checked that his fake badge was at the ready, and then donned his aviator sunglasses.

"Here goes nothing," he said under his breath.

# 49

## · LITTLEWOOD ·

### February, Kansas City

Littlewood, now in Khan's Kansas City warehouse with Everett and DaVinci, couldn't remember the last time he'd felt so exhausted. He reached for the cup of coffee Khan had handed him two hours ago and gulped the remainder of the now-cold beverage. The entire warehouse was cold. Freezing, actually, courtesy of Kansas City's northerly latitude. He'd take Florida's humid summers over this any day.

Along with Khan and Everett, Littlewood had labored through the night while DaVinci slept, having cried herself to sleep. Once the machine appeared to be functioning normally, Everett had insisted on making one journey before they used it to retrieve Jillian, who was due back first.

Everett made a quick trip to Alexandria's library and returned in the proper amount of time, after which Littlewood breathed much easier.

"It appears the journey went perfectly, using only the expected amount of power, wouldn't you say?"

Littlewood indicated a readout he wanted Khan and Everett to double-check.

"The readings are nominal," said Khan.

Khan had been on edge since they'd arrived. Understandable, of course. Perhaps Littlewood should offer him some praise in addition to the many thanks he'd already offered.

"You've done remarkably well on your own, you know, Jules," said Littlewood. "All we did tonight was a little fine-tuning."

A little fine-tuning that would make the difference between a functional and non-operative device, but Littlewood wanted to encourage Khan to continue in his currently non-hostile mode of behavior. He thought of something else for which he could praise his former colleague.

"The sound dampening you've achieved on your device is nothing short of remarkable, Jules."

A look of smugness flashed across Khan's face. "I value my hearing."

"If I'm honest, it never occurred to me to address the problem," said Littlewood.

"It *is* a great deal more pleasant," said Everett, "having the noise levels down during operation. Well done."

This, coming from a young man who'd been fired on by Khan, was rather generous.

"I take it we're ready, then?" Littlewood asked.

The other two nodded.

"Shall we awaken DaVinci?" asked Littlewood.

"I'm awake. I heard everyone talking," mumbled DaVinci. Although she was no longer crying, her pale face was pinched with worry. "So it's Jillian first, and then Quintus and Halley after fifteen minutes?"

"Yes," Everett replied gravely.

Littlewood tried to offer reassurance.

"The device is fully operational," he said. "I'm sure Jillian and the others will be back with us in only a few minutes. Jules? I trust you can do the honors?"

DaVinci's eyes narrowed as if she didn't trust Khan to do anything, and Littlewood hastily added, "I'll just be your second set of eyes, shall I?"

Khan nodded quickly and tapped the controls. The machine began to thrum again. The group watched the timer counting down the minutes and then seconds. From the corner of his eye, Littlewood noticed DaVinci swiping at her eyes. He retrieved a fresh handkerchief from the pocket of his Harris tweed coat and passed it to her, along with what he hoped were comforting words.

"All that is necessary for a successful retrieval is that the singularity device be up and running, my dear," he said. "The timer will merely tell us the window of opportunity for retrieval has come and gone. That is, ah, well, I'm sure it won't come to that."

DaVinci crumpled against Everett.

"Oh dear," said Littlewood, "please forgive me, I, ah . . ."

But he didn't finish his sentence, because at that moment Jillian appeared on the platform. Everett was at her side at once. It had worked! After everything that had transpired in the past sixteen hours, it had almost seemed too much to hope. Littlewood felt something wet tickling his cheek.

"Here," said DaVinci, returning his handkerchief with a huge grin. Then she sprang over to her friends, shouting with the sort of enthusiasm he associated with university football games.

Littlewood wasn't really a hugging sort of person, so he contented himself with smiling at the three happy young people before turning his focus back to Khan and the screen regulating the singularity device.

The machine was already cycling up for the second retrieval when Littlewood noticed something in his periphery. He turned. Despite the remoteness of this warehouse and the lateness of the hour, it appeared someone had joined them while everyone's attention had been fixed on the platform. That would never do! They had only a few minutes to get him out of the building, whoever he was.

Littlewood squinted at the approaching man. And then recognized him.

"Oh dear," he murmured.

Khan, who had noticed the man as well, muttered something considerably saltier.

It was Benjamin Nevis. In one hand he held a revolver and in the other, a Taser.

# 50

February, Kansas City

Khan had, for a brief moment, hoped he'd hallucinated the sudden appearance of Nevis, but he quickly realized this was no imagined visitation.

"What the hell are you waving guns around for?" he demanded. "These are my . . ." Khan paused, struggling to find the right word. Friends? Colleagues? "These are my *associates*."

His statement didn't seem to motivate Nevis to lower his weapons.

"Don't you think you're being a little overly dramatic?" Khan asked, lowering his voice.

"Do you know him?" Littlewood asked Khan, indicating Nevis.

Khan hesitated before answering, but then decided it was all going to come out anyway. "Yes," he told Littlewood. To his gun-toting associate, he said, "We're all on the same side here."

"I wish that was true," Nevis said to Khan. "But unfortunately we are *not* all on the same side. I'm on

263

the side where citizens are allowed life, liberty, and the pursuit of happiness, and the rest of you, unfortunately, are not."

Khan released a snort of laughter. "So, what—we're all under arrest?"

"Officer," began Everett, "I think there has been some manner of misunderstanding. I assure you no one here means you any harm."

"I'm not concerned about harm to me as an individual," said Nevis.

"Then would you mind with the guns, already?" demanded DaVinci.

Irritation flickered across Nevis's face. "I remember you. You showed up with that gladiator."

"He is *not* a gladiator. He's an *immunes* of the Roman army," said DaVinci, evidently offended.

Khan shifted his gaze back to Nevis. "What do you want? Money? Art? Jewels?"

Nevis shook his head, eyeing Khan as with pity. "You just don't get it. There are things that are more important than amassing riches. I took an oath to support and defend the constitution of the United States against all enemies—*all* enemies."

"With respect, sir, I've taken the same oath," said Everett, "in another time and place."

"Then you'll understand why this equipment must not be allowed to remain in the wrong hands," Nevis said coolly.

"So it was you that destroyed the other time machines?" asked Littlewood. "Do you realize what you could have—"

"Enough!" shouted Nevis. "You've invented something worse than the hydrogen bomb, professor.

It's a veritable Pandora's box, and the only course of action open to us now is to seal the box and bury all memory of it."

During these exchanges, Khan took the opportunity to inch away from Nevis, hoping to make other, nearer targets more appealing to his crazed associate. He was now near enough to the operations station to notice the machine was about to retrieve Littlewood's remaining friends. The unexpected appearance of several more people might distract Nevis and make Khan's getaway easier . . .

He used his body to block Nevis's view of the screen and its timer.

Then he had another idea. It was probably not a good one. A bit too . . . heroic. He wasn't exactly hero material. Actually, he wasn't even the sort of person who clapped for the hero.

Khan crossed his fingers, metaphorically, while Nevis continued his monologue about the greater good. While Nevis was still droning on, the room flickered with blue light and the time machine platform was filled with people, two of whom assessed the situation quickly enough to charge Nevis. How perfect! It was the distraction Khan had been hoping for. He spun around and began working the controls for one more journey.

## 51

### · *HALLEY* ·

February, Kansas City

As soon as Halley and Edmund materialized in the twenty-first century, Halley saw Quintus had been pulled back home, just like Jillian had said.

"Thank goodness," she murmured, pulling out of the kiss she'd been locked in.

It was then that she noticed two strange things. The first was that her friends didn't look nearly as happy to see her as she would have expected. The second was that the room they'd arrived in didn't look right. In fact, it was completely unfamiliar.

"Oh no," she murmured. Had they altered the timeline? But even as she asked herself the question, something else demanded her attention. Quintus and Edmund were rushing someone. Someone holding a weapon—no, *two* weapons.

The stranger fired at both men, with Edmund taking a bullet.

"No!" Halley cried, running for Edmund, who fell and didn't rise. At his side, Quintus shivered as voltage

from a Taser raced through him. DaVinci joined
Quintus at the same moment that Halley got to
Edmund. There was a bright bloom of blood. Was it
his heart? His shoulder?

"Face down on the ground," shouted the
stranger. "Both of you girls. Now!"

"You *coward*," shouted DaVinci.

Instantly another gunshot rang out.

"I didn't have to miss," said Nevis. "Next time I
won't. Face down on the floor!"

Halley threw herself over Edmund.

"Littlewood," said Nevis, "on your knees, hands
behind your head. Now!"

"Sir," cried Everett, "just tell us what you want.
You have our permission to destroy this machine—"

Nevis attempted to backhand Everett, but Everett
blocked him. The two struggled with Nevis gaining the
upper hand in seconds.

Everett slumped—or feinted—Halley wasn't sure
which.

Nevis's attention had been redirected, however.
"Khan, what the hell do you think you're doing?"

Quintus groaned beside Halley. "Wound . . .
needs . . . pressure," he grunted.

Halley nodded and pressed on Edmund's wound
for all she was worth. There was so much blood. She
felt light-headed. She looked away, trying not to let up
on the pressure.

Khan was engaging Nevis. It was obvious Khan
had basically no skill as a fighter, but at least he was
distracting Nevis.

Everett rose, shaking his head like he was clearing
it. He squared off to aid Khan. Nevis fired again.

Halley wasn't sure who'd been shot until Khan fell to the ground.

Everett tackled Nevis from behind. Jillian ran to help, but Nevis grabbed her and then threw her like she weighed nothing at all. Jillian hit the ground and didn't get up. Everett punched Nevis, once, twice, and then the two began grappling for possession of the firearm.

Khan, meanwhile, was crawling to the time machine's platform, a trail of blood behind him.

"Really Dr. Khan?" shouted Halley. "You're just going to run away?"

This caught Nevis's attention long enough for Everett to break Nevis's grip on the gun, but unfortunately he lost control of the weapon, which went spinning across the warehouse's slippery floor. Both raced for the gun, and it looked like Nevis would get there first, but then Everett shot out his foot, tripping Nevis, and retrieved the gun. Aiming at the ceiling, Everett fired all the remaining shots and hurled the weapon to the far end of the warehouse. He then raised both fists, ready to take Nevis on again.

Nevis, sneering, delivered a single kick that connected with his opponent's gut.

Everett went down like a rag doll.

"No!" cried Halley.

Nevis, meanwhile, twisted and raced back to Khan, shouting, "Khan, don't you dare!"

Khan had curled into the fetal position on the far end of the time machine platform with his arms protecting his head, probably a tempting target for Nevis. A quick glance to the control screen told Halley that Khan was going to get away. Nevis had realized this too, and sprinted for Khan, livid anger etched on his face.

Nevis leaped onto the platform. Moaning, Khan rolled just as an arc of blue fire lit the room.

# 52

## · HALLEY ·

### February, Kansas City

Nevis was gone.

From the moment Nevis had fired the first shot until the moment he'd disappeared into the past, only a handful of minutes had elapsed.

Halley heard a pathetic cry and traced its source. Khan, still curled into a ball, lay moaning where he'd rolled off the platform just in time for Nevis to travel alone.

"How long do we have before he returns?" shouted Littlewood.

Khan moaned even louder.

"How long, dammit?" demanded Littlewood.

"He's . . . gone," mumbled Khan. "Won't . . . be any . . . trouble to us now."

Quintus, seemingly recovered from the Taser, spoke to Halley. "Allow me to aid Edmund."

Halley, fearful and possibly in shock, shook her head, and kept pressing on Edmund's wound.

"Hal!" said DaVinci. "Let him save Edmund.

Quintus knows what he's doing a lot better than you or me."

Something in Halley seemed to snap, and she got out of Quintus's way.

"I require bandages," said Quintus.

At this point, Khan began calling loudly. "I've been shot. Someone needs to call 9-1-1."

Everett, his lips pinching unsympathetically, rose and crossed to aid Khan.

Halley realized she was shaking from head to toe.

"It's okay," said DaVinci. "It's okay."

"Bandages?" Quintus repeated.

"Here," said Halley, exposing her underskirt. Her hands shook as she tried to start a tear in the fabric.

Jillian joined her. "I've got this." She began tearing long strips from Halley's skirt while DaVinci held Halley, repeating that it was going to be okay, everything was going to be okay.

~ ~ ~

Before he'd started working for Littlewood, there had been two occasions when Quintus helped Father Joe taking the injured and uninsured to a crisis-care facility. At Quintus's suggestion, Halley located such a facility in Kansas City that offered mobile no-questions-asked medical care.

A large delivery-style van with medical markings pulled up within ten minutes, during which time Quintus had gotten Edmund's bleeding mostly under control.

While the nurse and EMT worked on Edmund, Halley saw that the mobile response driver was staring at what she and Edmund were wearing with a vaguely curious expression.

"You're probably wondering about our costumes," Halley said, tentatively.

The only response Halley got was, "Miss, believe me when I say we've seen everything."

They really were "no questions asked."

The medical personnel cleaned Edmund's entry and exit wounds swiftly and efficiently, patched him up, told Edmund to take Tylenol and avoid ibuprofen and aspirin, and drove off to their next no-questions-asked crisis.

After that, it was back inside the warehouse, where Quintus had dressed Khan's very minor bullet-graze. It was only then that Everett and Littlewood told Quintus, Halley, and Edmund why they'd ended up in Kansas City instead of Florida.

In the silence that followed, Halley noticed a vaguely familiar-looking lump. It was shriveled but recognizably person-shaped.

"Is that, *um* . . ." Halley broke off, feeling slightly queasy.

"Oh, yes," said Littlewood. "It would appear Jules Khan saved us all, at a not inconsiderable risk to his own life."

"Where did you send him?" Halley asked in a hushed voice.

"Antarctica," replied Khan. "One hundred years in the past. He will have died of exposure before making his return journey."

"Then . . . why is he mummified?" asked DaVinci.

"I shut off the power," said Quintus. "Just to be sure."

"Remind me never to cross you," Halley murmured with admiration.

"That's my badass gladiator," said DaVinci.

Quintus glared at her.

"Just kidding," said DaVinci, her hands encircling his neck. Then, with a quick leap, she wrapped both legs around his hips and gave him a very not-for-public kiss.

Jillian tittered and Everett looked mortified, but Halley turned and smiled at Edmund.

He shifted his uninjured arm, bringing a hand to her face, and then, drawing her close, he whispered, "It's good to be home."

After a few minutes of quiet, Everett, Littlewood, Khan, DaVinci, and Quintus marched outside to dispose of Nevis's remains. They returned just as the sun rose, shining weakly through the warehouse's east-facing windows.

DaVinci's stomach growled loudly, breaking the silence.

"So, I know this place with decent doughnuts," said Khan. "If anyone's hungry?"

## 53

Eighteen Months Later, Wellesley

Halley and Edmund were hosting their second annual Fourth of July backyard barbecue in Wellesley, Florida, where clouds chased blue skies on a balmy 82 degree afternoon. Halley was breaking in Edmund's Father's Day present, a gas grill, while Edmund strolled with their daughter Felicity, attempting to convince her she'd rather sleep than hang with her people. It wasn't going well.

Under the shade of a Halley-sewn awning, Quintus, DaVinci, Everett, Jillian, Father Joe, and Arthur Littlewood passed bowls of sliced watermelon, tortilla chips, and Jillian's latest attempt at the perfect teething biscuit.

"I don't get why Felicity isn't digging these," said DaVinci, grabbing another biscuit. "I could live on these things, I swear." She turned to the grill. "Hal. Get over here. Sit. I hereby order that chicken to survive without you."

Halley considered DaVinci's decree and decided

she could use a break, but on her way to Edmund's latest woodworking project—an Adirondack chair—she murmured to her husband to please keep an eye on the chicken. Taking Felicity from him, she sank gratefully into her chair.

Eleven-month-old Felicity Marie Mikkelsen-Aldwych was *not* sitting. Not in her mom's lap and not in her matching miniature chair. She'd done precious little sitting since taking her first-ever steps at 4:30 that morning. Now, having climbed out of her mom's lap, she began playing a favorite game: circling from person to person distributing her toys and books, and then collecting them and redistributing them. She steadfastly refused to go down for a nap, or even to nurse.

"I think she's weaning herself," Halley said with a tinge of sadness.

"That girl was busy *before* she figured out how to walk," said DaVinci. "There's no way she has time for the boob now."

"You should masticate a small quantity of roasted lamb or goat for her," Quintus said gravely.

"Masticate?" asked Halley.

"*Chew*," murmured Jillian.

"Oh, boy," said DaVinci. "Here we go again with child-rearing in ancient Rome."

"Pre-chewing is common in many cultures," said Jillian. "Not everyone has supermarkets and baby food aisles."

"Yeah," said DaVinci, "but there's no way Branson pre-chewed your food when you were a toddler."

Everett laughed just as Felicity plopped in

275

Halley's lap and said, "*Muh.*"

"Oh, goodness," said Father Joe, looking up from the rose beds he had begun weeding. "Did she just say 'mama'?"

"She has but one word," replied Edmund, returning with a platter of chicken. "'*Muh*,' which serves for all purposes."

While the rest of the group ate chicken and placed bets on what Felicity's *actual* first word would be, Halley began nursing her daughter. As happened every so often when she nursed, Halley found herself remembering Maria Lavenham, Countess of Shaftesbury. She always felt a little sad when she thought of Maria, or rather, when she thought of the price Edmund had paid to remain with Halley and their beautiful daughter.

And then she remembered something else.

"Oh." She brought a hand to her mouth.

A letter had arrived yesterday from England— from *Hensley Manor*, according to the return address. The old stone manor still stood, although it was surrounded by cricket pitches and Victorian-era brick houses instead of by fields. Halley and Edmund had talked about visiting the manor someday, maybe when Felicity was old enough to remember the trip, however old that was . . .

"My love?" asked Edmund, who had heard her quiet *oh*.

She shook her head. "I just remembered something. When everyone's gone, there's a letter we should open together."

Their quiet conversation was enough to snap Felicity back to full wakefulness.

"*Muh*," said the tiny girl, after which she wriggled out of her mom's lap and began walking from person to person, regaling them with books, toys, and lots of "*muh*'s."

"Come here, little one," said Everett, holding his hands out.

"*Muh*," said Felicity, turning her back on Everett. She wobbled uncertainly in the middle of the group, turning solemnly from face to face.

"Come see Auntie DaV?" asked DaVinci, wiggling a bright rattle.

Felicity grinned and clapped her hands together, but did not go to DaVinci, either.

"Auntie Jillian has your favorite book," said Jillian, holding up a Beatrix Potter board book.

"Uncle Everett makes duck noises when he reads it to you," said Everett, holding his hands out.

Arthur Littlewood only smiled at Felicity, whom Halley was beginning to think intimidated the heck out of the brainy professor. But he did take great pictures of her—with an actual *camera*, of all things. Father Joe, meanwhile, had started to weed Halley's cucumber bed. She'd given up trying to stop him from doing chores after Quintus had told her it made the priest happy.

Halley sighed and sipped her virgin strawberry margarita. The party was going just fine, in spite of its hosts' crazy-early morning of "baby's first steps."

Everett, across the circle from her, had started making duck noises, which he really was good at. Felicity was still wavering on whose invite she would accept.

"Who gives the best raspberries?" called DaVinci.

"You do," Quintus replied, treating the question as an actual question.

"*Ki-ki*," said Felicity. She took several steps toward the lounge chair DaVinci was sharing with Quintus.

"What does 'Ki-ki' mean?" Jillian asked, setting the board book down.

"We're not sure," said Halley. "She started saying it this morning when Edmund told here all of you would be coming over."

"*Ki-ki!*" repeated Felicity.

"Maybe it's her sound for fireworks," said Everett. "I've never seen a baby so taken with fireworks."

It was true, mused Halley. Babies were supposed to be terrified of loud noises like thunder and fireworks, but Felicity loved them both, squealing with glee over either.

"Fireworks," said Edmund, nodding. "Felicity? Do you want to see the fireworks?"

"Ki-ki!" said Felicity.

"How do you know if that means 'Yes,' or, 'No, idiot adults, I want *ki-ki!*' asked DaVinci.

"We don't," admitted Halley, laughing. "Felicity?"

Her daughter looked over her shoulder at Halley.

"What is 'ki-ki,' my little love?" asked Halley.

Felicity turned back to face the lounge chair. "Ki-ki! Ki-ki! Ki-ki!" And then, ignoring Auntie DaVinci's outstretched arms, Felicity marched to Quintus and began pounding her fists on his knees.

"*Ki-ki*," she said.

"Oh my God, babe," said DaVinci. "I think 'Kiki' is you!"

Quintus reached his arms out and Felicity grabbed what she could of his muscled forearms with her plump fists.

"Ki-ki."

DaVinci began laughing. "Uncle Kiki, *huh?*"

DaVinci leaned over to place a raspberry on Felicity's chubby thighs. Felicity tolerated this for about half a minute before shoving Auntie DaVinci away with a determined palm.

"Ki-ki," murmured Felicity, after which she buried her face between Quintus's chest and bicep and fell asleep.

"Babe. Can she breathe in there?" DaVinci asked softly.

"Assuredly I shall not permit her to suffocate," Quintus replied with a look of indignation.

Halley noted Quintus's hand was resting on Felicity's back where Quintus was keeping track of her every breath. She smiled softly. That little girl had one heck of a family. Uncle Quintus stood after a moment and began his "walk and rock," which he insisted aided the baby's digestion. Halley knew from experience that Quintus wouldn't stop rocking Felicity until she woke up, even if she napped for hours.

"So, ah," began Littlewood, "Khan reached out again to Everett."

Everyone turned to Everett.

"Seriously?" said DaVinci. "Gotta say, I don't get the whole connection you guys have."

Everett smiled enigmatically. "He's a very lonely man."

Jillian tilted her head. "Does Khan remind you of your father?"

"A bit," agreed Everett. "He's richer than my father ever was, but he's every bit as miserable."

"Money is useful, but it cannot purchase contentment," said Quintus.

"It purchased him an entire island in the Bahamas," DaVinci retorted. "I'd be willing to find out if that would make me content."

Halley chortled. DaVinci was always saying things like this, but like the rest of the group, she'd held off using Littlewood's new time machine to amass riches.

"We flew out to visit Jules last week," said Jillian. "His house is really something."

"She says," added DaVinci, "as a card-carrying member of 'Lifestyles of the Rich and Famous.'"

Jillian flushed.

"His house is remarkable," said Everett, turning the conversation away from his fiancée, "and it's stuffed to the gills with furnishings and art, but . . . it's empty. I suppose it does remind me of the home I grew up in."

"It's very kind of you to offer him friendship," said Father Joe.

"Seriously," murmured DaVinci.

"He's offered us the use of his island for our wedding," said Everett, smiling at Jillian.

"Oh my God. You're not actually considering the offer?" DaVinci looked around the circle of friends for support.

Halley shrugged and said nothing.

"This and other such visits allow us to observe Khan with proper vigilance," Quintus said.

"Next you'll be offering to spy on him," said DaVinci.

"I have already done so," replied Quintus, "but Everett and Dr. Littlewood object."

"So, *um*, is anyone ready for cupcakes?" asked Jillian, diplomatically heading off any further discussion.

At the word "cupcake," Felicity raised her head, mumbled, "*Muh*," and then crashed out again in Quintus's arms.

~ ~ ~

After ungodly amounts of food had been consumed, fireworks applauded, and leftovers refrigerated, Halley and Edmund collapsed on their futon couch, watching their Energizer-bunny daughter as she motored around the room calling for "Kiki."

"From whence comes a child's energy?" asked Edmund.

"They steal it from their parents," Halley replied, yawning hugely. She reached for her phone to check the time and inadvertently knocked a stack of mail off the counter.

"Oh," she said. "Here's the letter from England I told you about."

She picked it up and handed it to Edmund. "Tell me what it says. I'm too tired to comprehend written language."

Edmund, retrieving what looked like a dagger-shaped letter opener but was actually a dagger-shaped dagger, sliced the oversized envelope and removed the letter, along with another smaller and very aged envelope.

"Aloud?" he asked.

"Mm-hmm."

"*Dear Madam* . . ." Edmund looked up, saying, "I

281

think it's addressed to you."

"Just read it to me," mumbled Halley, eyes at half-mast.

Edmund returned to reading the letter.

*"During the past six months I have debated not sending this news, but my conscience has got the better of me. We share a common ancestor, my nine-times great grandfather Edmund Aldwych, second earl of Shaftesbury. The title was stripped from our family during the Civil War (England's, that is,) but my ancestors retained the manor itself.*

*Edmund Aldwych was an odd sort of man. In 1609, he created an early "time capsule," to be opened the first of January, this year. My wife, then living, was ill, so we did not wish for media attention. Thus, I might've kept its contents for myself, though they belong to you. Their value would have allowed me to carry out repairs to Hensley Manor which heavy taxation has prevented in my lifetime. I leave no heirs, unfortunately, to complete the work.*

*However, I cannot keep what is not mine. As to how my ancestor could have known the heir of a first, secret marriage would live in Florida in the twenty-first century (and research revealed you* do*), his children maintained he was blessed or cursed with second sight. That is the best explanation I can offer.*

*If you would care to visit a rather dull old man across the pond, I will convey the items. There is a collection of sermons by Geoffrey Aldwych and a very fine quarto version of* The Tempest *by William Shakespeare. Its authenticity will have to be vetted, of course, but its worth is likely something north of a hundred thousand pounds. The play and sermons are labeled, "For Felicity and the heirs of her bodie," and seem to have belonged to a daughter from his first marriage, from whom I presume you are descended.*

*There is a second item, not referenced in Edmund's letter to*

282

*his daughter. (I enclose the letter.) It is a 1623 bound edition of all Shakespeare's plays, which Edmund must have added to his time capsule later. An inscription reads, "Halley Mikkelsen," and not Felicity. As descendent of both women, you now own a manuscript worth many millions.*

*I hope you will forgive the delay in forwarding this news, but between the loss of my wife and the temptation to keep these riches for myself, well, it has been a difficult year. But I shall die knowing Edmund would have been proud of me. Perhaps he and I will discuss it over tea in heaven. I cannot for the life of me recall whether tea was known in his lifetime, but I feel certain that as a good Englishman, he will learn to like it.*

> *Yours most sincerely,*
> *Charles Aldwych*
> *Hensley Manor, London."*

Edmund looked up, clearly stunned.

Halley understood. She felt the same way. She wasn't remotely sleepy at this point.

"I don't believe it," she said, breaking the silence.

"Here is the other letter to which Charles Aldwych referred," said Edmund, handing it to her.

"It's not addressed," said Halley, taking the yellowed envelope.

"Open it, I pray," said Edmund, his voice soft as a whisper.

Halley lifted the broken wax seal and unfolded the letter, stiff with age. She frowned at the writing and looked up. "I can't read this." She handed it to Edmund.

"Ah. This is my handwriting as it appeared . . . then."

Halley couldn't tell if Edmund was about to laugh

or cry, but after a moment, he smiled. "The style of writing is called 'secretary hand,' and it looks as if the other Edmund wrote it in the rain."

"What does it say?" asked Halley.

"It's a letter to Felicity. Perhaps we should wait until—"

"No. Read it!" demanded Halley.

Edmund nodded and began.

*"My dearest Felicity,*

*Words cannot convey my gratitude for thy visite this past weke."*

Halley gasped. "What?"

Edmund, frowning, replied, "It would appear our daughter will time travel at some point in the future."

"There's no way," began Halley, but then she frowned too, and said, "I guess that's a moot point, huh?"

After shrugging, Edmund continued to read.

*"As thou didst guess my hart hath ben heavie with the death of thy half-brother James but to see thee and to heer that thou and thy mother do thrive—childe thou seest the tears that do blur mine ink. But it is well with my soule knowing thou shalt live and prosper."*

Edmund looked at Halley, his eyes wet with unshed tears.

"She must have gone to visit the other Edmund after his son James died," Halley said softly.

"James was born . . . after I returned with you. I never knew him, but our daughter must have returned to offer comfort to my other self."

Edmund's eyes rested on tiny Felicity, who had finally curled up on a rug and fallen asleep to the sound of her father's voice reading the letters.

"Is there more to the letter?" Halley asked after a minute passed.

"Yes—yes, of course." Edmund lifted the page again.

*"I have considered what I maye do for thee that is what gifte I might leeve for thee and the heirs of thy bodie and if thou shouldst marrie one day. It grieveth me and thy step-mother that we shall see thee never againe sundered by time and ocean as we must evermore be. Therefore we do ask thou wouldst accept this smale gift of a play by William Shakeshaft. The action of the play is the love of a father for his daughter sundered from her inherytaunce by his neglect but that he loveth her truly none maye doubt even as I love thee Felicity Mikkelsen-Aldwych and do ever praye for thy happyness and salvacion.*

*Edmund Aldwych*

*Hensley Manor*

*1609."*

Edmund looked up, a vulnerable look etched on his face. "What say you? Shall we visit my many-times-removed great-grandson, my love?"

"Of course," whispered Halley. "Yes. *Yes!*"

## Epilogue

### Three Years After the Letter

It was Felicity's fourth visit to modern-day Hensley Manor. It had taken nearly two years for the Aldwych manuscripts to be vetted, but only three minutes for the First Folio to be sold. However, several trips to England had been required, during which time Felicity became a favorite with the elderly Charles Aldwych.

This visit coincided with the anniversary of the death of Charles's wife Julisa. Felicity's laughter as she zoomed around the newly renovated Great Hall seemed to cheer the old man up considerably, which was more than Halley or Edmund had known how to do.

"My wife always loved when children visited the Great Hall," said Charles, half a smile on his wrinkled face. "And seeing the old place looking like this? She wouldn't have believed it possible. Do you know, I can almost imagine the old earl himself strutting about in a ruff and doublet."

Halley had to stop herself from laughing, because that was *exactly* what she'd been imagining.

When Felicity took Charles Aldwych's hand to

show him the musicians gallery, Halley took the opportunity to whisper a question.

"How are you doing, my love?"

Edmund's eyes shone, but he blinked and the sorrow was gone. "It is well with me."

Halley took his hand and squeezed it tight. "I'm so glad we made the decision to put the money to good use here."

"As am I," said Edmund. "More money can always be found, but more moments like this one?" He looked up to the musicians gallery from where Felicity and Edmund's nine-times great-grandson Charles were waving at him.

Felicity squealed, peals of childish laughter echoing in the large chamber.

"Are you sure you don't want to accept Charles's offer to live here?" Halley asked. "Felicity loves it so much."

"She wouldn't like being so far from Uncle Kiki," Edmund pointed out.

"True. Uncle Kiki and Auntie DaVee have made it clear they're Floridians for life." Halley hesitated but then asked the question again. "But what about you? Would you be happier here?"

Edmund turned to give her his full attention. "I will always be happy to come and visit, as long as Charles is alive. But this isn't my home anymore, Halley. Wellesley is our home."

Halley smiled. "Come on, 'fess up, Farmer Ned. You'd miss your orange groves too much, is that it?"

"I would miss crowning you with their blossoms in spring. I would miss squeezing fresh juice for you and our daughter. I would miss the heat of the sun on my back when I walk the groves." He drew her close. "But most of all I should miss our very ordinary, very under-renovated, very small house, because it is *ours*, Halley, in a way this will never be."

Halley felt Edmund's hand slipping around the small of her back. Her body still thrilled to his touch, electric in any century, any place. Edmund pulled her closer and lifted her face to meet his.

Felicity's voice rang out shrilly as she ran down from the gallery. "*Ew*, they're going to *kiss!*"

And they did. Then, and for all the years to come.

## THE END

For information on all releases by Cidney Swanson:
cidneyswanson.com

# Acknowledgments

Another series comes to a close with this fourth book. I know, I know, I've said that before and then returned to a "closed" series. I won't rule it out because of my track record, but if nothing else, I think the loose ends are mostly tied up here. I will certainly miss Halley and Edmund, Everett and Jillian, and DaVinci and Quintus (*hubba-hubba!*) I might even miss Jules Khan, who is just so much darned fun to write. In any case, I owe you, dear reader, a huge thank you for making it possible for me to write down these stories and get paid for it. *Thank you!*

The jaunt back to the late Elizabethan era was so much fun. It was made much simpler thanks to several excellent books. I relied heavily on Ruth Goodman's *How to Be a Tudor*, audiobook narrated by Heather Wilds, as well as Stephen Greenblatt's fascinating exploration of Shakespeare's life and times in *Will in the World*. For kicks and giggles, 1601-style, it's hard to beat Barry Kraft's *Shakespeare Insult Generator*.

As always, I owe my biggest debts of gratitude to my writing buddies for encouraging me when skies aren't blue, and to my family for always believing the next book will be finished, eventually. Special thanks to my husband, whom I like to call Dr. Science, for aid with the physics and math, and for believing in me the *most*-est.

# A Sword in Time

www.ingramcontent.com/pod-product-compliance
Lightning Source LLC
Chambersburg PA
CBHW021212250626
47155CB00008B/2783